TOO LUCKY TO LIVE
The First Somebody's Bound to Wind Up Dead Mystery

"In this entertaining, sexy debut, Allie is a sharp Stephanie Plum paired up with a hot partner. She quickly learns how adept a blind man can be in dealing with trouble. The original voice, humor, and unusual premise will appeal to Janet Evanovich readers."

—*Library Journal* (starred review)

"As the plot zigs and zags, readers will enjoy hanging out with Tom and Allie, whose quirkiness will remind some readers of Janey Mack's Maisie McGrane."

—*Publishers Weekly*

"Fast pacing, multiple plot twists, and humor, including a Stephanie Plum-like main character, enliven the story and keep the pages turning."

—*Booklist*

Murder to
the Metal

Books by Annie Hogsett

The Somebody's Bound to Wind Up Dead
Mysteries
Too Lucky to Live
Murder to the Metal

Murder to the Metal

A Somebody's Bound to Wind Up Dead Mystery

Annie Hogsett

Poisoned Pen Press

Copyright © 2018 by Annie Hogsett

First Edition 2018

10 9 8 7 6 5 4 3 2 1

Library of Congress Control Number:
2017954237

ISBN: 9781464209987   Large Print

Poisoned Pen Press
4014 N. Goldwater Blvd., #201
Scottsdale, AZ 85251
www.poisonedpenpress.com
info@poisonedpenpress.com

Printed in the United States of America

For Margaret, excellent mother.
For John, excellent son.
Love and gratitude always.

& In memory of Paul.

"So close your eyes.
For that's a lovely way to be
aware of things your heart
alone was meant to see."

— *"Wave" by Antônio Carlos Jobim*

Acknowledgments

Family first. To Bill, the committed partner in all this writer's dreams. To John, the best son, for love, joy, and road trips. For Vicky and Chet, sister and brother of the heart. Treasures. Yeah, Cujo. Fuzzy outlaw. You, too.

Much gratitude:

Poisoned Pen Press. Sherpas for my high-altitude journey. Lifesavers, all: Annette Rogers, Barbara Peters, Rob Rosenwald, Diane DiBiase, Holli Roach, Beth Deveny, Suzan Baroni, Raj Dayal, and Michael Barson, And of course, the "PPP Posse" of authors, a warm, kind circle of support.

My agent, Victoria Skurnick, for wisdom and patience. Even more wonderful in person.

Tina Whittle for reading the first of many final drafts, for solid advice from Day 1, and for the blessings.

Stacey Vaselaney, of SLV Public Relations, for PR miracles and fun. Meredith Pangrace, of MAP Creative for my beautiful website, and Bill, patient (mostly) webmaster.

Mary Lucille DeBerry— eagle eye on every line and hours devoted to protecting me from embarrassing myself. For raising the bar.

Thrity Umigar for being there and being you.

My Sisters in Crime, near and far. The tribe.

My book groups: You let me be "your author." And a launch party, complete with friends, flowers, and wine? A high point in a writer's life.

Bob Robinson, Car Man, for expertise and general encouragement, and Tech Guy, Chad Parker, for helping me create a tiny explosion in the plot. Bob, I assume you can start your car remotely?

Joe Valencic. (Jože Valenčič.) For helping me discover Lisa Cole's Slovenian roots.

Tim Ash and Claude Brewer for research on scrapping.

Mark Valentine for turning my debut novel into a leather-bound work of art.

Steve Gluskin for Braille and cows.

Vicky Shorts. Without that AAA map of Cleveland, everybody would have been lost. Especially me.

The sustenance of friendship! Elaine, Bob, Doug,

Thom, Laura, Maura, Kathy, Dan, Joe, Pat, and all the Lake-Dweller Neighbors of Shore Acres. For the "I Know Annie Hogsett the Author" Tee-Shirt Conspirators, and The Ripley Yippees, who baked me cookies in the shape of pencils. To Ms. Cece, of course, for turning Author Annie into a toddler Halloween costume. Truly, you all made this an amazing year.

And certainly not least, to Linn Raney for saying to me a while back, "I never go up Taylor. Way too many traffic lights...." Thanks, Linn.

Chapter One
Friday, February 24

Lady Obsession kills. She dumps the body of the climber into the blue crevasse. Chokes the arteries of the gourmand. Strangles the reluctant object of desire. Sometimes she kills by accident.
Sometimes she kills by design.
Sometimes, Obsession is a murderer's best friend.

Not every obsession is grand. Lloyd Bunker was driven by his need to avoid stoplights. Perhaps he couldn't bear the moments of self-criticism that pounced on him at any pause in his forward motion. Maybe Lloyd's demons could really get at him when he was backed up in traffic at the intersection known to the locals as Five Points, where East 152nd, St. Clair, and Ivanhoe come together in the shadow of Collinwood High.

He was happy to enumerate, to anyone who would stand still for it, the painful statistics: If you were heading south on 152nd, the total wait would be one minute, forty-five.

"And what's worse," he'd continue, the light of recollection firing his eyes, "that includes a full twenty-second lead allowed to oncoming vehicles, and all you can do is sit there and watch everybody else get to go. And don't get me started about just missing the light and having to sit through the whole thing twice."

Lloyd's fingers would flex as he related this, as if drumming on an invisible steering wheel. Most people, even people who liked Lloyd okay, even the one or two who actually loved him, would murmur something sympathetic at this revelation and back away. Many of them knew he had similar numbers for intersections all over town.

On the night in question, Lloyd was told to pick up a package at an address off Euclid Avenue in Euclid. He liked how the avenue and the city names were the same. "Symmetrical," he mused about it to himself. Satisfying how that all matched up.

The waiting was making him jumpy. Lloyd hated leaving the GTO outside unattended. They weren't making cars like his anymore. It was the nicest thing Lloyd had ever owned. A total classic. 1967. V-8.

440. Black vinyl, bucket seats. "Linden Green" exterior. He didn't think of it as green, though. Green was for grass. Linden was the name of a tree and the tree's color wasn't all that good either. He'd looked it up. Online had images of everything. No matter what anybody called the color, Lloyd's GTO was the color of wind. Or rushing water, maybe. Fast like that. Pontiac should have come up with a better name.

He shivered. This place was haunted by the ghosts of too many stolen cars.

The minutes ticked by while he stood, feeling like a goddam jackass, on the freezing, damp concrete. He was a courier tonight, they'd said, and it seemed to him that the courier should get more respect. Even if he wasn't permitted to know what he was courier-ing. He'd always felt, his whole life, that he'd come up painfully short in the Respect Department. Sometimes he could still hear his dad say, "*You're pathetic, Lloyd. What's the matter with you?*" He said that to himself sometimes, too. It made his eyes burn and his chest clench up when he thought how unfair—

But here at last was the man with the upfront money.

The envelope was fat. Lloyd had to stop himself from checking to see if it was all there. He'd never done a courier job before, but the deal was sweet. Whatever they were putting in the trunk of his car must be worth a lot to somebody. All he had to do was drive it down to Bratenahl, meet the guy, turn over the package, and the whole ten grand would be his, tax-free. It crossed his mind again that the logic, or lack thereof, of this plan might spell T-R-O-U-B-L-E. But he'd said yes and, anyway, he was already caught up in mapping his route.

The quick and easy way to get to the address would be to turn right onto Euclid, go a couple of miles, turn right on Noble, then right onto 152nd, and roll all the way to Lake Shore. From there, it was straight and smooth to Bratenahl and the gate, the long driveway, the porte cochère, where his package would be unloaded.

He'd looked up porte cochère so as not to appear ignorant, but as far as he could tell it was a glorified carport. He'd done a test run. Piece of cake. Empty-looking house. Lake view.

But now, at 11:45 on a Friday night at the end of February, everything grim and frozen, with a thin fog of snow in the air, that plan didn't have much appeal. For one thing, at the very heart of that route was the goddam Five Points Intersection.

Plus, with the Cleveland Fifth District Police Headquarters parked, like, two blocks away, and who-knew-what in the trunk of his GTO, Lloyd could be stuck in a risky situation for a minimum of one minute, twenty-five.

A lifetime.

So Lloyd altered the flight plan he'd filed with the guys. When he got to the Noble intersection, he kept going straight. Due to the late hour, a lot of the cross streets were blinking amber. Plus he proceeded to hit it lucky a couple of times. He was booking on toward downtown. Except for one pair of dim headlights behind him, he had the road to himself.

The snow picked up with bigger flakes and the swirl of rising wind. He'd better pay attention to how he stepped on the brakes now, but—good news!—he mostly didn't have to even slow down. He was moving smoothly, slightly over the thirty-five-miles-per-hour limit. Green. Green. Green.

Occasionally he pushed his luck just a bit for an amber, but so far, he was pitching a perfect game. A near thing at the corner of Euclid and Mayfield, but all good. Lucky. His heart was pumping, his fingers, lightly resting on the steering wheel, tingled pleasantly. He felt alert, happy, almost powerful. Definitely in command.

He noticed, with a little grin, that the car behind him was closing the distance. Probably wanted to see what it was like to do an all-green run with a pro.

When he passed Severance Hall, before the turn to Chester, Lloyd told himself that when this job was done, he'd take Loretta to a concert of The Cleveland Orchestra. You didn't refer to it as the Cleveland Symphony if you didn't want to sound like a dumbass. Lloyd knew that for sure. He could learn.

He'd buy himself a good suit. Fancy shoes with a little bit of lift to them. A fine, thick topcoat that would camouflage the spare tire. He'd always felt ill at ease, almost scared, around rich people. But not this time he wouldn't. Loretta would be impressed, too.

The sad feeling was sneaking up on him. She was so pretty. So smart and sweet. All the women who'd turned Lloyd down, and suddenly here was Loretta, saying she loved him. "Her Lloyd." Even though she knew him pretty well. When he took her to the concert, he'd say it back this time. *I love you, too, Loretta.* He blinked. His eyes were burning again.

And, anyway, how many of those classical dumbasses ever had five-thousand dollars in their glove compartments? Not too damn many, he figured.

Severance was dark. The richies were tucked in all safe in their mansions by now.

He eased down onto Martin Luther King Drive. Right turn on red with a perpetual green arrow. Sweet. Still going strong. The perfection of this run must be an omen. Lloyd's life was on a roll, ready for a big change.

He sailed past the VA Hospital and its shadowy parking garages. Lloyd never rode roller coasters and hollered woo-hoo, but he imagined he could be having that kind of moment now. He wasn't one of those stupid, crazy, out-of-control guys, though. This was dead serious.

In his preoccupation with his mission, Lloyd was oblivious to the beauty of MLK on this night. How the boulevard snaked through Rockefeller Park, tracking alongside the icy black coil of Doan Brook. How the massive stone bridges hovered. Under the dim glow of streetlights, the statues and monuments in the cultural gardens were apparitions cloaked in snow. In India's garden, Gandhi, frozen midstride with his staff in hand, wore a robe of white. None of this touched Lloyd because he was about to realize his lifetime goal of a one-hundred-percent Green Light Run.

He'd forgotten about the five-thousand dollars in the glove compartment and the five-thousand he

had coming. Of his package he had no consciousness at all. He knew that, after the VA, there was
one, single, solitary light on all of MLK and that
was before the last bridge. No matter if that light
was yellow, or even dead red when it came into his
view. On a night like tonight he could slow down
until it turned. If it was green, he could simply
speed up. His heart was racing now.

He tried to calm his breathing, not think too far
ahead. As he rounded a turn, he could make out
the last bridge. The light was red. Good. That light
was only fifteen seconds. An easy stretch of road
with the brook a meandering shadow on his right.
He was golden. He slowed, just enough. Nothing
could stop him now—

As if in response to that thought, the unthink-
able happened.

The GTO made an odd, muffled sound like a
small backfire, and the engine died.

Chapter Two
Saturday, June 17

I read a book once about Einstein's $E=mc^2$ formula. Before that, I'd never understood that you can't go faster than the speed of light. No. Truly. You cannot. I assumed that Einstein foolishly ignored the fact that you can always press down a little harder on the accelerator. Apparently not. The laws of the universe do not allow for this.

Period.

I have a corollary to that law: There has got to be a thread-count of sheets that is the most threads you can ever jam into a single sheet. After that, add a single teeny thread more, and nuclear fission or fusion, one or the other, occurs. However, that maxed-out sheet, if you can afford it, is the very epitome of sensuosity. I know "sensuosity" is not a real word, but there's a certain level of sensuousness that requires the invention of a whole new vocabulary.

My significant other, Thomas Bennington III, PhD, can afford a Speed of Light Formula Sheet such as the one I've described. In fact, as a five-hundred-fifty-million-dollar-MondoMegaJackpot-winner, he could probably afford a stack of sheets of this quality about a mile high. That's how crazy rich Tom is. And I am, by default. Since I share his sheets and much, much more.

I met this Thomas the III, hot, blind, associate professor of English literature, in the middle of Lake Shore Boulevard in Cleveland, Ohio, where he was standing dazed and vulnerable after being honked at by an impatient woman in a Hummer. I rescued Tom and his groceries, plus his lottery ticket, from the street, and took him and his sexy white tee-shirt home on the bus to my run-down but charming cottage.

That first twenty-four hours changed everything. It was the Bulldozer of Fate. We had dinner and fell immediately, if not in love, definitely in like and absolutely, no question, in lust, and got started kissing out by the edge of my lakeside cliff, within the sound of my neighbor Ralph's annoyingly loud TV.

The kissing which, let me say, was everything kissing should be, got all interruptus when Ralph's TV blared out a number Tom recognized as the exact one he'd played to prove to a kid that you would not win the MondoMegaJackpot, even if you picked your very own, special, lucky numbers. Oops.

After that, the Mondo Ball really got rolling, and before the night was out, there was mayhem spread all over the place. But the Bulldozer of Fate (hereinafter, BOF) also delivered another opportunity for kissing and much, much more before the dawn went ahead and broke on the next day, which is when the news of the murdering began to break, too.

Before the BOF moved on, Tom and I were in love. That hadn't changed. We were also in danger most of the time and that hadn't changed either, but it was not as much in our faces right at that moment as it was during our first Mondo month. No surprise, however, that Jackpot = Chaos in Tom's universe. I myself am ambivalent—on the more positive end of the scale.

I now knew, however, that, great sheets aside, there are many things unlimited money can't buy. Real security, for one. Another day of life if someone is holding a gun on you. True love.

On a more mundane level, it could buy me a world-class glamour haircut, but, ten minutes post-salon, Glamour Girl would be gone. Again. And there'd be the ordinary, brown-eyed, friendly-as-a-golden-retriever-and-not-entirely-a-dog Alice Jane Harper. Cute, yes. Glamorous, no. But, once upon a recent time, I didn't have enough money to get my car fixed and now here I was with a Tom Bennington. The Third. PhD.

I could deal.

Back to the bedding news. We owned only two sets of the $E=mc^2$ sheets. One in white. One in a sage-y green, which I particularly admired. Tom didn't care about the color but the man appreciated thread count. And the senuousity of it, too.

The sheets are pertinent to this report of the first case of the newly established T&A Detective Agency—of which I, Allie Harper, am The "A" and The Recording Secretary—because this case began for me right there between those sumptuous sheets. With yet another extremely disconcerting interruption.

It was eight a.m. on a gorgeous, warm Saturday morning in June. Tom and I were lying side by side between the aforementioned sheets in our temporary, but over-the-top-vast-and-luxurious rented mansion in Bratenahl, Ohio, a highly upscale, lakeside village, surrounded on three sides by the City of Cleveland. A watery-smelling breeze was moving the curtains gently in and out of the open windows, and I could hear Lake Erie right outside, murmuring a few suggestions about some wicked stuff Tom and I could be getting into soon.

Since this report is mostly for my own benefit—and possible memoirs—I should make a note here that if you are lying naked between Einstein-quality bedding, not only is the fabric that touches you thicker and smoother than anything you can imagine, but your own skin feels incredibly velvety, too. The infinitesimal interface between your skin and those sheets just vibrates with electrical heat.

Trust me.

Add to that the thought that your skin—all of it—is about to meet the skin—all of it—of someone you're absolutely out-of-your-mind in love with?

Red alert, Alice Harper. But in a good way.

Imagine: I was lying on my back, allowing the top sheet to caress my entire front. Tom was lying on his front under that same top sheet. He reached out his arm and slipped one warm, highly welcome palm onto my bare, pink, sheet-caressed front. I let him do this. Gladly. Tom may be blind, but he always knows exactly where his hands are.

I am shameless.

"Mmm," he proposed.

"Mmm, Mmm," I replied, stretching deliciously so as to improve contact.

And then?

The doorbell chimed.

Chapter Three

The chiming of that bell was the death knell of a unique, irreplaceable interlude. But Otis was on door-duty, and Otis was constitutionally unable to turn anybody away unless they brandished a gun or looked otherwise suspicious.

I could hear his deep voice and a higher-pitched voice. The cadence and the pitch of this voice suggested to me that the woman talking was upset about something. Otis answered her, his chocolatey bass a steady counterpoint to her squeaky, staccato soprano. They went back and forth like that for a minute or so. Then I heard the front door close and Otis' heavy feet tromping up our majestic, sweeping staircase. Drawing near.

I got out of bed, with an unhappy glance at the handsome back of my beloved, grabbed my robe, and poked my head out the door of the master suite, trying to look sleepy rather than frustrated. I don't think Otis was fooled for a second, but we glossed over that by mutual unspoken agreement.

"Ma'am—" he began. Otis was a Cleveland cop for twenty years before he saved my life in a parking garage, and became our bodyguard and a fully licensed private investigator in the State of Ohio. He was accustomed to referring to any woman, no matter how skanky and out of control, as "ma'am."

For my part, when Otis called me ma'am, I was afraid he was about to ask me to step away from my car and keep my hands where he could see them. I'd mentioned this to him, but old habits die hard. Reminded by the quizzical arch of my brow, he backpedaled.

"Allie. There's a lady here to see you. Says she's a former colleague of yours. Ms. Loretta Coates? I woulda told her you were busy—" At this, Otis and I both diverted our gazes to somewhere safe.

"But she's cryin'."

I clenched my teeth. This was not going to be a quick and easy fix. Loretta Coates, at her best, could be high-maintenance and time-consuming. Loretta Coates crying? Could take all day.

"Give me a minute, Otis," I sighed. "I'll be right down. And can you make some coffee, please?

He nodded. "Okay, Allie."

Fifteen minutes later, I was dressed and sitting across from Loretta in the downstairs study as if nothing had happened.

Which it had not.

The sunlight from the front windows stretched out in bright oblongs on the Persian carpet—"Priceless," according to the rental agent. It reminded me of the ugly red-and-brown thrift-shop paisley dress I hated when I was about fourteen, but I hadn't mentioned that to the agent. Just nodded politely and made a mental note to drink only red or brown things in that room.

Out back, Lake E was a steaming blue. Loretta and I both had big mugs of brown coffee. She wasn't drinking hers. She was telling me about Lloyd, her boyfriend, who'd disappeared one snowy night in February, and who, she assumed, was dead.

"At first," she was saying, "I figured he'd taken one of his crazy routes home that night and run off the road somewhere slick. Lloyd has this obsession with avoiding stoplights. I even broke up with him one time for about six weeks because he took us all the way to Strongsville on the highway to get us to a party in Chardon."

I reviewed this itinerary, using the map in my head. The phrase "way 'round Robin Hood's barn" came to mind. Understatement. I also noticed that Loretta was vacillating between past and present tense when she talked about Lloyd. Which suggested to me that, in Loretta's mind, he was sometimes dead. Sometimes only missing.

She paused, sniffling wetly for about the fourteenth time, as Otis—thank you, God—appeared with a box of tissues cradled in his large brown hands. She looked up to him in gratitude, took one, honked apologetically, and crumpled it daintily in her hand. Otis set the box down on the end table, said, "I'll just leave these, Allie," and withdrew.

Lucky him.

Loretta picked up the thread. "He was kind of OCD about that, you know? I swear, he could tell you the exact duration in seconds of every stoplight in Cleveland. It drives me absolutely batshit crazy. He was a terrible pain in the ass. But I loved him. I did. I'm pretty sure he loved me back. And he's dead. That's all there is to it. He has to be dead."

She plucked another tissue from Otis' box and pressed it to her eyes. I was nodding along, still composing my face around my surprise at having heard Loretta say "batshit" and "pain in the ass."

Loretta worked at the Memorial-Nottingham Branch of the Cleveland Public Library. For a while after I moved to Collinwood from Shaker Heights, having righteously divorced D.B. Harper, dickhead lawyer and philanderer extraordinaire, and before I met Tom and became happy and accessory-to-a-massive-jackpot all in one day, I was a part-time librarian there. At Memorial-Nottingham, Loretta was a fixture.

She was mid-forties and pretty, but her attractiveness was impaired by the fact that she looked worried. A lot worried. Most of the time. Her blue eyes were perpetually widened by concern. Her eyebrows tucked in toward each other in a tiny wrinkly frown. Her lips, a lovely bow when she relaxed enough to smile, stayed pursed up.

Loretta worried about everything. She worried about global warming and crime lords. She worried that the teenagers who stopped by the library after school only checked out DVDs or that, when they checked out books, they chose the ones she found inappropriate for teenagers. She worried that her biological clock was approaching figurative midnight, and that it might rain before she figured out whether she'd left a window open at her apartment so she could call a neighbor and ask her to close it. She worried that the neighbor might not be home.

Like I said. Every. Thing.

This was a problem for me because being around a worrier *par excellence* like Loretta tended to drag my normally upbeat, confident self down a negative rat hole. When Loretta was puckering, I would catch myself surveilling the History & Geography section for crime lords, and feeling annoyed with myself. And with Loretta.

Of course, Loretta was entirely justified in being worried about Lloyd. I myself experienced an extra stab of concern when she said, "And, Allie, I had this feeling he was up to something. Something that was making him too excited and happy for his own good."

I probed for more info from the "up to something" index, but she seized another tissue and wept into it some more. When she emerged, pale and bloodshot, she could only shake her head in response to my "Something? Like what?" questions, which I phrased three or four different ways. Until I ran out of new ways. And patience.

At that moment, I heard Tom coming down the grand staircase with the smooth assurance of a man who's honed his remaining four senses and added on what he calls the "blind man Spidey sense." That one has proved to be almost superhuman from time to time. But mostly, he's just really paying attention.

His arrival was a welcome interruption. Loretta was distracted by Tom's tall, tan, fit, and handsome appearance—dimple and sexy white tee-shirt included—and the irresistible attraction of his intense interest. Nothing is so captivating to an unhappy human being as someone who truly, deeply listens to what's on her mind. It helps that Tom empathizes at the drop of a hat. And, as noted, he is way hot. One look and Loretta stopped sobbing.

I gave Tom the short version of Loretta's concerns about Lloyd maybe being over his head and getting into some sort of trouble, and he pressed her for "anything at all you can remember."

For Tom, she thought extra-hard.

"I don't have anything specific. You need to know this about Lloyd. He was the sweetest man. He had a kind heart. But something made him feel… oh…not good enough. Even though he was very smart, he had a problem with that.

"A couple of weeks before he disappeared, I sort of blurted out that I loved him. And he—I could see he really wanted to say he loved me, too. But he couldn't. Right after that he started talking about being more of the kind of person I deserved. Who could give me things. Take me places. Allie, you know me. I don't want to go places. I'm scared to travel. But I think those things Lloyd was talking about…they usually cost a lot of money."

She was crying again and I was wishing I could go back and be a better friend to Loretta in our Mem-Nott days.

She got out another tissue. "That's all I know. Just that bad feeling of Lloyd trying something dangerous and maybe doing that for me. I can't remember anything more specific. Except feeling terribly, terribly worried. You know?"

I knew. I nodded and she told Tom and me about the last time Lloyd was seen on Planet Earth.

"He was on Euclid, headed west, at 11:52 p.m., Friday, February 24th. He ran the stoplight at Euclid and Mayfield. The flashy camera got him."

Chapter Four

When I'd first suggested—while under the influence of love and champagne—that Tom and I might become the T&A Detective Agency and use his money to help people solve their mysteries, he recommended we put my initial first, so as to prevent folks from assuming we only investigate in strip clubs.

By now, though, we realized that we would never be a detective agency with a logo and a business card, so I decided we should leave it the way it was. It gave us something to chuckle about. Which is always an asset in your business name, as far as I'm concerned.

The T&A was a work in progress. Apart from locating a missing Volvo for my former landlady and best friend forever, Margo—ill-advised teen joyride in the first degree—we'd yet to have a real assignment.

Therefore, The Lloyd Case was big. And an excellent example of the sort of case we had in mind. Mysteries of the heart. Answers for the kind of unanswered questions that leave cavernous holes in people's lives. And since we would never have to worry about running our agency in the black, we figured we could make up the rules as we went.

One obstacle to my plans for free-for-all rulemaking was Otis. Tom was the T, and I was the A, but Otis was the only actual P.I. His status and expertise as a former Cleveland Police Officer made him a shoo-in for accreditation. At that moment, Otis was the man standing between me and my rightful *cartes blanches* for rule-making and breaking. Otis actually knew the rules, and he fully expected us to follow them. Right then, I was thinking of a rule I wanted to break that very afternoon.

After Loretta left, Otis, Tom, and I convened in the breakfast room to discuss what the T&A Detective Agency could do to help Loretta find out what happened to her poor, stoplight-obsessed, almost-certainly-dead boyfriend.

While Tom and I enjoyed some waffles and bacon with juice and coffee, and Otis had his usual spartan yogurt and fruit, I was describing to Tom the view of the lake, which was shimmering like a cocktail dress in the mid-morning light.

View Narration is part of my job description in our relationship. I give him my eyes. He's responsible for giving me his ears and his sixth sense for knowing when someone—unfortunately, me in particular—is telling a big fat fib.

I love my job.

Just then, though, he was frowning. "A cocktail dress? I'm having a little trouble visualizing."

"You do remember sequins?"

I said this, knowing that Tom could rely on an extensive inventory of things he'd seen before he'd lost his sight to a stroke that doctors called "anomalous" in a twenty-five-year-old, but which did him permanent damage anyway.

He grinned. "Ah. Sequins. Thank you, Allie."

Otis was frowning. "Our job is to find out what happened to Mr. Bunker so Ms. Coates can have peace of mind. But we don't have much to go on. Okay. We know his car was on Euclid at the intersection with Mayfield at 11:52 on the night of February 24th." He shook his head sadly. "That's it."

"If that's what we've got, let's take a look." I swiveled on my chair and opened the top drawer of the breakfront that stood like an icon of French civilization against the wall. On top of the impressive array of silver cutlery which came with the house was a map of the City of Cleveland. It's hard to find a paper map these days. I procured this one—perhaps the last in the known world—from the Cleveland Office of the Triple A. I valued it more than the silver spoons, which didn't belong to me anyhow.

I spread out my map on the table. "Help me think about where Lloyd might have gone."

I placed my finger at the intersection of Euclid and Mayfield. It marked the epicenter of University Circle, with its hospital complex, Severance Hall, the Cleveland Museum of Art, and, of course, Case Western Reserve University—whose University it is the Circle of.

I have to confess that at that moment, in my skeptical mind, the map was about as untrustworthy as a Ouija board. It's a big world. How could we ever know where Lloyd got himself to that night? My confidence level was low. I was considering how easy it was to *think about* being an amateur detective, compared to actually needing to figure something out.

"Let's at least assume that Lloyd was behind the wheel. Otherwise…" I moved on.

"So. All we know for sure about Lloyd is that he had an unusual aversion to stoplights and that he was here." I tapped the map. "Where he actually ran one. Not by much, I don't think. Somebody who organizes his life around not wanting to stop at an intersection obviously believes he's supposed to stop on red. I bet he was sure he made that one.

"Tom? This is your campus, your territory. You don't drive it every day, but you don't have to think about driving when you're there, and you sure seem to know where everything is. Tell us what you see, too."

The very first day we met, right before we were run down by the Mondo BOF and the onset of true love, Tom suggested that we agree to "cut to the chase on all the sight metaphors." This saves a tremendous amount of conversational gyration.

"Close your eyes," he answered me. "Let's build us a mental picture."

I obeyed, allowing myself a quick peek at Otis to make sure he was playing along.

Unnecessary precaution. Otis' calm black Buddha face was dutifully closed up for serious concentration. Back behind my eyelids, I smiled into the murky night of Friday, February 24th. Otis and Tom were pretty much always on the same page.

"I'll start," I said. "We know it's dark. And probably snowing. I got that from Loretta and I checked online. Two to four inches and another two to four after midnight. We can be confident that Lloyd stayed on Euclid here. Since he ran the light."

I squeezed my eyes tighter. "It's late, it's dark, maybe the streets are getting slick. If you keep going, there's Church of the Covenant on your right and then Severance Hall."

I pictured them both, majestic and beautiful, shrouded in falling snow. Euclid Avenue, four lanes wide, stretched out ahead, unfurling itself westward toward downtown. On a night like that, the landmark buildings of the Cleveland Clinic would be glowing. Hazy but iconic all the same.

"The Lloyd we know wouldn't have turned up the hill, it's a snare of lights and slowdowns."

Tom was nodding along. "Agreed. Stop and go. He could have turned right at Severance onto East Boulevard. Go that way and you can circle by the Art Museum and on down to MLK. It's pretty narrow and winding, but there are no lights until you get to the VA. He might have turned in there."

"Well, for sure, I don't see him heading on down-town." Otis threw in. "You have to stop a good bit, no matter if traffic is light. Even if he were headed somewhere in the city, I think he'd turn at Chester and take MLK because…"

I reached out, found his arm, and gripped it tight as realization struck. I knew that light. I myself loved its "free pass to MLK" arrow a lot. Now it was pointing the way. Here was a sign and a portent.

I got a shiver. Our Ouija board was working, after all.

My eyes popped open and February morphed back into June. I tapped the magic map again.

"Otis, you are a genius. And, anyhow, whether Lloyd turned at Severance or here, there'd only be a couple lights at the VA Hospital intersection. That time of night he could adjust his approach and be home free to the Shoreway. I think there's only one light total on MLK between Chester and the lake. It's all the way at the end."

"And so many places down there for a man to disappear." Tom mused.

We sat and thought on that one for a while.

Chapter Five

Otis rumbled into our thoughtful silence. "Maybe we don't know anything for sure, but at least we can ask Tony about any reports from MLK between the VA and the Shoreway that night. We already need him to find out if anything turned up on the missing person's report Loretta filed back in February."

Tony Valerio was a Cleveland cop, and he'd been a major player in last summer's MondoMega crime-spree drama. In spite of his extreme aggravation with my meddling in official police business, we'd emerged as somewhat uneasy allies. He liked Tom. He already knew Otis. He could just about put up with me.

We wanted Tony on our side, but I also needed to keep him out of my sandbox for another couple of hours.

I cleared my throat. Tom and Otis shot me simultaneous facial expressions of sudden, profound suspicion.

"Uh. Before we call Tony? Loretta had a key to Lloyd's house. That's how she got his ticket after he disappeared. She left her key here with me." I paused to craft my next couple of sentences for maximum nonchalance.

"Maybe we should go there today? Since Loretta gave me her key." I arranged my expression to exude nonchalance and glanced at Otis. Sideways.

"That would be legal, wouldn't it, Otis? Since Loretta has given us her permission. And her key…"

I was mentally reviewing the number of times I'd said "key" so far. It seemed weak to me, but that key was all I had. I let my voice trail away and went to silent running.

Otis scowled into the bottom of his fruit and yogurt bowl. "That's a very gray area, I'd say."

I locked my gaze on him until he looked up, met my eyes, and caved. "Okay. All right. No apparent downside. It's not like anybody's tearin' up the neighborhoods searching for Lloyd. I figure the place has already been eliminated, assuming they even found somebody to go there. Tony would agree. Chances are, if we don't find Lloyd, nobody

ever will. We can go look around without getting
into trouble. I just hope—"

I paid him off with my warmest love-you-Otis
face and moved on. Briskly. "We'll need you to
drive, Otis"

Signed. Sealed. Delivered.

A word about the official T&A vehicle. Tom
didn't feel that money was the absolute root of all
evil, exactly, but he'd had plenty of bad experiences
of late to make him leery of its temptations.

His blindness rendered him mostly impervious
to the lure of the glittery, flashy, and overpriced.
However, he did have some weaknesses that I was
more than willing to exploit. When it came to
the selection of a car for our transportation and
security, he was as vulnerable as any man to the
voluptuous embrace of a luxury automobile. This
went double for Otis, who always secretly envisioned himself either being or transporting a rock
star.

All of which explains how we came into possession of the Ice Black Cadillac Escalade. Bose
sound system and the leathery fragrance of luxury
for Tom. Navigation and general cushiness for me.
Every single thing about it for Otis. Besides, it
looked very safe. Actually, it looked impenetrable.
I like that in a car.

● ● ● ● ●

Lloyd lived in a one-family house on Ridpath Avenue in Collinwood. A street of modest-sized houses, mostly carefully maintained. Flower boxes. Bicycles in the yards. One notable junker car, an ancient Chevy sedan with an insouciant mustache of rust emblazoned across its hood, parked facing the wrong way. Older folks walking their dogs and sitting on their porches. Kids everywhere. Idle hands on a warm summer afternoon.

I noticed I felt more at home here than in Bratenahl. I also noticed that the Escalade was broadcasting "movie stars or serious drug deal" up and down the block. Almost before Otis silenced the purr of the big motor, the vehicle was mobbed by eager boys and girls. Otis sighed. I knew he was envisioning ten pairs of grubby hands pawing his meticulously applied shine.

He stepped out and loomed over the kids in all his big, dark, well-dressed officialness. Otis still knew how to "do cop" when he needed to. The children were not easily intimidated—they were growing up in Collinwood. But they stepped back.

Otis made eye contact with the tallest of the boys and signaled him to move closer.

The kid stepped up.

Otis leaned down. "Nice car." Not a question.

The boy nodded.

"Give me your hand."

This was almost too much. The boy took a step back but then made contact with the force field of his cohorts behind him. His reputation was at stake. He braced his shoulders and reached forward. Otis took the small brown hand in his huge one and gently turned it palm up. "What's your name?"

"A.J."

"You know about fingerprints, right, A.J.?"

The boy bobbed his head vigorously.

"That's good. Well, look."

He selected the kid's index finger and placed it gently but firmly on the shiny surface, gave it the obligatory side-to-side roll, and then returned the hand to its owner.

"See that?"

A.J. peered at the smudged print on the gleaming Ice Black door. He nodded again, his expression hovering between fear and excitement.

Otis nodded, too.

"That's your own fingerprint, A.J. Nobody else's anywhere is like yours. If you never put your hands where they're not supposed to be in this world, your prints won't ever get you in trouble. I'd like that. Wouldn't you?"

The boy eyed the smudge, worriedly, and looked back up at Otis. "I guess so."

Otis pulled an immaculate hanky from his back pocket and buffed away the print.

"Now. You and your friends are welcome to admire this car. But not to touch it. And if you do, I'll know. And don't assume you can just rub out your prints, like I did. Somebody always misses one. Okay?"

"Okay."

"Good. You're in charge, A.J. Don't let your friends do anything stupid."

He glanced at Tom and me where we stood, well back of the car ourselves, somewhat intimidated by this performance. I was resisting the impulse to bury my own guilty hands in my pockets. Otis acknowledged our deference with a satisfied nod. "We should go."

We went.

Chapter Six

Lloyd's house was on the north side of the street and differentiated from its neighbors by its lawn, a tangle of grass at least a foot tall. The three of us stood on the front walk like we were waiting for an invitation.

Everything about the scene spoke of months of neglect. The windows were opaque with grime. The blinds, splotched and sagging, were pulled all the way down. The porch was layered with the debris of winter, the pollen of spring, and the dust of summer. A heap of newspapers by the door was slowly recycling itself. For at least a couple of weeks, the *Cleveland Plain Dealer* delivery person must have pretended Lloyd was still reading his paper.

The old-fashioned porch swing appeared functional but pathetic, nonetheless. Behind it, a climbing rose still scrambled up its trellis, still blooming, still dispensing its perfume, as if it remembered that happier, prettier days had transpired here.

I imagined Loretta showing up in early March, before the rose offered one bright spot of hope. Finding Lloyd not around. Worrying.

The street was all quiet now. The children were standing as close as they dared to the Escalade, but even they were subdued, like visitors viewing the body at a wake. I could hear the shush of cars on 156th and a bird talking some birdly trash, but the rest was silence.

I was experiencing the eyes-boring-into-you feeling I'd learned to call "Creepy Eye" when the MondoMegaMadness was in full swing last summer. The watchers may have been out of sight, but I could feel their gaze, fixed on the back of my neck. I was also entertaining the very uncomfortable awareness that Lloyd was missing and only presumed dead. What if he were at home and receiving visitors? Alive and waiting, armed against intruders. Or home and dead. Possibly long, long dead. Either way, I was not reassured.

Tom was feeling the tension, too. "Allie. There's something…"

He was doing what I was learning to think of

as "Tom's Full-Body-Listening." Stripped of the supreme distraction of sight, he was free to absorb everything in his environment—sound, smell, taste, vibration, proximity, and much, much more.

"I'm a bat," he'd say without embarrassment. "I can't see. But I feel what's around me. A lot better than most sighted people do. I have my own radar."

This bat thing always sent me straight to, "Mmm, Dracula!" and that thought would devolve into fantasies of Tom biting my neck and changing me into a creature who would live forever in his darkness, probably naked, and be able to make love to him for all eternity. I never talked about this idea but I believed he intuitively knew.

However, right now, Tom wasn't using his blind radar on me.

"I hear…water. And there's a smell, too. It's thick. Musty. Woodsy. I can—I can taste it."

I took a deep breath. I could smell it now, too, and I did not want to taste it. I fished in my purse for the key. Otis stepped up, hanky in hand, to turn the knob. I wondered if his junior detectives were noting that Otis was the enemy of all prints everywhere today.

The door was designed to open inward, but it was currently hung up on something. Otis put his shoulder to it and pushed until it gave way enough that we could see inside. The smell rushed out to meet us.

Mildew, mold, decay, thick and pungent enough to make my eyes sting. And the sound of water. Water dripping. Water everywhere. It trickled down the walls from the second story. It stood in puddles on the floor. Saturating—no, make that supersaturating—everything. The wallpaper was peeling right off, the plaster under it dissolved, revealing bare lathe. Sodden carpet and swollen flooring blocked the door. Ruin everywhere.

Otis was the first to speak. "Damn. He's been scrapped."

Chapter Seven

My heart sank as I took in the moldering destruction. The expression "scene has been compromised" didn't do this justice. Anything I hoped to find—telltale paperwork, incriminating answering machine messages, any useful anything at all—was toast. Or whatever the soggy opposite of toast might be.

Plus, even if I might be game to slog on in there and have a look-see, Otis now had me firmly by the arm.

"No, Allie. It might have not been a crime scene before, but it totally is now. I have to call this in. And if you put a foot inside that door, it will be obvious that you did that. On the floor. On you. You don't want that kind of attention for something that's going to get you nowhere anyway."

"Hell, Otis. Okay. Can we at least sit in the swing until the cops show up?"

He unpacked the slightest suggestion of a smile. "You and Tom can, Allie. I'm not sure it would hold the three of us."

When they arrived, the cops appeared to share Otis' assessment of the usefulness of a premises search. After squeezing in and sloshing around enough to make sure Lloyd was not in residence, they came back out and focused their attention on Otis.

They were deferential to Tom, and didn't regard me with much suspicion. I appreciated that. I'd attracted considerable unfortunate attention up at Fifth District Police Headquarters the previous summer. If Tom was now unofficially identified in the community as "The Blind Mondo," I was for sure "his nutso girlfriend."

They took down some information. They promised to inform City Services about the situation. Then they nodded politely, got back in their squad car, and departed the scene. They did not trouble us—or themselves—with the "And why were you here?" question. I figured Otis was enough for them.

After a few minutes, the neighbors who had been lured out by the arrival of the squad car dispersed. Even the kids were gone by the time we got back to the Escalade. One was still hanging around, though.

A.J. was standing a judicious distance from the SUV, his eyes fixed on Otis. "It was scrappers, wasn't it?"

This got Otis' full attention. He squatted down so they were eye-to-eye. "You saw something."

The boy nodded. "Yeah. Maybe a month ago. Before school let out. Some guys in a beat-up brown van. My mom is part of the Neighborhood Watch thing, but she doesn't watch much. Too busy. But I saw them. And a light was on overnight, too. It was raining a lot that week. Nobody outside to see or hear anything."

"What did the guys look like?"

"Guys. Three or four. One black guy, couple of white. Maybe. I only ever saw their backs as they were leaving. Skinny. Grungy. Boots."

"And you didn't say anything?"

He shrugged. "Didn't want to say and then be wrong and get in trouble for snooping around. Nobody seemed to care."

Otis fished in his jacket pocket and brought out a card. "Listen, A.J., if you see anything else around that house, this is my phone number. Call me. 24/7. Don't DO anything. Guys like that—you don't want to mess with them. Just call me, okay?" He handed the card to the boy who looked at it like it was LeBron's autograph and then tucked it carefully into the pocket of his jeans.

"If I help you sometimes, could I maybe ride in your car?"

"Sure. Your mom would have to say it's okay. But remember what I said about calling me and not DOING anything?"

"I got that part." And he strolled away, cool. Little cucumber. He made me think of Rune, the kid Tom was trying to dissuade from gambling when he bought the one and only lottery ticket of his life.

A.J. showed the same wary intelligence, the same intrepid curiosity that made Rune so great. Rune, who lived in Pittsburgh now with his Aunt Iona, Uncle Clarence, and his four cousins. Hidden away from Mondo notoriety. And danger. Iona arrived at the precise moment Tom and I were hoping to adopt him. Iona was a wonderful lady and it was right for Rune to be with his family, but that was still a sore spot for us. We missed him, but we knew he couldn't be safe with us right now. Not even for a visit.

Tom talked about marriage before the Rune disappointment, but he hadn't mentioned it since. When I applied Allie's Full-Body-Listening, everything I could see, hear, taste, touch told me Tom and I were forever. But it was only natural to ask myself sometimes if I was the blind one in the Allie + Tom equation.

I couldn't inquire about that so instead I jumped to another question that was top of mind. "Otis, what's a scrapper?"

● ● ● ● ●

Ten minutes later we were scrunched into a booth at Chloe's, the diner up on 156th. The lunch crowd was cleared out so it was the three of us with our burgers and handcrafted chips. Afternoon sunlight glinted off the Escalade outside the front window. It rippled artfully down over the sculpted front of Tom's still pristine and awesome white tee. Close enough to touch and yet so far—*Lordy, Allie. Get a grip.*

We respected Otis' desire to eat his Chloe's Special Burger in peace, but he was slowing down now, so Tom repeated my question for me.

"You said Lloyd was scrapped, Otis. And A.J. said the people he saw were scrappers. I've heard of it, but what's scrapped about what we found there? I call it 'drowned.'"

"A mess. That's what it's about, Tom. About folks so screwed up in the head and so desperate they'll trash a whole house—do maybe a hundred-thousand dollars in damage—to pry loose a hundred bucks' worth of scrap metal. They break right into walls. Drag away fixtures, appliances, whatever they can break loose. Sell them for…something. Pennies."

I was having trouble shaking off the sight of dripping walls and green sludge everywhere. "But, Otis, why turn on the water? That seems unnecessarily malicious."

"Nah. Scrappers aren't—" He frowned and fished around for the perfect word. "They mostly aren't aware enough to be malicious. They didn't turn on the water. They just didn't bother to turn it off when they cut into the lines. And it worked well for them. Who's going to slop around in there looking for prints or evidence? The scene is destroyed. Totally."

This sent me right back to how morose I was feeling. How our chances of finding anything more about what happened to Lloyd were slimmer than none. And how I was going to have to break it to Loretta about the house being ruined.

I was staring sadly down at the remains of my lunch and considering a piece of Chloe's peach pie for comfort's sake, when the street door opened and Tom said, "Hello, Tony."

Chapter Eight

I looked up. It was Tony Valerio, all right. In his "I am an officer of the law and you most assuredly are not" uniform. He paused inside the door, hands on hips within easy reach of his weapons—Glock, Mace, Taser, the works. He was packing his stern face, too. Especially for me.

I needed a distraction.

"Tom!" I exclaimed with a cheery interest I did not feel. "How on Earth did you know it was Tony?"

He grinned. "Right after the car door slammed, a guy out front said, 'Hey, Tony.'" He gestured to the vacant spot in our booth. "Have a seat. You want something to eat? I believe Allie is thinking about pie."

This did amaze me. "How did you know?"

"Babe. I do not have to see you to know what you're thinking."

Too true.

Valerio slid into the booth next to Otis. The monobrow formed a veritable ledge of disapproval. "Word has it you were apprehended at another crime scene, Ms. Harper."

"'Apprehended' is not a fair word."

"You got a fairer one?"

"I think it would be more appropriate to mention that when we merely showed up on Mr. Bunker's porch and discovered that intruders had been in the house, I encouraged Otis to alert the proper authorities."

"Merely showed up? With a key."

"Mr. Bunker's—I paused. "Girlfriend" didn't do justice to what Loretta had been to Lloyd, or what his memory was to her now, but maybe I was a bit oversensitive on that point. "Mr. Bunker's friend, Loretta Coates, a former colleague of mine at the library, gave me the key so we could check to make sure—" Tricky here. "—to make sure he wasn't… uh…home. Would you like some pie, Tony? The peach is really good here."

"I'm going to say one more time that getting mixed up in official police business is a leading cause of death amongst wannabee P.I.'s."

"I would take that very much to heart, Tony, if I wanted to be a P.I. I do not."

I felt comfortable with this. It was even the truth, for a change. I wanted to do all my investigating while standing safely in the shadow of my real P.I., under the protection of his gun, with no need at all for any gun of my own. I wanted the investigating done by me to be more of an intellectual adventure. I'd already been shot once and I hadn't liked it.

Reassured to be wearing the righteous armor of the truth for a change, I pressed on. "And as far as I know, there is no ongoing investigation into Lloyd's disappearance. He's missing. That's all. Gone, but not forgotten by Loretta Coates. As far as I can see, nobody else is thinking about Lloyd anymore."

Tony sighed. "Pass me a menu. I need pie."

I chalked that up as a victory for The Wannabee. Tony, being an honest but realistic Cleveland cop, would have to gloss over our modest misbehavior, given that I was right. Nobody at the CLE PD had the leisure to figure out what happened to Lloyd.

I ordered the pie, too, à la mode.

Things got more congenial after that, and everybody at the table had pie with the à la mode and coffee to go with it. I waited for the sugar to kick in and then I eased another inquiry into the chit-chat. "How come I've totally missed this scrapping thing?"

The question wiped all the pie happiness off Valerio. "You don't want to know. It's a mess, Allie."

I nodded toward Otis. "I heard. But how does it work? How often does it happen?"

"Way too often." Tony held up his coffee cup and the waitperson came and refilled it.

"You're stonewalling me, aren't you?"

"Every minute of every day."

"I'm curious, though. How come I've never heard of this?"

"Lucky?"

"Do you really want me to do research on my own?"

I had him. I knew it. I waited until he was completely done with the long, drawn-out, aggravated-yet-somehow-resigned sigh.

"Okay. But only to keep you out of it. Right?"

"Absolutely."

"One absolutely might hope."

Sarcasm. But I'd set him rolling now.

"Scrapping got big because of one of those perfect storms." He sighed again. "First, there's the drug addicts and minor criminals. They need small or large amounts of money virtually every day and their lives are too disorganized for jobs or…or anything. Scrapping is who they are most of the time.

"Then, as if that could be worse, regular folks,

kids a lot of the time, but grown-ups who should know a lot better—" He was in his head now, his expression cramped by disapproval and pessimism.

"They get themselves hooked on prescription painkillers, which are cheap if your doctor prescribes them after your major surgery and crazy expensive—thirty…fifty dollars a pill expensive—if you buy them on the street. And guess what's cheaper? Heroin, is what. So now there are all these rich suburban idiots driving around our neighborhoods looking for H. And overdosing. And getting shot by dealers and common muggers. That's a mess almost nobody saw coming."

He was pushing the last forkful of pie around on his plate. I was thinking maybe he'd fallen off his train of thought entirely, but he shook his head and started up again.

"On top of that, times are still tough around here. People drift out of the marginal ne'er-do-well category and into the desperate-need-of-money/ no-job-available category.

"Then—concurrently—the housing market took that dive. And in Cleveland it was already down, so that hit hard. Scams. Bank fraud. Foreclosures. Vacant houses. Easy pickings. And about the same time, the demand for scrap metal went up. So the money got better."

"How much money are we talking about?"

"For a while copper hovered around four bucks a pound. It's not there now, but still it's money, and heroin is cheap and available. Couple of hours of trashing a house and you can at least get a fix. They go after other metals, too."

"Like?"

"Brass. Bronze. Aluminum. Steel somewhat."

"But where...?

"Girl, you would not believe. Besides vacant houses? Manhole covers. Cemetery flower urns. Somebody swiped a three-thousand-pound Buddha out on the West Coast someplace. Catalytic converters have platinum in them, so suddenly your car starts running extremely loud."

"But that would—"

"Cause problems for people? You think? Manhole covers cover up big deep, dangerous holes, right? City is starting to weld them in place now, which is major ass-pain for guys who have legitimate reasons to go down in there. Oh, and power companies really need their copper wire that the electricity runs through. And the miserable sons of bitches who are swiping the metal out of transformers and substations get themselves fried—which I could almost feel sorry about—and that knocks out the power, too. It's one, giant—"

"Mess. I'm beginning to see."

"It's ugly. It's dangerous. Sometimes people go away for a weekend and come back to the sort of thing that happened to Lloyd. For what? For nothing."

"But Tony, somebody somewhere has to be making major money on this. Where's the real profit?"

He clunked his mug down hard and iced me with a look. "Nowhere I would ever expect to find you, sweetheart."

I let it drop. Apart from my own nosiness, I couldn't see how the scrapper angle was relevant to what happened to Lloyd before or during his disappearance. The house thing was bad, and I knew it would be disheartening for Loretta, but assuming Lloyd was dead—which I was thinking he most likely was—he was beyond caring about the condition of his home. I needed to let that one go.

I shifted gears.

"Otis mentioned you might have seen the missing persons' report that Ms. Coates filed in February. Can you tell us anything at all that might give us some insight into what might have happened to him?"

Ha! Diversionary tactic. I'd intercepted Tony at the point where he was about to start yelling at me and knocked him off-kilter so far that, after a short disoriented pause, he simply answered my question.

"We didn't find anything, Allie. I looked at the file before I headed down here. I passed the Escalade on my way to Ridpath Avenue." He risked half a smile. "I know how you can't go by pie without stopping.…

"Officer checked out his house back then. He wasn't there and it hadn't been touched, as far as she could see. Ms. Coates had already contacted every hospital and doc-in-a-box in town. More than once. Early morning on the night Lloyd went missing, someone called in a blue/green vintage GTO broken down and being towed away by a non-tow-truck-type vehicle on MLK. Thought it seemed funny. You may have heard that 'seems funny' doesn't cut it with the 9-1-1 folks? It was gone by the time a car got a minute free from actual crimes to drive by. Could have been a hijacking in a pinch, I suppose."

I nudged Tom and kicked Otis on the ankle. MLK. That much we had some evidence for. Oblivious to our moment of detective triumph, Tony continued.

"By the day the Coates lady filed her official report, and somebody connected the dots, there was nothing to see down there. It snowed ten inches that weekend. Then thawed early the next week, low forties, pounding rain. The brook was high out of its banks. Everything bone-cold and sucking mud. Nobody looked too hard or too long. And that was it. No other calls. Nothing."

I scouted around for a facial expression that would indicate to Tony that I was discouraged and losing interest. I didn't have to look far. I could feel it on my face.

Tony recognized authentic disappointment when he saw it. "Well, I gotta get back in the car. Still some shift left." A sad smile. "The 'f' is silent."

He extricated himself from the booth and groaned as he straightened out his knees. "Enjoy the rest of your day, Allie. I'm looking forward to not seeing you around."

Chapter Nine
Sunday, June 18

I would have preferred to spend Sunday morning at my leisure. In bed. Reading the Sunday funnies to Tom. That's a euphemism. So I was dismayed to find myself, after barely twenty-four hours, back in the company of Loretta. It felt as if she'd hardly left the house and here she was back again. Not crying nearly as continuously, though.

It helped that I invited her for brunch and that Otis was cooking. I had a hard time remembering my life before Otis became our full-time, live-in bodyguard, P.I. Guy, and aspiring Food TV chef. It seemed very far away and Otis-deprived. Otis was happy, too. He had his own wing, which equaled a house in luxury square footage, and complete access to both the main and second-floor kitchens where he exercised his chefly skills every chance he got. Plus his salary was Arco Security Guard x 4. With excellent benefits. Win/Win/Win. All around.

Loretta and I were sitting at one of the tables on the pool deck surveying a spread that included French toast, lightly dusted with powdered sugar and a taste of maybe cinnamon, a compote of fresh fruit, a side of bacon, and of course Otis' premium coffee. The big, numerous flower boxes were flowering in color-coordinated pink and rose. The lake was shimmering all sequin-like again.

If I could have swapped in Tom for Loretta and Otis, my morning would have been complete. As it was I was only marginally okay. I was getting to the part about Lloyd's house and that was bound to change the tone of the day for the worse.

When I added up everything we had on Lloyd, it totaled less than nothing. Without a paper trail or any other possible evidence I might have discovered in Lloyd's swamp before it got to be a swamp, there was nothing to investigate. In the figurative search for the needle that was Lloyd, we had not found even an intact haystack. Tony Valerio would have been delighted by what a bust at mystery-solving the T&A was turning out to be.

I fortified myself with a sip of Otis' high-test brew and slogged in. I explained about the GTO maybe having been seen down on MLK, figuring that for sure Loretta would have called to check on her missing persons' report—multiple times—and already knew. She had. She did. I wondered why she hadn't mentioned that the day before, but then I remembered her state of mind on that occasion and my own reluctance to probe. At last, I turned, ever so gently, to a description of the condition in which we discovered Lloyd's home.

I was surprised. She took it well. Granted, I didn't lay it on too thick about the flood, the sludge, and the mildew, but I made it clear that Lloyd's place was a teardown. She found the whole scrapper thing as confusing and terrible as I did, but she held up to the news without crying. Maybe knowing that Lloyd had nothing to come home to now, made his disappearance more palatable. Or more final.

She actually patted my hand. "You tried, Allie. I appreciate that. I do. Maybe it's time for me to admit he's gone and he's not coming back. I'm probably never going to find out where or how."

Wouldn't you know? Right when Loretta starting letting Lloyd go, I started hanging on to him. Maybe I was realizing this was going to be an inauspicious start for the T&A. Maybe I was getting all chafed about how Valerio was going to show me his most irritating, self-satisfied face the next time I saw him.

I could have let the whole thing drop and gone back to bed with Tom for the rest of the day.

But no.

"I was hoping we'd discover some real evidence at the house. Paperwork. Pay stubs. Banking stuff. Tax info. Address book. Something. Anything. Now that avenue is closed to us and I don't…"

Loretta's expression hushed my mouth.

"But Allie, I have all that stuff about Lloyd. Why didn't you ask me?"

Ah. Why, indeed?

I'd glossed over the most fundamental truth about Loretta: She was a librarian, for mercy's sake. Information was her stock in trade. And any information she had access to would be expertly collated, filed, and safeguarded.

I'd let my estimation of Loretta as an over-emotional worrier blind me to her indisputable value as an excellent practitioner of her profession. I didn't want to upset her with a lot of questions. Worse than that, I hadn't thought to ask.

I sent my brain a mental reminder to also follow up on the "I had a feeling Lloyd was up to something" dead end, too. For an irritatingly dogged person, I'd let an inexcusable ton of stuff slide.

Loretta was our first, best resource regarding Lloyd, but I was focused on him, what he'd had, what he'd done, where he'd been. I'd been focused on me, how clever and capable I was about to be. And on Tom, how smart. And hot. And I'd neglected to ask Loretta some of the most rudimentary questions. In other words, I'd been stupid.

"I don't know why I didn't, Loretta." *False.* "I should have. I wasn't thinking." *True.*

She patted my hand again and I tried to hide how much worse that was making me feel. I sat up straighter and began afresh. "So. Tell me what all you've got."

She settled back in her chair with a smug smile that reminded me how close to get-out-of-jail-free-and-back-in-bed-with-Tom I'd been.

Too late now, Alice. Suck it up.

"Well, first, you'd have to have known Lloyd. He was an interesting guy. I wasn't joking about the OCD thing. Not that it's anything to joke about, but you know how challenging…although apparently he was actually OCPD. I guess that means he had obsessive compulsions, but believed that was a good, smart way to be. Oh. Wait. I just remembered."

She vanished into her purse, which, from what I could see, was eons better-organized than any purse of mine, and pulled out a small manila envelope. Handed it to me. Teared up. "I wanted you to see—this is Lloyd."

I took the envelope from her and extracted the photo.

Lloyd. Our case. Loretta's lost love. I smiled into his anxious expression. He looked right past me. No eye contact. It could have been a fifth-grade school photo if the guy in it wasn't fifty-something and wearing a real suit and a tie that didn't clip on.

Lloyd was the boy in every elementary school class I'd ever been in—the kid with the clean, round cheeks, slicked-down thrice-combed hair, and the worried, self-conscious blue eyes. The smart one who never had the answer when he was called on. Too insecure, too beaten down by something or someone, too wounded to let the smile creep into his eyes.

Or to say, "I love you, too, Loretta."

Damn. Lloyd broke my heart.

Oh, Loretta.

I blinked hard before I looked up. Not that Loretta would mind if I cried about Lloyd, but I didn't want to threaten her hopes about how he might still be playing the slots in Vegas.

"Oh, Loretta. He's handsome. And very smart. Even I can see that.'

She was nodding. Smiling, even while she was still blotting some tears. Happy, in spite of everything, that it was so obvious to me why she was so proud of Lloyd.

"He got an economics degree from John Carroll and he was a CPA, too, but he—" The smile faded. "It didn't help him very much. He had these weird ideas and wasn't the least bit shy about sharing them, so he could never hold down a job very long. Until recently. I mean, people could only be patient for so long. I don't know how I—"

She stopped herself from speaking disloyally of the almost-certainly dead. I jumped in to give her a hand, "You said, 'until recently.' He got a job?"

"Yes. He said it was 'security work' for some big company. Odd hours. Lots of nights. I figured, maybe, night watchman? You can see how that would be perfect?"

I could see. "And he liked that?"

"He was so relieved to find work he could actually do and not get fired. It didn't pay much, at least to start. But it was steady. Regular hours were good for him. And recently, they'd given him other assignments. Things he was good at, but could do on his own. The way he needed to do things."

"If he was an accountant, how come he gave his paper stuff to you? Even his address book?"

"He knew I'd take care of it all and he could get it from me at any time. The whole accountant thing left a bad taste in his mouth, Allie. You can imagine. He felt he was very competent, but his clients kept leaving him. And all the while he assumed everything he was insisting on doing for them was absolutely necessary and worth any extra cost involved with the extra stuff. They weren't grateful. He never understood that.

"I was so delighted—and amazed, too, I'll tell you—that he was able to stop handling his own paperwork. There wasn't much but he handed over everything. I paid his bills. I have his W-2s. His financial picture was not complex. Although lately I could see he was getting cash under the table for some of the things he was doing. Which worried me. But I didn't want to get him going, so I didn't make a big deal about it."

"A lot of cash?"

"Not a ton. A decent amount, in addition to the salary. That was not bad either. It all added up. And he was expecting more. He was so pleased about that. I suppose I should have asked him about it but I was trying to be…I don't know, Allie. Let him do his own thing. Not worry so much all the time."

There it was again. The something Lloyd might have been up to that got him disappeared.

A big payout, on top of his salary, and some non-negligible cash-under-the-table. I'd follow up on that now.

I patted her hand. Feeling better.

"No worries, Loretta. We'll figure this out."

"Thanks, Allie. You can keep the picture. I have lots of copies. Lloyd was such a handsome man."

Chapter Ten

By one-thirty I was following Loretta down Lake Shore. She lived in a tall lakefront building not more than a mile from our own luxury Bratenahl estate. This amazed me because I thought Loretta would concoct all kinds of concerns about living high up. I shouldn't have given that any consideration. Her apartment was second floor and not on the lake side. She explained it was cheaper like that and less likely to get, in her words, "lashed by storms."

I was secretly relieved when we found the door appropriately locked and her place in apple pie order. I'd been primed to consider breaking, entering, and general destruction to be the order of the day. This was all Loretta. Tidy and cozy with lots of books, naturally, and a pleasant view out to lawn, river, and trees. I sank down on a plump couch, admired my surroundings, and savored the normalcy.

For about a minute. That's how long it took for Loretta to put her fingers with unerring certainty upon the spot where she'd filed the Lloyd papers—but not find them where she'd left them.

Let me say one thing for the record: Hell hath no fury like a librarian who can't find something she's looking for. Her search devolved from a harpist's delicate pluck straight to shuffle, pummel, and paw. Her long years of discipline did not permit her to start pitching things out of the drawer as I would have done, but she was close. At last, she turned to me in quavering consternation. "Allie. The file is gone."

This, I had deduced.

"Are you—?"

I started to ask if she was absolutely sure about where she'd put it, but stopped myself when I heard my survival skills screaming.

Mouth brakes. Sometimes they save our lives.

"—aware of anyone who might have a key to your place? Besides you."

"And Lloyd?"

Oh, well. Him. I bet Lloyd would have one of those labeled key chains. With Loretta's name and address right on it. Probably said, "Lloyd's files are here" too. So anybody could—

Anybody?

That pulled me up short. Who was this so-called "anybody?"

I figured Lloyd, being probably dead, did not come here and snatch back his file. My neck tingled. Who would have connected Lloyd—and his papers—to Loretta? And how? And when?

I tuned back in as Loretta continued her review of key holders. "—And the management people do. In case you lock yourself out. Or die."

I tried to hide my despair while sorting an unmanageable number of puzzles. Here was yet another lesson on how vast and unruly the real world of crime is. As opposed to the world of crime fiction. Whatever happened to a standard tidy handful of relevant clues?

I reminded myself to have the T&A's second case work out more like the plot in a TV show. "Father Brown," maybe. Short, to the point, easier. With murderers who smirked and sneered rather tellingly.

I dragged myself back to Loretta's list.

"Anyone else?"

"My friend up on the tenth floor, lakeside. Lisa from Channel 16."

At this, Loretta's rage and despair eased ever so slightly. She had a celebrity friend.

Ah. Coincidentally, I knew Lisa, too. Except I always referred to her as HummerWoman. She was the one who honked at a blind man in the crosswalk in front of Joe's Super Market last summer and changed my life to unrecognizable.

In gratitude for her having hooked me up with the man of my dreams and five-hundred-fifty million smackeroos, I forgave Lisa and vowed never to reveal the circumstances of our meeting. We were getting to be pretty good friends.

For Loretta, I projected mild intrigue.

"Oh, really? The reporter?"

Loretta beamed. "Yes. She did such a wonderful story about the Memorial-Nottingham Library, and we discovered we both lived here. Now we run into each other in the bar downstairs a lot. It's a happening place."

Loretta, I hardly knew ye.

All this was more information than I could collate. I stuffed the list of key holders into a file drawer in my head. I hoped this file drawer was more secure than Loretta's.

"Look, Loretta. You need to change your lock. You can give a copy of the key to Lisa."

Why I trusted Lisa, I don't know, but after that one breach of humanity, she'd stood up like a mama lion for us.

"And give one to me. That should handle your getting locked out."

I did not add "or dying," but I saw it cross her mind.

I walked over to where she was sitting—scared, sad, betrayed by her own private Dewey Decimal System—and packed as much comfort as I could muster into a teensy shoulder squeeze. "Don't worry, Loretta. I bet you have a lot of those details in your head. Now's not the time, though. You need to recover. And change that lock."

She nodded. "I'm sorry, Allie. I thought I could help you find Lloyd, and I lost it all—"

A human face is a fine-tuned instrument. Right then Loretta's was playing me the opening bars of "*Except for one thing.*"

"What? Loretta?"

"The address book, Allie. It's a book. Not a file. So I put it on…"

"The shelf."

Of course.

She didn't even have to show me where. I was a teeny bit librarian myself, after all. I walked over to the bookcase and pulled out a small volume, bound in black leather.

It was filed under B. For Bunker.

Chapter Eleven
Monday, June 19

Lisa Cole, intrepid reporter for Channel 16, was reading aloud to me from a notebook she'd pulled out of her purse. By focusing, laser-sharp, on the page, she was avoiding my eyes and ignoring the fact that I was moving my head, slowly but firmly, from side to side.

"Listen to these quotes, Allie:

'I wish it never happened. It was totally a night-mare.'

'The money came in and the love walked out.'

'If I knew what was going to transpire, honestly, I would have torn the ticket up.'"

She looked at me. "Is that how Tom feels, Allie? Do you?"

"Lisa," I dragged her out of her notebook with the iron grappling hook of death in my voice. "I'm sure I don't need to remind you that you yourself played a role in the "Lottery Miracle on Lake Shore Boulevard." A role you would not want to see—how shall we say?—highlighted as 'Ms. Honkin' Hummer' in the blockbuster movie about me."

I had her there.

She'd been bugging me for weeks to have lunch at her expense in exchange for my human interest story about the Mondo. This was naiveté on her part. I could no longer be bought with a lunch. She could not even have bought me with a lunch in Paris, France.

Unbeknownst to her, we were there because I thought she might cast some light on the Lloyd situation. I moved to make my position even clearer. "Lisa, I'm paying for this lunch. I'm only ever-always paying for lunch."

"Can I quote you?" The reporter vanished and who was left, grinning mischievously at me, was my new friend Lisa, who'd been born in the neighborhood and changed her last name from Čebulj to Cole to shake loose some consonants.

I returned the grin. "Oh, I think that's universally understood. Not news anymore. And, yeah, I read those quotes in the *Plain Dealer*. You left out the ones from the friends and associates of the dead winners. Like 'He didn't deserve this.'"

I didn't add that I was an admirer of the honest man who said, "I regret the drugs. I can't say I regret the women."

She shrugged. "It was worth a try. So it was you who maneuvered me to this lunch?"

"True. But luckily it's a good lunch."

It was, too. We were hiding out in an under-occupied section of the patio at The South Side Restaurant and Bar in Tremont. Nobody, as yet, had identified us as Minor TV Star and Slutty Mondo Girl, respectively, and come over to just say hi. I was deep into the Cobb salad, which was creatively deconstructed into delicious bits of perfectly grilled chicken, roasted onions, applewood-smoked bacon, and general yum. I love to dig for the happy bits in a salad. And a Bloody Mary never hurts either.

"So what do you want to know?"

"I'm looking into a disappearance for a former colleague of mine."

"This the T&A in action?"

"You don't know about that. You never heard a word. On pain of complete ratting out on the Hummer incident."

"I know. I know. But I love the idea. It's The Justice League. Solving crimes. Righting wrongs. Finding out the truth. What I thought being a reporter would be like back in my ignorant childhood." I considered this for a moment. Only Otis—handsome, black, muscles-all-over from the post-heart-attack weight-losing and working out—was Justice League material. But Tom did have the secret powers of his Spidey sense. And Valerio did fill a role of the insider guy with dark knowledge and hidden skills. The concept fell apart when it got to me. I had nothing. Bad hair. Easily accessed heart. Perhaps too easily accessed much, much more—

I aimed my blush at the remains of the salad, until the warmth receded somewhat.

When I resurfaced, Lisa was grinning again. "You were thinking about Tom. Is it true what they say about blind guys…?"

"Reading your body like Braille? Off the record?"

"On my mother's *žganci* " She crossed her heart.

"What is that?"

"Grits. Not important now."

"It's true."

"Ah, God. And he's handsome and über rich. You are so lucky."

"I'm not sure I want the likes of you too close to the T&A League, Miss 'Ah God.'"

"No. You do. Tom would never give me a second glance. Er…moment of attention. Except as a friend someday, I hope. He's got reason not to like me much."

"True. But I keep telling you he's over that. It could happen. If you're kind and helpful to me."

She got all down to business then.

"Who's your former colleague? And who's missing?"

"The colleague is a friend of yours. Loretta Coates."

"Oh, Loretta. I like her. We're friends. She's a sweetheart. Worries too much, though."

"Well, not this time. The missing person is her boyfriend Lloyd Bunker."

"She has a boyfriend?"

"He's been missing since February. We have reason to believe he's dead."

"Wow. That completely sucks. But, Allie, I don't know anything about it. Loretta's missing boyfriend is not sensational enough for 16. Unless there's oh, I dunno, a serial killer or maybe Democrats practicing witchcraft involved. What are the details?"

"There are no details. His car, a green '67 Pontiac GTO was seen, apparently unoccupied, down close to the last bridge before the Shoreway on MLK in the early hours of Saturday, February twenty-fourth. After that, *nada*. All I have, besides that, is the fact that his house in Collinwood was scrapped and Loretta's file with his stuff was swiped out of her apartment. So, except for his address book—What?"

On the word "scrapped" Lisa's expression changed for the much more interested.

"Scrapped? I know some stuff about scrapped."

"Great. I want to know some more stuff about scrapped, but, even then, I'm not sure it's related to Lloyd's disappearance."

"It's related to every kind of crime you can imagine. Drugs. The heroin kind of drugs. Meth, too. Cocaine. And now there's fentanyl. Plus B&E. Vandalism. Murder. I—"

At that very moment, as things were getting juicy, the inevitable happened. Lisa's cell went off like a bomb. "Heart of Rock and Roll." Huey Lewis and The News. Naturally.

After that she was instantly answering, standing, walking, saying good-bye to me.

"Yes? Sure. Got it. I'll be there. Give me ten. I'll meet the van. Sorry, Allie. But listen. I have a file. I'll have it copied and get it delivered to you tomorrow. Thanks for lunch. Bye."

Film at 11.

At least I still had some chicken. And the Bloody Mary.

Chapter Twelve

**Glorious mornings! Amazing sunsets!
"At home…lakeside."**

"This remarkably designed, gated estate overlooks Lake Erie and offers breathtaking water views and spectacular gardens on 2 1/2 impeccably manicured acres. Magnificent pool with 3 levels of expansive, connected decks. Private sand beach. This French-Revival masterpiece, circa 1914, designed by one of the legendary architects of his time, is listed in the National Register of Historic Places.
A treasure.
Fully equipped, completely updated gourmet kitchen, with every modern amenity and convenience feature. 10 spacious bedrooms, 8 splendid baths. An extraordinary walk-in

sky-lit shower is the gem of the sumptuous master suite. The last word in luxury. 9000+ square ft, 5 fireplaces, fully-equipped fitness room. Lake views from your treadmill! Central air. Five-car garage. Gatehouse. State-of-the-art security system by Magna-Protect, Inc. Ask about leasing possibilities."

Like many, many advertisements, the realtor's listing sounded way too breathtakingly magnificent to be true, but back in late March, we were desperately looking for a big, safe place to hide. The rock-solid construction, walls, and gates, plus the impermeable security system fit the bill. And renting beat buying, even though we certainly had three million to spend.

So here we were. Palace of Versailles, Cleveland, Ohio.

When I was married to my philandering dickhead lawyer, we lived in a pleasant four-bedroom Colonial in Shaker Heights. So during those interminable years I'd experienced what I would formerly have considered spacious surroundings.

That place was a lot roomier than the cramped ranch where I'd been raised in the company of my mom and dad and my big brother who grew up to be a narrow-minded, pain-in-the-ass fundamentalist preacher. No disrespect. There were only the four of us but that house felt like the cabin of a space shuttle—all the attendant problems of choreography and waste disposal without the thrills of weightlessness.

Aggravation makes the space grow smaller, I say.

But nothing prepared me for occupying a rental house the size of Times Square. Nine thousand plus square feet is, like, five metric tons of feet. I could have dropped our entire small-town shuttle into the master bath. Given that we were renting and the true owner spirited a lot of his irreplaceable items into climate-controlled storage, much of the house consisted of immense, gorgeously paneled, heavily fireplaced but under-furnitured spaces that took a while to merely walk through.

Whenever I gazed into the living room, which opened directly into the dining room, which opened into—wait for it—the ballroom, the word "skateboard" skipped through my wicked brain.

We'd rented the mansion—in spite of our discomfiture with the yawning emptiness and over-the-top opulence—based on its availability and our need for kickass security, which this place was touted as having. Once Tom's mental map of it all was complete, he'd shrugged and said, "Well, at least there's not a whole lot to trip over. And the security system is intense."

So why on that Monday afternoon after my Lisa Lunch—with Tom and Otis off on some professor-related mission—was I not feeling secure? Why was I, in fact, feeling like an ant captured by an eight-year-old in a very big jar?

A storm was moving in, churning the lake dark and wild, and a relentless wind made the old joists creak and groan. I was holed up with the only surviving copy of Lloyd's address book in a tiny study located at the top of the main staircase. It was my favorite room in the house—although I liked the master bedroom a lot, too—because it was sized for coziness. According to the real estate lady, it was devoted to the storage of the household linens back in the day. 1914 was very, very far back.

The room was almost entirely paneled in cupboard doors but it sported one built-in space filled with ranks of fat, wooden rails, over which, I presumed, the family's freshly ironed linens were hung. Why it was up here, so far from the basement laundry, I couldn't fathom. Unless nobody cared that the servants had to traipse up and down the back staircases. There were two of those.

For me it was like time-traveling to a moment in history when I'd almost certainly have been the one ironing tablecloths and traipsing. Fortunately for everyone involved, there was now an excellently appointed full-scale laundry room on the first floor. One on second, too. So those bases were covered.

I loved my tiny getaway for its thick rug, its lovely arched window, and the small desk with its old-fashioned green-glass-shaded lamp. Except for the ghosts of pissed off maids, the room had a friendly vibe. The scent of lavender still lingered after all these years. It offered all the makings of a cozy library. Unlike the one downstairs that only required stone lions by its double doors to fully realize its pretensions.

I paged through Lloyd's book, wondering where to start, and also wondering how he could have brought himself to leave it with Loretta. I answered myself that it must have been his backup, with his most current info stored in his now long-missing phone and his waterlogged, rusted-out computer. Lloyd was a man who would have wanted backup out the wazoo.

He was also a man who liked to check and recheck the pages in his book. Some showed signs of being more over-handled than others. I was most interested in those, but I decided to start with the A's and be systematic in my research. In memory of Lloyd.

Trying to pay attention to the search, and ignore the storm building at my back, I arrived at a well-thumbed spread in the Cs. I pictured Lloyd returning to it often, checking and rechecking. Making sure. Other than a listing for Crispy's Tasty Eats with phone number and the neatly inscribed notation, "Crispy's carryout menu in top right desk drawer," these two pages were dedicated to something called CyCLE, Inc. with landlines and cells all duly labeled. E-mail addresses and after-hours details, too. Was this the corporate employer Loretta mentioned?

"Cy" sounded cyber-ly computeresque to me, and the CLE, uppercased like that, had to be the Cleveland International Airport designation that was the brand of the city before LeBron James made it popular for us to call our town "The Land."

A big Cleveland tech outfit would certainly need a night watchman.

In my mind I constructed the large, cold, many windowed hulk of an office complex. I saw Lloyd in a drab—but very neatly pressed—uniform walking a long, darkened corridor. The narrow beam of his watchman's flashlight swerved from wall to wall, making creepy shadows everywhere. This image spooked me out even more. My neck tingle was back.

The thunder was getting closer. When the wind rose enough to chill my actual neck, I got up to look. The lake was navy blue, shot through with whitecaps, but the horizon had vanished and the murk of the oncoming downpour was already blanking out everything in its path. Trees on the lawn were slashing around like mad. When lightning stabbed the lake right in front of me, I stepped back and closed the window. That lowered the volume considerably.

Right then, in the semi-silence I'd created by shutting out the uproar, a door slammed downstairs.

For a precious ten seconds, I stood dead still, listening for another sound and trying to talk myself out of having heard the first one. This did not work. The atmosphere was still vibrating from the force of that bang.

Someone was in the house with me. I was a sitting duck in this tiny space. To punctuate that thought, another flash of lightning killed the power. With the light doused, the room felt even more trap-like.

That flushed me out. Padding as silently as I could, over floorboards that creaked with age, I let myself out into the hall. Left? Right? Up? Down? So many directions to choose from. So little time. I figured I needed to pick a bedroom and a closet and go with it. Hopefully, my intruder would be as confounded by the multiplicity of choices as I was.

So. Not the master suite. Too obvious. I turned away from it, blanked my brain into randomness, followed the hall past one, two, three sets of closed doors, and picked the fourth one on the side away from the storm.

The furniture in this dim space was blanketed in dust covers. There were three doors, lined up. The first one creaked when I touched it and revealed floor-to-ceiling shelf space. The second opened into a bathroom. The third one was exactly the closet I wanted. Large. Long and narrow with the door at one end. And full of long, formal dresses I'd bet had been left here since 1925. Even in the dim light and my panicked state of mind I couldn't help but observe that they were arranged by color.

I eased my way deep into the closet and slid myself down. My back was jammed comfortingly against the wall and my arms were embracing my jellied knees. Immediately I needed to pee. Immediately after that I told myself to shut up about peeing.

Hiding in that closet, wholly in touch with how passionately I hated Hide and Go Seek when I was a kid, I rediscovered something: There is no sound scarier than no sound at all. Bad as it would have been to hear someone sneaking toward me, it was way worse to, like, dilate my ears for the teeniest whisper, the slightest, most muffled step, the softest nearby inhalation. And hear nothing. Staying put and not running out screaming, I would argue, was the practice of patience at its highest level.

I sat. I waited. The floor was hard. Time passed. The dresses smelled of a sickening combination of heavy perfume and cedar. The air was stuffy. I still had to pee. I wished I'd learned to meditate. I wished I could slow my heartbeat and put myself into a trance like those cool operatives in thrillers. I wished I had a Memory Palace I could escape to. I sat and breathed as calmly and soundlessly as I could. Sometime after all that—I cannot believe this myself—I fell asleep.

I woke up an unspecified time later to hear someone hollering my name. Tom. I staggered to my feet, pawed my way out of the hovering clothes, ran out into the hall and into his arms. It was almost like nothing had happened.

The storm was over.

The power was back on.

Tom and Otis were home.

I checked in my cozy study. The address book was gone.

Chapter Thirteen

Dusk had fallen on one of the longest days of the year, which was working out to be one of the longest damn Mondays of my life. Tom and Otis were trying to cheer me up. Otis drove the Escalade up to the Beach Club Bistro in Euclid and brought home two large Arcadia Club Pizzas. The Arcadia boasts the undisputed Chewy Crust Ruler of this galaxy. And on that sublime foundation the Bistro people layer red sauce, asiago, sausage, meatballs, pepperoni, ham, bacon, and provolone. No kidding.

There are times you truly need to eat something that will shorten your life.

Otis also made me his signature cosmopolitan, with extra vodka, fiercely shaken until tiny ice crystals formed inside its pink wonderfulness. In a large shiny cocktail glass. With a slice of lime.

All this was not Michael Symon's Lola or the

Velvet Tango Room but it was doing the trick. One bite and one sip at a time, I was getting better. But I still felt able to complain. This was not cracked up to be a one cosmo night.

I took another sip and let Otis' pink magic seep deeper into my elbows. "My record on this whole case is so sucky." Even I could hear the loathsome self-pity. It sounded faraway.

"First, it never occurred to me to ask Loretta for any serious information about Lloyd. I only wanted her to stop crying. Then when I got around to it, it was long gone. I lost his house. I lost his file. Now I lost his address book. And it's only been, what?" I counted on my fingers. "Three days? And that's counting today. I need more pizza."

Otis passed me a new slice, and Tom said in an annoyingly soothing voice, "Allie, you did not lose Lloyd's house."

"Feels like it." I applied more delicious pinkness to my gray mood.

"Maybe it feels that way to you, but as far as we know, that scrapping thing is totally unrelated. Lloyd's house was an easy target for those guys because it was abandoned."

"Which…" I pointed an accusing finger at Tom and then realized he couldn't be intimidated by that. I put the finger away and proceeded, ignoring

Otis who was suppressing a definitely obnoxious smile. "*Which* he abandoned by having been made dead. On purpose.

"Somebody else's purpose," I added with as much dignity as I could find, "as we now know. Almost for sure."

"Still not your fault. And only about twenty-four hours elapsed between the time Loretta first came here with her problem and the time you both went looking for Lloyd's papers."

"But what if they'd still been there after only twenty-three hours elapsed?"

"What if you'd discovered whoever took them, still in Loretta's apartment. Taking them?"

"That would have been bad. Very bad. I wasn't prepared for that guy. I didn't have Otis."

Otis patted my hand. "I'm glad you appreciate my value for those occasions. Next time, I'll be there."

I narrowed my eyes. "Are you patronizing me, Otis?"

"Maybe a little. Here. There's a drop more in this shaker."

"That was a splash, Otis. I know a splash when I see one. I forgive you, though."

I took a long sip and returned to my whining. "But now we don't know anything. This right here—where we're sitting now, in this exceedingly gigantic kitchen at this tremendously massive granite bar—is square one.

"We're back at square one. Again. It's embarrassing. I myself am embarrassed. Got any more cosmo in there?"

Otis pushed the cocktail shaker out of my reach. "No, Allie. This is not square one. First of all, you've learned a couple of very important things in only three days."

"Such as?"

"Such as somebody definitely doesn't want you to find out anything about Lloyd. Which means that you now know almost for sure that Lloyd didn't just run off the road back in February. Because that's exactly what Tony would like you to think."

Tom was frowning. "That's what I would like you to think, too, Allie. But clearly Otis is right. And now—"

"And now what?"

"And now that somebody or somebody related in some way to that somebody has stolen Lloyd's papers. Unless you think Loretta mislaid them."

"Librarians do not mislay."

"But even if she did, through some un-librarian-like aberration, you now have definite proof. Because somebody knew enough about Lloyd and Loretta to break in and take the file. And now somebody, who knows enough to come here, came here today for the address book. And—let's not forget—is somehow capable of bypassing our crack security system."

Here was critical and troublesome information that needed serious processing, but I wasn't quite done beating up on myself.

"I should have taken it with me into the closet."

"No. I'm glad you didn't. I'm glad you took yourself into the closet and stayed there."

"Asleep."

"Alive."

"You don't think that person would have killed me, Tom? Not dead."

"Allie. Wake up. Somebody killed Lloyd. Oh, maybe he's out there somewhere, on the run, or—"

"Playing the slots in Vegas! That's what I was hoping, Tom. Although Loretta wouldn't approve, I don't think…"

Tom tabled my Vegas theory and went on, "But if that's the case, why not tell Loretta he's alive, at least? Let her know. Highly unlikely, I'd say. So now we know there's somebody who doesn't want us to find out anything about him. Maybe they came here to get the book and now they have it, they're satisfied. I sure hope so, but you should know as well as anyone that murder breeds murder, and it keeps getting easier on down the line."

He had me there.

"I remember. And, also, there's the big, foggy, danger…part…you mentioned. That somebody is one step ahead of me. Us. All. The. Time. To know to steal Lloyd's file from Loretta. To know I had the address book. To know all everything. Somebody's psychic or…something. That's just—Crap. I'm too…sleepy to talk about this anymore."

"I agree. You're right. It's all too much for tonight. Let's go to bed."

"Mmm. *There's* a good idea."

Otis quickly occupied himself with clearing off the remains of dinner and Tom and I guided each other up the stairs to the bedroom, where I shucked off my clothes in record time and hopped into bed.

Tom joined me shortly thereafter and I was dismayed to see that he was wearing his PJs. Anyhow, he still looked sexy.

I told him so.

"You look sexy in your PJs."

"I assume you do, as well."

"No I don't. I am not wearing any PJs."

"Why am I not surprised?"

I threw my arms around Tom's neck. My head was all warm and fuzzy and untroubled by the sorrows of the world, and my entire body was answering his powerful gravitational pull. I kissed him so as to communicate willingness. He kissed me back in a warm and friendly way, but then he unwrapped me from his neck and other parts and kissed me again, in a pleasantly firm, nighty-night sort of way.

Bummer.

"Oh, no. I figured you would want to make fabulous love to me. It's been decades."

Tom pulled our lovely silky sheet over both of us. It felt very sexy. "I'm painfully aware, Alice. But I feel I should only make love to you when your mind is in your body."

"Really? Seems kinda stupid to me. You were so sexy when you said 'un-librallian-like abbleration.'"

"I'm glad you liked it. But there we are." He kissed me that friendly kiss again. "Goodnight."

And that was the end of Day Three in The Case of Lloyd Is Missing.

Chapter Fourteen
Tuesday, June 20

The Komatsu PC300LC weighed seventy-seven-thousand pounds. It was either old, or, having been exposed to the elements at their most formidable for most of its working life, it merely looked old. Its bold yellow was faded to a sickly ochre and big patches of rust had broken through all along the back of the cab. The kid wasn't paying attention to any of that. He was enraptured by the Komatsu's brute strength.

The man in the cab wasn't even wearing a hard hat. The big excavator was resting on two long slabs of splintered wood that formed a parallel track for it to run on. This track was in the middle of a big old rusty barge. The barge was floating on the lake, about ten feet out from shore. It couldn't float away because two big poles that looked to the kid like

I-beams, were stuck down through the deck and into the lake-bottom.

The only other occupant of the barge besides the operator of the Komatsu was wearing his hard hat and using a motor to make the poles go up and down so the barge could turn and move. If the pole didn't go in far enough, the guy in the cab would raise the shovel high in the air and bang right down on it.

The shovel looked to the kid like a dinosaur head. A Tyrannosaurus Rex. Big teeth. Slobbering silt and water. He thought this was the best part. He waited, hoping to see it again.

At the moment, however, the claw was submerged in the lake, fishing for rocks that it was moving to make kind of a break wall. With the long, slender, yellow neck extended to the water and its head below the surface, it looked almost defenseless. As if the dinosaur, worn out from its day of roaming about, spreading death and carnage all over the Cretaceous, simply bent to refresh itself. The kid knew his dinosaurs.

He dropped down in the grass and kicked off his shoes. His mom told him this was a beautiful summer day and that he should go on outside and spend it doing whatever he loved to do most. And not to get hurt and wreck his whole vacation and miss out on everything. That was his mom. In church when the preacher said, "The Lord giveth and the Lord taketh away," the kid would substitute "Mom" in his head for "The Lord."

He'd wandered around for a while, trying to figure out what he loved to do most, without getting hurt, of course, and then he had drifted on down the street toward the park by the lake, feeling out of sorts and lost.

Now, though. Now, he felt awesome.

The operator in the cab gave him a wave and brought the claw out of the water, its teeth bared and dripping. They didn't get many rocks this time. The kid stood up and walked closer to the bank, peering in, trying to get a better look at what was there.

When he started yelling and pointing, the guys on the barge didn't pay much attention. But when the dinosaur's head was up higher, way above the cab, they could see what the kid had spotted first. The thing that was nestled in the giant metal teeth. Something with a bony foot.

Chapter Fifteen

CyCLE, Inc. The cyber-people.

I calculated that, between one thing and another, on Monday night, my brain was functioning at twenty-percent capacity. It was worthless. I was trash. Except, as I drifted off to sleep, I had a thought.

On Tuesday morning I felt as if I'd been steamrollered by the Big Cosmos—that's spelled with the capital B&C—but I'd hung on to my thought. The address book was gone but I'd stored one clue in my head.

Miracles happen. I still had CyCLE.

I was back on the hunt, but, first, I needed to jumpstart my body. And reattach my mind to it.

I had a plan for this.

Our master bath had one truly off-the-charts

magnificent feature. The shower. The "sky-lit" shower that was "the gem" of our "sumptuous master suite." Sky-lit *and* big. A person could have parked two Escalades in that shower.

You could go in there and sit down on this lovely wooden Zen-like bench, under whatever sky Cleveland was providing that day, and let warm water pour over you from about one thousand different shower heads. I did this. It felt great. Like a cloudburst in a tropical rainforest. All it lacked was parrots. The sky Cleveland had on offer right then was a cloudless blue.

Close at hand, in a perfect Zen-like wooden bucket, I kept my upscale, excellent-smelling, Jo Malone Lime Basil & Mandarin Shampoo, which I could afford by proxy.

Even the description was sexy. And I quote, "Peppery basil and aromatic white thyme bring an unexpected twist to the scent of limes on a Caribbean breeze." It was also supposed to leave hair looking naturally glossy. I was still waiting for that, but I'd bought the matching conditioner, too, so there was always hope.

Tom's sandlewood-ish soap was in the bucket, too. It made me think, shall we say, kindly of him. One of the first things I'd noticed on the day we met, before the Mondo fell on us, was that he smelled like good soap. That exact sandalwood soap. Being here in the shower with Tom's actual soap from Day 1, a day on which I woke up and went to work and didn't even know of him yet, made me feel like my life was a wonder. Also I figured Tom's soap contained extra-added pheromones, which didn't hurt a bit.

In that shower of perfection, I scrubbed until I felt my mind and body hooking up again. Then I turned up the cold to cement the deal. When I stepped out, I was clean and awake and only slightly dizzy. I slipped into my terrycloth robe, toweled my hair into damp disarray, and went back to the bedroom to don my body armor.

Tom was standing in front of his closet, getting dressed for his teaching job. His hot associate professor attire was maybe as—or possibly more—sexy than his dazzling tee-shirt attire. The white shirt, good jacket, no-tie combo. Mmm Mmm. That tan. I bet the young ladies in the front row of his classes—

My armor would have to wait. I walked up behind him, opened the robe, pressed my bare front into his jacket, slipped my arms around him, and inhaled his own freshly showered soapy goodness.

"This is to notify you that I am now *compos mentis*. And much, much more."

"I am so excited to learn of this. And you smell very tempting and…hot." He turned and used his bat radar to put his mouth exactly on mine.

To quote a recent bulletin from Channel 16: "*Ah. God.*"

But I gently disengaged myself. Payback for last night.

Stupid.

"You don't want to be late for your class."

"Oh, no. I do. I very much do."

"No, you don't. What I have in mind would make you late for tomorrow's class. And we both have responsibilities. I wouldn't think of disrupting your day."

Liar, liar, panties on fire.

At that moment when the morning was hanging in the balance between duty and one delicious fantasy after another, duty hollered up the staircase.

Otis.

"Tom," his voice echoed. "I got the car ready. When you are."

One last tantalizing kiss and Tom whispered, "Damn, and I am so…"

But he located his cane, and left the room.

Ah. God.

But this was good. It didn't seem at all good in the moment, but I remembered my earlier intention.

Today I would get the T&A back on track. I slipped into my jeans and tired old blue shirt and let the allure of a tropical paradise all go to waste.

I couldn't bring myself to return to my study. Too many fresh memories of spookiness. After a penitent's breakfast of fruit and yogurt with the barest sprinkling of granola, I treated myself to a refill of the Otis Premium Blend and carried it into the security room, closing my mind to what the coffeemaker would have said if he'd have seen me bringing "food or drink" into his sacred space.

The room was windowless, shadowy, and crowded. I didn't see much space anywhere to put one's "food or drink" safely down. It reeked of technology—that unique, unnatural, intoxicating, techy smell. Metal, plastic, and the Internet. All the high-end, obscenely high-priced devices winked their banks of colorful lights in an intimidating manner. They seemed to be broadcasting, "Don't Spill On Me!" And, possibly, "Death to Scofflaws."

I decided to set my coffee on a shelf next to the door and only visit it from time to time.

I was trying to understand why, when a genuine intruder entered the house yesterday, our state-of-the-art security system was out to lunch.

On a number of occasions, Otis had tried to acquaint me with all the technicalities of the

Magna-Protect Custom 9,000 Home Security Package. It was supposed to monitor, 24/7, for burglary, fire, smoke, high levels of carbon monoxide, high and low temperatures, and medical emergencies. How come all this so-called monitoring dropped the ball on the rudimentary, "Hey, Allie! There's a guy in your house!"

But it hadn't. At least not completely. The system not only transmitted video of the outside perimeter of the house to right here—the location where monitoring was conducted—it also stored it digitally for the client's own perusal on the monitor in this room. When I brought up the recordings for yesterday afternoon, located the one from the cameras scanning the back of the house, and fast-forwarded through the hours between 1:00:00 p.m. and 3:00:00 p.m., I saw the storm come.

Wind ruffled the surface of the pool, lightning flashed, rain began whipping the lens. A short, rain-blurred guy in a black slicker that hid all his identifying features, slipped in the door from the kitchen deck as the door got grabbed by the wind and blown shut.

My whole body still sizzled with the electric current of that slam.

Right after that a particularly bright flare of

lightning was followed by black screen and an attempted reboot that flashed on the kitchen door again and, finally, a rolling pattern of nothing a person could make out at all. So much for "Battery Backup" and "Instant System Reboot."

But what I still didn't get was why—with the system fully functional at the instant the guy opened the door—didn't the alarm go off, alerting me and Magna-Protect, and summoning the Bratenahl police? I knew Otis armed the system as he and Tom left the house, because he had called up to me as he always did, "Allie, I'm arming the system. Don't forget to turn it off if you want to go out."

Well, duh, Otis.

But I had not turned it off.

I backed up the footage and watched the guy come in again, revisiting the prickle of the door slam and reliving the icy gut-clench of my flight to the closet. The police didn't arrive in answer to any alarm, silent or otherwise, and, after it was all over, there wasn't anything to see except a fritzed-out security system. The officers who showed up when Otis called them were unimpressed.

We agreed before they got there not to over-emphasize the missing book. It was gone, in my opinion, far, far beyond the reach of an after-the-fact routine follow-up where no one was dead. I didn't want to get us all tangled up in official police business—AKA Tony Valerio—unless I absolutely had to. And Otis supported me on that. Based on my own comparatively recent Mondo-break-in experience, the investigation of a B&E where nothing of value—in fact, nothing verifiable at all—is taken, can't help but go nowhere. We mentioned that the address book seemed to be gone but we didn't play up its possible significance.

I visited my cold coffee and came back to the chair, trying to shake loose some perspective. How could I find out if the system was on when the guy came in? *Ah. Wake up, Allie.* There was a log, too. A document you could print out or read onscreen. A resourceful woman such as myself should be able to find it without screwing up Otis' world.

Emphasis on the "should."

It was a crapshoot.

I peered at the menu at the top of the screen, recalling the Magna-Protect Promise of user-friendliness. I pulled down the one marked "Functions."

Here was something I had not considered: an option entitled "Remote Access." I'd forgotten we'd been told we could use our iPhones "from anywhere on the planet with phone service" to turn the heat up or down, the lights on and off, or who-knew-what all.

We could also disarm the system. "For example," the guy from Magna-Pro explained when he came out to acquaint us with the workings of the system, "if you wanted to let somebody in. IN AN EMERGENCY." All caps emphasis. The Magnafolks loved to invoke the idea of Emergency, Capital E. Making you feel dreadfully insecure and then using their merchandise and services to soothe you back to complacency was their stock in trade.

So maybe our remote-access had been hacked?

I scrolled around and pulled down some more tabs until I found our log. Bingo. There it was. At 3:25:26 the system was deactivated remotely.

Geez. What else could these creeps do remotely? Unlock the doors? Spy on us? I remembered the other cameras. They were all aimed at access points and not the living spaces. In theory. I was sure there were none in the master bedroom because I'd made Otis check. Under some pretense we both recognized for what it was.

My neck was wide awake and crawling again. I was starting to think that our big, fancy refuge might be about as safe as it felt to me yesterday.

Ant in a jar. That was me.

So naturally, at this very moment, the doorbell rang. Lucky me. If I had been holding my coffee cup, there would have been "drink" on the ceiling.

Chapter Sixteen

I tiptoed down the hall, mindful of Tom's warning which somehow penetrated the fog of the previous evening and got stuck in my brain. "Murder breeds murder. And it keeps getting easier on down the line."

This was even more unsettling today in the bright light of not-drunk.

The entry hall of the mansion was in keeping with the oversized and over-the-top grandeur of the rest of the place. The massive, elaborately paneled front door was a paragon of sturdiness. However, it was flanked by tall, unfortified sidelights. This inconsistency had flitted through my consciousness once or twice before, but it was front and center for me now.

The alarm panel on the wall by the door was twinkling busily. I suspected that its situation-room display of multicolored lights was working hard on impressing the client. It was a formidable array, though. The protective layer of "many-lights-mean-business" always made turning it off cold turkey daunting for me. If I was alone in the place, I usually hid and waited for the chime ringer to go away.

My heart was hammering, "*Run, Allie, run, run.*"

But this person was jamming on the doorbell with no sign of letting up. This didn't strike me as stealthy murderer MO. Reviewing the killers I'd met, I decided that annoying and rude did not fit the profile.

The appearance of a mop of curly red hair and a young, rather freckly, face—hands cupped around the eyes, and the eyes peering through battered round wire rims—pushed me over the edge. I entered the code and opened the door to a boy—you couldn't call this a man—of maybe eighteen. Jazzed, if I were guessing, by proximity to the biggest, fanciest house he'd ever seen.

"Whoa. You live here?" Hard emphasis on both the "you" and the "here?" Also on the question mark. He looked me up and down with serious dubiousness. Once again I remarked to myself on the sad, but probably good, fortune that Tom would never see the real me. Still, I was slightly torqued off.

"Nah. Squatting."

"Huh? Oh. You're kidding. I get it. I mean is this your house? Like, you're not a…servant or anything?"

"Can you even see daylight in that hole you're digging yourself into?"

"Huh? Oh. Sorry. I didn't mean to insult you or anything. I'm Andy. Andrew Riley. Intern at Channel 16." He held out his hand and, in spite of my offended self-image, I shook it.

"Lisa Cole gave me this package for you. If you're Allie Harper?" He appeared to seriously doubt this for a couple of seconds. Then he shrugged, reached into the messenger bag slung across his chest, and handed me out a padded manila mailer. The blue-and-white "Channel 16 It's News to YOU!!!" logo was emblazoned on the return sticker.

I took the package and fished in my pocket for a tip. I couldn't help myself. Interns need money like flowers need rain. Plus, I kind of liked the kid. He was such an unrepentant doofus. The bill in my pocket turned out to be a ten-dollar one. The kid's eyes widened and he started to ask something, reconsidered, stumbled over a thank you, fled down the steps and into a battered Jeep parked in the drive, and screeched away.

Cool. I'd provided beer money to an underage idiot with a Jeep.

I closed the door, reset the alarm, and stared down at the package in my hands. Here was a fresh opportunity for a T&A screw-up. Emphasis on the Allie.

Four days into the Lloyd case and I'd already lost three significant pieces of evidence—one of which was a house, one of which was a file I'd never even seen. The other was the address book I'd only started to delve into. That one had been in my hands, as substantial as the package I now held. My fingers were still twitching from the phantom pain of my severed grasp on that book, which was now reduced in my mind to two ambiguous words: CyCLE, Inc.

For all the obvious reasons, my first impulse was to hide the mailer. My next impulse was to take my new screw-up-in-waiting out of the big bright, window-infested entry hall into a dark, enclosed space and open it there.

Back in the Magna-Protect security room, I ripped open Lisa and Andy Reilly's package. Well, damn. It didn't look all that exciting. In fact, it looked a lot like research. I pulled out maybe thirty pages of a script.

The first scene was described as a long shot of a police car rolling down a snowy drive toward a well-tended suburban home. I didn't need to look at the voiceover column, to get a chill. Bad news for somebody. Tragedy. Dread.

I set the script aside and reached back in for something happier. Not much luck there, either. I shuffled though about ten pages of copied photos. Scrapped houses. They could have been taken at Lloyd's if the light in there were better.

Gaping holes in drywall exposing the stump-ends of severed pipes. A porcelain sink smashed to pieces in what must have been a fit of pique, a burst of exuberance, or a clumsy accident. More holes were knocked in smooth plaster to get at wiring. Still more holes, more severed pipes. Standing water pooled on tiles popped loose by lying a long while in standing water—was I having fun yet?

No. I moved on.

The last two pieces were a DVD disc and a note from Lisa.

"Hey, Allie. I grabbed this stuff for you. If you're one of the last humans to have a DVD player, here's a copy of the video made from the script. If not, you can stream it off our site. Let's talk when we have a minute. xo L."

The URL was there, but there was an actual DVD player right in front of me. I popped the disc in. Watched the squad car from the script roll down the drive, heard the crunch of snow, imagined the wife, or the husband, or maybe the parents at the back of the house having a regular morning that would end forever when the cop made her way up the front steps to ring the bell.

I hit pause. Delaying the delivery of somebody else's terrible news.

More cold caffeine would prepare me for this scene.

When Otis opened the door, I was standing right next to it, raising my contraband cup to my irresponsible lips. I jumped, of course. Cold brown liquid rained down the front of my shirt.

I didn't lose my grip on the cup, though. And I'm proud to say my shirt and I soaked up almost every drop.

Otis looked me over. Made note of the fact that the drink wasn't in the immediate vicinity of his equipment.

Sidestepping seemed to be my best defense.

"Otis," I said, "hi. I thought you'd be interested to know that the Magna-Protect Alarm can be operated remotely."

Chapter Seventeen

Fortunately—and, it turned out, also unfortunately—Otis had bigger fish to fry right then than my predictably careless behavior. But he had to try.

"Allie." He glanced down over me to a splash of brown liquid on my bare foot. "You must have a guardian angel or somethin'. I suppose you and Tom can afford to replace thousands of dollars' worth of high-tech equipment. So," he shrugged, "no worries."

I circled us back to higher ground. "But did you know that? About the remote access?"

"I did. I studied all the manuals. And Tom listened to them on his laptop. But access to that function is supposed to be protected. Like dead-protected. It would be a serious breach. Somebody could—"

I started filling in the blank. "Somebody could—" *Open the back door and walk right on in, climb the stairs, look for me, not find me, but find where I'd been sitting with my juicy clue and*— There I was. Right back in that stuffy closet again.

Otis noticed.

"It would be bad, Allie, but it should be impossible. At least I think…hope so. The owner of the house, maybe. But Magna-Protect rebooted the whole system, last thing before we moved in. In April. And I changed the codes."

We considered this. After another couple of frowns and a headshake for the possible complete breach of our so-called security system, Otis refocused his attention on me.

I prepared myself for something not good.

"Allie, there's been a development. I got a call from Valerio."

"Valerio? Tony? Why would he—?" I thought of a couple of reasons. Neither of them good. "Otis?"

"Remains have been discovered. A crew was out with one of those big excavators—a big shovel—to repair the break wall. In the lake west of here. Pretty close to where MLK turns into Lake Shore. East of the park, and—"

"They think they've found Lloyd."

"They think so. Not much le— not much for ID. But there was a gold chain. Not real gold, of course—"

"And it's Lloyd's?"

He nodded. Sure looks like it. "Ms. Coates put it on the list of identifying items he might have had on his person. She'd given him a chain. From her description, that chain. Tony thought it might be best if you gave her the news."

Terrific. Tony had finally come up with a use for me.

● ● ● ● ●

The Memorial-Nottingham Branch of the Cleveland Public Library used to be a school and it shows. Bright expanses of glass, and crayon-green beams create an open, friendly space that raised my spirits during my stint as a part-time librarian there. Before I met Tom and became gainfully unemployed.

That was the period of my life which I'd characterize as the Post-D.B. Harper-Lonely-Broke-Crappy Epoch. Before Tom (BT). Besides all that, I was ill-suited for the position, especially since my MA was in English literature, not library science, which made me a part-time *bogus* librarian.

Coincidentally, the library is home to the Ohio Library for the Blind & Physically Disabled, providing audio and Braille books and many other services. Tom uses it. Has for years. He and I might have crossed paths back then. Maybe we did. Something about that gives me a queasy feeling. Vertigo. As if our brushing by each other in a different reality could have erased us from each other's lives.

So one might appreciate all the mixed feelings I had about Mem-Nott. Especially that afternoon, when I was going there to give Loretta The Bad News.

Lloyd was a complete stranger to me four days ago, but he was in my life now. For keeps. For some reason, the phrase "carryout menu in top right desk drawer" kept sneaking into my head. Crispy's Tasty Eats. In the Cs. Lloyd was a person to me now and my throat was crammed full of sobs I was trying my hardest not to let out.

When I came through the door into the big main space I was relieved to see that Velma, not Loretta, was behind the main desk. I figured that Loretta, upon seeing me, would not think, "Oh, look! It's Allie."

She'd think, "Lloyd is dead." I tried very hard to arrange my face for the former, but I knew that would surely make everything worse.

Velma was my favorite fellow employee at The Branch. She and Loretta were both full-fledged, degreed librarians. Both of them were kind and supportive of me, in spite of my bogus standing. But they were day and night, those two.

Where Loretta was pale and worried, Velma was black and spunky. She favored bright colors and hairstyles that worked exclusively for her. She was always twinkling about something, eyes bright, smile at the ready. If she worried, she made a point of never letting it show.

I was extra glad it was her at the desk because she took one look at my meticulously arranged face and said, "Allie! What's happened? What's wrong?" And then, "Oh, no. Is this about Lloyd?"

● ● ● ● ●

After a few minutes spent wanting not to have heard what I'd told her, Loretta calmed down. Velma was right there with me for the news-breaking—which Loretta, of course, read right off the front page of my transparent expression.

It was Velma who pushed through Loretta's desperate resistance to the truth of what I'd told her. Velma, who delivered heartfelt words of faith and comfort, a warm hug, and a handful of tissues with the deft touch of a tough, kind-hearted woman who'd dealt with sad realities more than once in her life.

Quentin, the branch manager, a big, compassionate guy, gathered Loretta up, relieved Velma of duty, and turned temporary command of the library over to a young, possibly bogus, Part-time who looked thrilled to have some power for a change. I gave her a glance of solidarity.

Quentin drove Loretta. Velma followed Quentin. I followed Velma. It was a humble funeral cortège for Lloyd. Maybe the only one he'd ever get.

On that drive, alone in the last vehicle of Lloyd's parade—except, of course for Otis, who followed me at three car-lengths almost everywhere I went these days, whether I liked it or not—I kicked my original pledge to Loretta up a notch.

As we'd left the library, she'd taken my hand in both of hers. "Allie, I don't want you to feel bad about how this turned out. I asked you to find out what happened to Lloyd. Now I know. I can't thank you enough."

I'd hugged her and mumbled something that seemed half appropriate to how sad and mad I felt without upsetting her more. What I was thinking was, *not a chance, Loretta. No way.*

I wasn't done. Not even close. Nothing was solved.

One question was answered for sure. Lloyd wasn't in Vegas playing the slots. He didn't accidentally veer off some deserted road. Between the intersection of Euclid and Mayfield—where Lloyd ran his last light and the spot where his earthly remains were fished up from Lake Erie by a wretched shovel thing—was a real crime. A true mystery. I'd wasted a lot of time so far, feeling incompetent and blaming myself for clues that got away.

Somebody—maybe more than one somebody—was out there today. Probably not very far away. That person or persons unknown possessed the means, the motive, and the opportunity to end the life of Lloyd Bunker. A somewhat peculiar human being, with wounded, blue, school-boy eyes, who liked to get carryout from Crispy's.

Right there in my little red car I exercised my power as a Name Partner—or at least an Initial Partner —of the T&A Detective Agency, and took it upon myself to upgrade our investigation from The Case of "Lloyd Is Missing," to The Case of "Who the Fuck Murdered Lloyd?"

Chapter Eighteen

We'd been assured by everyone from the realtor to the landscaper that our Bratenahl mansion was blessed with a refined and gracious history. I was way more intrigued by its current owner, who—we'd also been told several times—supervised, on our behalf, the selection of every stick of furniture—of which there was not much—to replace stuff that he'd put in storage. Stuff ordinary people would need. Like a dining room table. And chairs. This, though, this suite of dining furniture, the realtor had told us in hushed tones, was from his private collection.

Wow.

On Tuesday night, as we, the three detectives of the T&A, took our seats for the very first time at the massive, dark, highly polished, hand-carved, roughly six-by twenty-foot table in the proportionally vast paneled dining room, I was wondering, not for the first time in the last few months, what that dude was all about.

"Despot" was the word that leapt to mind. "Dark Lord," maybe. Tom ran his sentient fingers over some Rococo-esque curlicues and winced. "How big is this furniture, anyhow?"

Otis had already settled himself into the throne at the head of the table. He grinned. "Daddy Bear-size, Tom. It's tacky as hell, but it sure is roomy."

The night was chilly with billowing rain. The airy breakfast nook felt all wrong for this serious and possibly hazardous occasion. Heavy, fringed drapes that muffled even the sound of the rain struck me as about right. Bulletproof drapes would have been welcome.

We were here to enter into the sketchy evidence we'd compiled up to now the fact that Lloyd was indeed dead, almost certainly murdered by a person or persons unknown. And to make our solemn declaration that—in spite of the sobering nature of this certainty—we, the T&As, were rock-solid about finding out who that was.

"I don't know what sort of man Lloyd was." I stopped to consider that "unique" might be the kindest word. "He may have been involved in something he shouldn't have been. But Loretta isn't a woman who would fall in love with a dangerous man. A bad man. She's—she pays attention to details like that. I realize this is turning out to be more than we bargained for as our first case, but—"

"Allie." Otis pressed his lips together. He was gearing up to be diplomatic. "Allie, I know you've got guts. More than is healthy for you a lotta times. But listen. Tony asked you to help out with telling Loretta. Right? He knows you better now—"

Uh-huh. I waited.

He waited.

"Otis?"

"Allie. Let me finish up this thought. You want to find out who killed Lloyd. And probably you'd like to know why. Although that's not—"

"I understand."

"I'm not sure you do, but here's what I'm thinking. You want the information. You want—"

"I want justice. For Lloyd. And answers for Loretta."

His mouth tightened up more.

"That's what this is about. Yes. But the way I see it, we can find out what there is to find out and maybe that'll amount to getting justice for Lloyd. And answers, too.

"But you and Tom are still front and center in a lot of crooked minds around town. You aren't anonymous citizens anymore. Everybody's seen your photos. The stuff on TV. That MondoSecrets website is down now, but months too late. You can't wander around 'being detectives.'"

"Tom. Otis just used finger quotes on us. You should know."

"I heard them, Allie. I agree with him. For the most part."

"Traitor."

"Cut it out, Allie." Otis said, "Listen now. I'm not trying to stop you, I only want— You guys don't have to do all the heavy lifting on this. You can get what you need for Loretta without—number one—making me nuts. And two, big major two, making Tony more nuts.

"He owes you one now, Allie. You've got him. Tony's given a lot of folks bad news over the years, but telling somebody like Loretta bad news she's been holding her breath on since February? That's like sticking needles in your eyes. Sorry, Tom. I should pay more attention—never mind. It would be like that.

"Tony knows you're smart, Allie. He almost trusts you sometimes. He'd never say so but—You need to tell him everything you've found out and everything you're thinking and let him take on some responsibility for this one.

"Talk with Tony. Coordinate with him. You'll

still have the satisfaction of helping build our case. If—*when* we find out what happened to Lloyd, you guys will be the ones to tell Loretta whatever we find. Which I gotta say is not going to make her jump for joy anyhow. So don't expect that."

"No, I don't. Will we need to go to the Fifth District Headquarters to talk with him? I have kind of a reputation up there."

Otis smiled for the first time since he'd sat down, so happy in his Daddy Bear chair. "Girl, I think you can probably lure Tony here with a pizza."

Chapter Nineteen
Wednesday, June 21

Wednesday morning, Otis drove Tom to a meeting at Case. Tom's expression as they left the house was grim. I watched him go. Jaw tight. Shoulders locked. He was radiating anger and despair. I had nothing for this. No words to lift his spirits.

The first night of the Mondo, I'd told Tom that his winning five-hundred-fifty million dollars with a number he and Rune had cobbled together from birthdays, on the one and only lottery ticket he'd ever bought, was an act of God.

"Like a tsunami or an earthquake," he'd said.

I didn't have a clue. We'd met barely eight hours before, but I was beginning to realize that Thomas Bennington III could be my own personal act of God. That it was him I'd been praying for at the bus stop, when I thought I was merely hoping the #30 would be on time.

So there he was in the crosswalk. Courtesy of Lisa Cole and her boss' Hummer. Associate Professor of English literature, Dr. Right, PhD. Smart, funny, kind to my BFF Margo, and, yeah, hot. Way hot. What warmed my D.B. Harper-demoralized heart, was that this great guy appeared to be attracted to me, even though he'd never seen me and never would.

The jackpot felt like a bonus to me on that magical evening. We kissed and the Mondo Ball dropped five-hundred-fifty million dollars, like fireworks, over Collinwood. I don't blame myself for not seeing all the possible complications. The murders didn't even start until after midnight.

Tom, though, saw trouble coming that first night. His vision for that was 20/20. This morning's meeting would be the final payout of Tom's five-hundred-fifty-million-dollar nightmare. In the grand tradition of lottery winners everywhere, he was on his way to quit his day job.

Last night's meeting was the tipping point. The T&A's first case was not some minor mystery. Not a quirky missing person. As we suspected from the start, Lloyd was murdered. And not because somebody decided to jack his car. Murdered on purpose. *With* purpose. A plan. That was bad enough, but now the elements of the case appeared to be moving all by themselves. Shifting. Connecting. Circling back to us, maybe. To the money, maybe.

Our impenetrable security system had been shut down remotely. Evidence was stolen from two separate locations. One of those locations, my own cozy study. Hard as it was to admit, we were all way beyond business as usual. Otis was flat-out insisting that we lock ourselves down more. He'd described Tom's regular Monday-Wednesday-Friday teaching schedule as some unknown criminal's "appointment with a sitting duck."

Danger was reshaping our lives again. Our world was shrinking. Tom's hard-won, rewarding career came to a dead stop with the discovery of Lloyd in the lake.

● ● ● ● ●

I wandered around for a while. Indoors, of course. With the security system armed. For all the good that might do. Fingers crossed.

In my folder for Tony of our efforts on the original "Lloyd Is Missing" Case was a list of evidence we didn't have anymore—a house, a file, an address book—which was about all the evidence there'd been. Gone. Lost. Stolen. Embarrassing. I had Lisa Cole's scrapper file, but that was all. And nothing there was news.

"CyCLE," though, might still be a viable clue. Maybe Lloyd worked there. I'd pictured him with his night watchman flashlight, walking the halls of a computer company. This could be it. Or a dead end. Maybe I was all "cyber" because tech was so in my face right now. Okay. Maybe a bicycle or motorcycle company? Unicycles seemed farfetched, even to me.

My salvage of that name was the only item on my list I could do something about myself, right now. I stopped myself from worrying about Tom and went online. I looked up CyCLE, Inc.

Here it came again: That unnerving rush of a bioelectric device going bonkers behind my ribs.

CyCLE wasn't computers or bikes.

It was scrap.

• ● ⬤ ● •

After the revelation that CyCLE was primarily in the business of buying and processing scrap metal, the first thing I wanted to do was call them up and ask them if they had a Lloyd Bunker on their payroll. I'd moved him out of the dark corridor in my mind and stuck him in a hellish setting of twisted metal and slavering junkyard dogs.

I could ask—

But no. That was last year's Allie Harper. This year's model was working on ditching her "gotta know/gotta go" compulsions.

I started with the Internet.

We'd already heard from Tony about the ties between the yards and the scrapping-for-dollars craze. At best they were a legitimate way for enterprising citizens to make some money. At worst, they'd been accessory to all kinds of crime and misery.

Right away I found new regulations designed to put a stop—or at least a slow—to some of that. For example, if I wanted to sell my big length of copper pipe in the state of Ohio, I'd need to present my driver's license, give my scrapyard person the make, model, and license number of my vehicle, and get my photo taken. With my copper pipe. The yard would keep my transaction records for a year.

Sounded good in theory. But this was Cleveland, after all. We can be pragmatic about that sort of thing.

CyCLE, Inc.'s website was nothing fancy, but the bare bones were clean and clear enough. They'd buy your scrap. They'd come pick it up if it were big and heavy. I smiled. *Ah. My three-thousand-pound Buddha.* They'd give you a fair price and handle everything responsibly.

"Call for details!"

They had three locations in Greater Cleveland. For my convenience. Now that I knew what I was looking for, I realized that I'd driven by CyCLE #1 about a thousand times. I wanted to go right then. Drive by. Take a peek. Maybe look around a bit and—

I took a hard line with myself.

No. Just, no.

But wait. Loretta! Surely Loretta would remember hearing the name of Lloyd's employer. She'd mentioned he'd finally gotten a job he liked. How wrong would it be to call her up and ask? Jog her painful memories.

Hassle her in her time of grief?

Yeah, okay. Got it.

I couldn't call Loretta. At least not until tomorrow.

I didn't have to wait, though, because right after lunch, she called me.

She thanked me again, tearfully, but not as sad as yesterday, for our help in getting answers about Lloyd. So she could move on "at some point."

Then she asked me to be sure to tell Otis and Tom, too. "Your helpers." I realized that Loretta, although she'd been our first bona fide client, never learned the name of our firm. Just as well.

After a bit, during which she shared that she was going back to work tomorrow and not staying home to "brood," I spied an opportunity.

"Loretta, I don't think I ever heard who Lloyd was working for. Did he tell you?'

Loretta's mom never raised any slowpokes.

"Allie! You're not still trying to figure out who—" She choked on the words. I jumped in.

"No. No, Loretta. I was closing the file, and I realized that was something I didn't know about Lloyd. I mean, we'd talked about how he loved his new job, but you never..."

I threw as much wistful sorrow as I could onto that "never."

She sniffled. "Oh. I'm sorry, Allie. Of course. Thank you. You've been very kind. Now what was it? Something with boats..."

"Boats?" *Really?*

"Not, boats that he was working on. Boats in the name. Floating. Float...something." I sensed the pucker developing between her eyes. And then, *pop!*

My fragile cord binding Lloyd to employment at CyCLE snapped.

"Flotilla! Flotilla. Corporation? Something. But Lloyd always calls—called it 'Flotilla.' I think it was a bunch of little companies, like small boats in a…you know. A flotilla. But Lloyd worked at the biggest one. 'The flagship,' he liked to call it. Thought that was funny. An office building, with several floors, I never even knew where—" Another sniffle.

I wanted to let her go. Let her mourn her loss far from my self-serving interrogation, but I needed to salvage something from this disappointment. "And he was a night watchman there?"

"I'm pretty sure. I know he didn't want to admit to me that's what he was. But he worked nights, all by himself, in what must have been a big empty building. What else?"

I'd made her cry enough for one day.

"Loretta, take care of yourself. You need time—I guess it's good you're going back to work. You shouldn't be alone with this."

She bounced right back, almost happy. "Oh, Allie, I'm not going to be alone. My friend Lisa Cole from Channel 16 is throwing a celebration of Lloyd's life—a wake, I'd guess you'd call it—in the bar downstairs. After her bit on the six o'clock news. We're going to drink Lloyd's favorite. The Manhattan!" Her voice perked up more. "I may not go back to Mem-Nott tomorrow after all."

"Good for you, Loretta. That sounds lovely."

God bless you, Lisa Cole. You deserve something a lot better than 16.

So Lloyd got both a cortége and a wake. How cool was that?

Chapter Twenty

In honor of the first day of summer, we were holding our meeting with Tony Valerio on the deck closest to the lake. Two of the four of us were a cop and an ex-cop, so I figured we might be fifty percent safe outdoors.

On this, the official longest day of the year, the sun was miles from setting. The wind had calmed to a lazy waft, the air had warmed to balmy. I like that in an evening.

I was encouraged to see Tony arriving in his off-duty attire. Loafers with no socks made him almost human in my book. Not trendy, maybe, but still. Plus, he was bearing a social-looking bottle of red. I wasn't letting my guard down, though. The wind could change.

Otis, our in-house ex-cop P.I. and official liaison with law enforcement, brought two large Beach Club pizzas to the table. One was the well-named

Utopia—red sauce, pepperoni, sausage, bacon, poblano peppers, onions, mushrooms, provolone. The other was my personal fav, the Wildwood Club—pesto, fresh spinach, bacon, mushrooms. With chicken.

Chicken was my idea and cost extra. My close personal relationship with one-hundred-ninety-million-after-taxes was easing me off my thrifty upbringing. I tried not to think of it as trading Tom's life's work for some chicken. As a sore point, today was very sore.

There was beer from the Great Lakes Brewery as well. No salad. Salad would have been frivolous at our business meeting.

Otis allowed us a few minutes for edgy pleasantries and pizza, and got down to it. "Tony, Allie has a list of some theories we had and some"—he slowed to pick a good word—"things that have happened that we believe relate to the disappearance and death of Lloyd Bunker."

He wiped the pizza off his hands, produced my skinny file, and covered my list in a small number of concise words: MLK. Lloyd's house key. Scrapping. The loss of Lloyd's financial file from Loretta's apartment.

Tony's brow lifted.

Otis raised both palms, a surrender-like gesture

designed to invoke the spirit of one cop guy to another. "I looked at the scene, Tony. No sign of a break-in. Nothing disturbed. And although Ms. Coates is a tidy and well-organized person, I had to consider the likelihood that the file was simply…mislaid. I wouldn't have enjoyed calling that one in."

Lordy. On "mislaid," I grabbed another slice of the Wildwood and treated myself to a sip of beer. I hoped Loretta was not feeling a disturbing ripple of librarian disrespect in the air.

Have another Manhattan, Loretta.

Otis didn't downplay our own break-in and the theft of the original address book, though. We'd reported it to the Bratenahl PD, he said, since it was their jurisdiction. But with no evidence except the absence of the book and my needing to hide in a closet—the brow ascended again—they'd been attentive but unimpressed.

"Allie went through the security cam footage yesterday morning and found a shot of the intruder. I made you a copy of what there is in the log. But again. Not much. We believe the security system was turned off remotely. That's a major problem for us, like you'd think, but I'm working with the security people. You'll know when I do."

I'd thrown a copy of Lisa's scrapper coverage in

with my lists, but that was all old news to Tony. He barely glanced.

"So." He tipped his beer bottle toward me.

My ballgame now.

"Tony." I took a beat to breathe and corral my points, and he jumped into the vacant space.

"Allie."

Drat. I'd already lost control of the ball.

"What?"

He huffed out a sigh. "Look. How about a—I hate to say 'truce' because that might cause me to let my guard down."

"Oh, yeah? What about my guard?"

"Okay. I get that. We've been in each other's hair and on each other's nerves, Allie. But I've got the experience and the authority you don't have and you've got the fresh point of view—and the funding—I don't have. You guys can pay for…things. Hell, you can pay for two pizzas. That's out of reach of the Cleveland Police Department's budget most of the time. Otis has proposed, I guess, an alliance. Shit. I cannot even listen to myself saying that without needing another beer."

I grabbed a bottle of Great Lakes' Grandes Lagos© from the cooler and slid it across the table. Used the distraction of a pale lager to slip a fragment of peacemaking under the door. "You can imagine how embarrassed I am about the evidence that got swiped, Tony."

He nodded and then reversed course and shook his head.

"No. I don't think you—Allie, I hear you. It would have been…better…to have all that stuff. But you're a novice so you're missing a very important point. Three key pieces of evidence have been stolen."

Okay, let's go ahead and sue me for being a novice, Tony.

"Yeah. I'm aware."

"No, really. I don't—You still don't get it. Three. Key. Pieces. Of evidence, Allie. *Have been stolen.*"

Wow. He was really rubbing it in. And Tom was nodding. And now Otis was nodding.

"Thanks for making this so clear, Tony. I don't think I could feel much worse about it than I do, but I'll try—*oh.*"

"Exactly. Oh. There's a fourth piece and it's probably the biggest deal. Why don't you tell me what it is since you just finally figured it out for yourself?"

I started in slow and picked up speed as Tony's revelation revealed itself to me. "Each of those missing pieces…is missing because…it linked somebody to Lloyd's murder! The trashing of the house. The theft of Loretta's file. The break-in for the address book. Equal and opposite clues. 'Have been stolen' says that somebody knows Lloyd's murder is bigger than Lloyd's death."

"Well, finally. What's more, your memory of CyCLE, which links scrapping to Bunker's house may be the most important bit. Don't exactly know how yet. But you should feel pretty good about that. Not to encourage you. Don't let it go to your head. And make you sloppy. Sloppier.

"Truth is, and this is why I'm here, the T&A didn't help us find Lloyd's body. He just showed up. But your investigation has filled in some blanks that we'd likely have missed. We're in a better position to pursue this now."

I nodded, speechless, partly because Tony was saying something encouraging about the T&A's contribution to a stagnant case, but mostly because he'd said "T&A."

I glared at Otis.

Otis wasn't looking at me.

I looked back at Tony. He was grinning.

"So here's what I suggest. You work your leads—relying on Otis for common sense—until they start involving your usual craz—uh, ill-considered crap—" He read my face. "What I mean is you doing anything that would be more dangerous to your person—and Tom's person, let's not forget—than you merely being yourself on any given day."

That wasn't much better but I gave him a D+ for trying. His using Tom as a weapon against me was mean, but it worked. Tom was my weak spot, my irreplaceable gift from the Goddess of Luck. I knew that goddess. She and the Bulldozer of Fate were sisters. I'd watched her spin her Fickle Finger.

Win. Lose. Dead.

Tony could tell he'd hit home. "You know what's at stake. You, of all people. So here's my non-negotiable rule: You listen to Otis. Do what you do. Make sure he knows what you're up to. Take his advice. And when he says, 'It's time to call Tony,' call me. Got it?"

I didn't say, "Yes, sir" because I didn't want to make him that happy, but it all seemed reasonable. If insulting.

I nodded and shot him my evilest smile. "I guess this makes you a member of the T&A, Tony."

"Did we shake on that?"

"No. Not yet."

"We're not going to, either. Don't forget what I said."

He left. We had another round of Grandes Lagos and sat for a long time while our own Grande Lago lost itself in the luminous haze of evening. The breezes eventually picked up like they do when night comes in over big water. The gulls made their ritual day-is-done flight out toward the horizon. *Why?* I asked myself. *Do they sleep out there?* I'll never figure out what makes gulls do all the incomprehensible things gulls do, but it's fun to watch.

That was it. We gathered up our stuff and went inside.

Chapter Twenty-one
Thursday, June 22

Otis and I had a plan to pay a visit to CyCLE to find out whether they were aboveboard or underhanded. For that, we needed a story, a beat-up truck, and a catalytic converter, AKA a "cat." That last thing was the challenge. Especially for me. My knowledge of those stopped at "need to have a working one to pass your E-check."

My inability to raise the cash to replace the one in the my salsa red VW Bug, The Flying Tomato, grounded her last summer. Which was how I came to be sitting in the bus stop at the exact moment Lisa Cole and the borrowed Hummer honked at Tom. This confluence of coincidences should explain why I was so antsy about the doggone Luck Goddess.

The cat we were looking for needed to be a good one which, in theory, could bring us as much as two hundred dollars at the yard. We wanted it to be original equipment from a newer model car. It was also important to us that there be ambiguity in the area of its having been legally obtained. Otis went on a mission and came back with the item we needed. He did this, according to him, without stealing it, but he wouldn't tell me anything about where or how he got it.

Fine.

I adored the truck Otis got us. Even before I climbed up into the passenger seat, the disreputable red Ford pickup took me on a nostalgic ride down some old country roads. It was red. It was ancient. It had a standard transmission, of course. It looked like it'd been driven 250,000 miles through mud holes and over ruts. It was dented. It was filthy. It smelled like sweat, dirt, and motor oil.

Home.

We explained our plan to Tom, having invited him into a balmy spot on the deck and plied him with one of Otis's fine Margaritas. I stayed generally un-plied so I could be a more effective persuader. Tom listened to this plan and let his expression speak for him. It said, "I have serious doubts about your half-assed plan." Actually, it said, "No way in hell." But I scaled that down to something I could manage before I answered.

"Tom. I will be with Otis in a public place."

"A mall is a public place. A restaurant is a public place. A scrapyard is a shady place. Marginal. Dogs. Guns. Who knows what? Did Tony approve this idea?"

I threw Otis a silent plea for backup.

"No, Tom. I didn't go to Tony with this. He couldn't give us the go-ahead for the plan without calling attention to the T&—To our arrangement. But I wouldn't take Allie there if I thought it would be dangerous. It's probably at least as safe as malls. You want to run into a bunch of rowdy teenagers and some actual criminals, go shopping on a Saturday. In the 'burbs."

I jumped in. "Tony said, and I quote, 'Listen to Otis.' We can trust his judgment, Tom."

"Will you be armed, Otis?"

"Tom. I am always armed. I'm armed right now.

Chapter Twenty-two
Friday, June 23

I created Lee Ann Smith out of a pair of wrecked cowboy boots and some washed-out jeans, packed away from a time in my life so alien I could barely find myself in it. Pre-Ohio State. Pre-Ohio. Before Tom Bennington. Before even D.B. Harper. Lee Ann was the me I'd been trying to grow out of. Or maybe retrieve.

Even if Tom had been able to see me for all of our time together, he still wouldn't have recognized this Allie Harper. The boots. The jeans. The plaid flannel shirt with the threadbare elbows. The hair pulled back and tamped down. The glimpse of an ill-considered tattoo. A little wild. A lot out of control.

Otis looked more like himself. There was a steady, always been Otis, presence about him. I owed him my life. I owed Tom my life. Something about that gave me confidence for assuming the identity of Lee Ann. One more time for a good cause.

We had our cat. We had our truck. We had our story.

We were ready for the scrapyard.

●　●　●　●　●　●

"Smith," I said to the guy. "Lee Ann Smith."

"Rexroad. Howard Rexroad." A grin with some disrespect attached.

He discounted my "Smith," I could tell, but wasn't going to make a big deal about it. No picture ID required for me. I already knew more about this outfit than I did going in.

"Well, now. What you got for me here, Lee Ann?"

"Catalytic converter. Grand Cherokee 2014. I…a friend bought it at a tag sale. Gave it to me for…" I met his eyes. Embarrassed but not much. "for being a good friend in his time of need. I looked it up online. Seems like it would be worth something. Maybe a lot."

The thing was awkward with pipes and bends. It weighed a ton and I'd been holding it on my lap in the truck for what felt like a year. I hoped

Howard Rexroad would take it off my hands. No questions asked.

Then we'd know what kind of enterprise CyCLE was.

I held it out. He didn't take it. Too bad for me.

"I tell you what, Lee Ann. Tell your friend to park over there and let's you and me bring this around back. I got equipment that will tell me more about what you got here."

Crap. I was not so enthusiastic about following old Howard "around back." I sized him up. He had maybe a hundred pounds on me and a lot of gratuitous tall. I had agility and desperation on my side of the equation. Didn't give me a lot of confidence. But I gave Otis a little directional wave and a teensy frown of dismay Howard couldn't see, and then I followed him, lugging my cat and its questionable provenance in my aching arms.

The yard was tidier than I expected, but not in any way attractive. In my opinion, severed body parts from the corpses of worn-out, run-down, wrecked-up vehicles, stripped of all their elegant functions, make the ugliest kind of trash. This was a graveyard for dead metal. Pieces sorted into bins. Stacked up rusted bodies, still on wheels but going nowhere. Random piles. Towering. Leaning. I'd sure hate to see my Flying Tomato end up here.

It reassured me no end to see the rusty Ford pickup with Otis at the wheel, slow and reliable, easing into view. Trailing me and Howard Rexroad around back. Howard, however, was less than thrilled.

"Hey, Lee Ann. What's your friend doing bringing that truck back here? I told you to leave him out front."

"Ray has a mind of his own, Howard." I couldn't resist. "Also, he's real jealous about me and other guys."

Howard digested this information, swinging his stare from Otis to me and back. He shook his head.

"Huh. How'd a cute little redneck like you—?" He glanced back at Otis, up behind the wheel—looking big and not white—and let the question hang off an insulting smile.

I activated the Allie Harper who was both the real me and the me who was Lee Ann wearing my old clothes and riding in a truck with her black boyfriend. Both us ladies were simmering.

"I'm sorry, sir. You just insulted me and everything I care about. I can find myself another junkyard. No sweat. Dime a dozen."

I swiveled, and my boot heel made a satisfying sound in the grit on the pavement.

Howard grabbed my arm. The one that wasn't

weighed down by the catalytic converter. The cat that I was considering swinging at his head if only I could lift it up that high. "Aw. C'mon. That ain't what I—"

The door latch on the truck went, "Chunk." Howard dropped me and put both his hands in the air where "Ray" could see them.

"Miss—*Miz* Smith. Let's back up here. I apologize to you and your friend. That was ignorant. I was…just flirting a bit. That's all. How about I make it up to you by offering you a hundred and fifty dollars for that heavy ole' thing you got there?"

It was a welcome offer. The "heavy ole' thing" was pulling my arms off my body. I could manage it for another minute, though.

"Let's say, two hundred, Howard. And I'll wave to Ray and let him know to stay in the truck. The sight of money chills him out. Otherwise…"

Howard didn't blink. He reached under his vest, into his back pocket, and pulled out a roll of bills. The hundreds were on the outside. He shucked me off two of them. Waved to Otis. Took my ton of bricks and trotted away.

I was back in the pickup in five seconds.

Otis turned the key and started backing out, while keeping one eye free to give me a look. "What was that all about?"

"He insulted our relationship. I implied, by my demeanor, that I was unwilling to sell my catalytic converter to a bigot, and that you would come back after dark and kill his ass. Okay?"

Otis cranked the truck around and peeled out, slinging a lot of small stones that made an even better racket than boots on grit.

"Works for me."

"Nah, Otis. It would work for my 'Ray.' But you're not him. You have a leveler head."

"I wouldn't count on it, Lee Ann." His mouth was set. "I wouldn't bet the farm."

Chapter Twenty-three
Saturday, June 24

"So what do we know about the CyCLE place this morning that we didn't this time yesterday?" Tom was still edgy, but at least his curiosity was up and running.

"Not much, Tom. But we do know the guy didn't ask our Lee Ann here to show her ID. Didn't insist on accepting the catalytic converter at the front of the lot. Or provide any kind of paperwork for the transaction. Took no photos. Nothing for the record. Maybe all we know is that Howard found Allie irresistibly attractive, even though, in my opinion, that wasn't her best look. Except for the boots, maybe."

I let that pass. "But Otis, he sure didn't act like someone who'd never done that kind of thing before. So at least we've observed that he's comfortable bending the rules. And that he's a jerk.

"If he'd given me one look and said, 'Ms. Smith, I'm going to need to see your picture ID,' then we'd know something different. Doesn't prove anything, but I'm glad we went because I got to see a scrapyard. Some stuff you need to experience for yourself."

Tom was leaning back in his chair now, relaxed and relieved. Only a small residual amount of pissed-off about how worried he'd been. This was a pattern for him and me, starting last summer when I was less mature than now.

We were on the pool deck waiting for the guys from Magna-Protect to come and report on their "intensive review" of how come our expensive security system welcomed an intruder like it was old home week. It was sunny and hot. Plus muggy.

I thought our getting sent not one but two guys on a Saturday morning was a sign of how affluent this house, with its lakeside deck, house-side deck, pool deck…all those intersecting levels of decks with the flower boxes strewn everywhere…all of the everything it displayed so lavishly made us look to the security outfit. And, yeah, like everybody else in the uncivilized world, they knew about the MondoMegaMoney.

"Anyway," I started up again, "what we didn't find out is why CyCLE was front and center in

Lloyd's address book. Of course, it was in there toward the front because it was in the Cs. But of the listings I'd examined up to then, it had the most contact information: landline, cell phones, e-mail, a bunch of stuff. And it was one of the parts of the book that fell open when I paged through. So we at least know that Lloyd had some reason to contact them."

Tom was wearing his serious listening/thinking expression. Focusing his attention on his thoughts. Not streaming them slap-dash, free-association-style, the way I did. Unrolling them, one at a time, in slow motion. Freezing the one that counted. The one that might give him an answer. Or an unexpected new question.

"Let's ask something different. Look for another connection entirely. Something that could help us link Lloyd to that place. Besides the address book. And the fact that his house was scrapped. How about maybe he needed parts. What kind of car did Tony say Lloyd's was?"

Otis didn't have Tom's magical thought process, but he made up for it with his uncanny memory. "A blue/green vintage GTO. The '67."

We all got there at the same moment. Even old scattered me. My neck buzzed. All those corpses of cars. Howard, a guy who'd know the value of a vintage GTO. A verified rule-bender-guy. With acres of room to hide a treasure he didn't want to crush to bits. Just yet.

Otis was nodding along to the beat of the idea. "A vintage GTO. Lloyd's last ride. It would connect whoever was towing it to his murder, and if it's at CyCLE, them too. It's a reach, but all the stuff that fits—"

I jumped on. "Plus, it might be hard for someone who knew its value to give it up. Especially something that would go straight to pennies-on-the-pound if you demolished it. And you could hide a circus train in the back of that yard. We can check the—"

I was about to say, "We can check the registration. Nobody could have stolen or hidden that. We'll know exactly what we're looking for."

But before I could finish the sentence, a lilting voice from the stone walkway around the side of the house pealed, "Yoo-hoo! Anybody home?"

The guys from MagnaPro were both women. Score two for girl-power.

Chapter Twenty-four

After their bright and cheery greeting, the Magna-Pro women, Sandy and Margaret, were all business. They had the paperwork, an explanation, and a fix for "the glitch" that put out the welcome mat and opened our back door to Mr. Slicker.

Sandy, the spokesperson for the duo—business-y dress, sensible heels, neatly coiffed hair to match her name: body armor for The Smart Woman in GuyLand—was straight up and straight on.

"We were hacked," she said. Telling it like was. Like it should not have been. "Specifically, your system was hacked. Something about the way the owner transferred the system to Otis—Mr. Johnson—created a vulnerability. No fault of the owner, or Mr. Johnson, I can tell you that for sure."

My back went up. "We didn't need to hear that about Otis. The owner—"

The owner had antagonistically obnoxious taste in furniture. It antagonized me, at least. That's all I knew for sure. No crime there, I supposed. The jury was still out for me, though. I left the sentence dangling. Sandy didn't pick it up.

"Our theory is whoever got in here—" The pain of saying "got in here" put a cramp in Sandy's professional bearing. She winced, a bit. Around her eyes. "Person or persons unknown to the owner and to us. Those people knew a lot about you, Dr. Bennington, and your…good fortune."

Tom did a better job of containing his reaction to an unwelcome phrase than Sandy. He merely nodded at his "good fortune."

"The way they were up-to-speed with your arrangements here? Makes us think they may have been keeping track of you all. For months, maybe. It takes time and significant planning…"

Otis frowned. Sandy moved on.

"You and Ms. Harper were both out of the country. Mr. Johnson was recuperating from his heart bypass surgery. They were out there. Somewhere. Waiting."

Otis glanced up and shot her a dagger re: "invasion of privacy" on the matter of his surgery. He let that one go, too.

"And then, once this place was all set up for

you to move in, the system was rebooted. Right on schedule.

"At that moment, they—whoever they are—had somebody—this is embarrassing for us, distressing in every possible way—located…uh…embedded, with Magna-Pro."

I was all ears on this one. "You mean, like a *mole*?"

Her face twitched again. This was a great example of the kind of pressure that builds ulcers and heart attacks. She got her control back and continued.

"I guess you could characterize him that way. The culprit provided an excellent file: degree, job history, references. All very expertly manufactured, but not—He's gone. Like he never existed. If he's within a thousand miles of here, we can't turn up even a trace. And believe me, we've tried. This was professional. At the level of a government contractor. At least.

"Dr. Bennington, you should know that people were let go because of this. Their jobs were to not permit something like this to happen. Ever."

She shrugged. "Collateral damage."

I knew Tom. He was not a bloodthirsty guy, but he accepted that news without comment.

Sandy produced an expensively designed binder. Tasteful, in a power-play way. The embossed logo was restrained to the point of invisibility. It drew the eye from the leather-like expanse to the company's name, aggressively small in the corner. "Needs-no-introduction," its size declared. The tagline below Magna-Protect, Inc. was way too tiny to read. Probably something innocuous and not true. "We'll keep you and all your stuff perfectly safe." Catchy like that.

I gave up and listened to Sandy.

She opened the book. Oh, cool. It was an upscale version of a Trapper Keeper. As in junior high.

I stifled all comment.

"This is how we propose to make you whole. First, we are refunding all the fees you've paid to Magna-Pro from day one of our relationship to date." She smiled and her voiced warmed. Tom would not see the smile, but he would hear it. "I believe it's a case of 'this is going to hurt us more than it would you.' But we wouldn't have it any other way.

"As soon as you can be ready, we will send a select, fully vetted team of three specialists to completely examine, redesign, and reboot your system. Everything will be replaced and secured. Hardware. Software. That will take twenty-four hours. I'd suggest you go somewhere for that period.

"I assure you, with my own job as collateral—" Her voice faltered as she heard herself saying "collateral damage," in that dispassionate voice, not two minutes ago, about some other folks, but she grabbed her composure back. "Your home will be perfectly secure during your absence. We'd like to start as soon as possible."

"Monday morning at eight," Tom said. "We'll be out. And we'll be back Tuesday at nine. I'll give you the extra hour." He warmed his voice a couple of degrees to acknowledge her professionalism and all she had at stake. "Thank you, both."

They left. Margaret, serious and alert, had played surgical nurse to Sandy's high-powered surgeon. When Sandy put out her hand for a Trapper Keeper, Margaret slapped it on there. They were a well-oiled machine, but Margaret never said a word, unless the opening "Yoo-hoo" was her.

Chapter Twenty-five

"So. What do you think, Tom?"

Both he and Otis knew what I wanted. Tom had a gift. It was part of the discipline he'd invested in putting his life back together—as a student, a teacher, and a man—after he became blind at twenty-five. He often could tell when someone was lying. I called it his deFIBulator. It worked best, unfortunately, on me.

The tight focus he brought to listening came fully loaded with information: the timbre of a voice, small, awkward breaks, an intake of breath. The concentration it takes to keep a lie aloft, like flying a kite. Tom could read these. He wasn't one hundred percent accurate, but it gave us a boost sometimes.

I wanted to know if he thought Sandy was lying. He shook his head. "There was something. She wasn't lying on purpose. She was very direct and there was nothing of a practiced liar in her. She's good at softening the truth, making it more palatable, of course. Job description for her."

Frowning now. "But it was like she herself had a question that wasn't answered to her satisfaction. She was hoping we wouldn't ask about it, maybe. She bumped into it two or three times. Something about what happened at our reboot? Something about their 'embedded' guy. And the plan to rebuild every single thing in one day. Those could be about technology she doesn't understand. Or the timing. Whether they can really get the job done in twenty-four hours. And I don't think she likes the owner of our house any more than you do."

"What? Tom, I never said—"

A grin. "You hate his chairs, that dining room. You believe only a pretentious prick could want furniture like that. Except for Otis' Daddy Bear Chair, which you're prepared to make an exception for."

"Glad to hear that, Tom." Otis was trying not to laugh. I could tell that with my eyes wide open.

"Whatever. I can't help it." I burst in. Indignation was giving my chain a yank. "The guy who made that room such an—arrogant spectacle. Him. And you're right. I hate his taste. I know I'm not being rational. But as far as I'm concerned, he's gotta be a Grade-A dick."

I heard my unladylike, and probably unwarranted, snarkiness, but before I could backtrack and acknowledge I wasn't being at all kind, and that possibly the poor fellow had a difficult childhood, was a sensitive lover, and so sweet with his children, the Universe delivered her retribution.

As so often happens, she used my phone.

It rang. My ringtone for the incoming caller was the drum intro to "Sympathy for the Devil." *Damn.* I picked up. And got what I deserved for being mean-spirited.

As advertised by his own special tune, it was D.B. Harper. My despicable ex.

The ringtone ratted him out, so I led off with my usual irritated, "*What?*"

"Allie," his voice oozed into my ear.

I considered how it would be at least ten-seconds'-worth of fun to drop the phone into the pool.

"D.B., what brings your nastiness here to mess up this lovely morning?"

"They call it a cell phone. You could break yours right now, but I'd get back to you sooner or later."

God. He knew me so well.

"Tell me what you want and let me see if I can salvage anything from the day."

He sighed. Fifty percent annoyance; fifty percent evil satisfaction. "Alice, I'm worried about Rune. Rune Davis? I'm concerned he may need additional protection. If the word should happen to get out about his location. With his folks in Pennsylvania. And all—"

Every circuit in my body shorted out and set my arms and legs set on fire. My brain got disconnected from its common-sense regulator. My mouth was on her own.

"D.B." My voice froze so hard both Tom and Otis startled. Even I was surprised. And delighted by how my state of mind had forged this well-honed blade.

"Get this, Duane. You know the resources I have at my disposal. If anything happens to Rune because of your acting like the asshole you so hopelessly are, I will have you fucking killed. I'm pretty sure I can figure out how to do that. It would give me great pleasure."

I hung up on him.

Otis was horrified. Tom, too.

"What? Otis?"

He shook his head, "Allie, you know how you always say those folks who have a couple drinks and go online late at night and tweet outrageous stuff and then get fired are dumb?"

The answer I was supposed to come up with was right there on his face.

I sighed. The adrenaline was amping down and I could now hear what I'd said—into D.B.'s phone which was probably set to record every death threat ever made against him. I hoped there'd been a lot.

"You're right, Otis. That was six kinds of dumb. But with my luck, no one will murder D.B. And I'll be off the hook."

And disappointed.

Chapter Twenty-six

Chastened. That was the word for my state of mind. Once my head cooled and Ms. Twitter-Mouth recovered her sanity.

"I'm sorry, you guys. I apologize to both of you. In advance. For the fallout my stupidity is bound to bring down upon us sooner or later. I should know better. I'd backtrack with D.B. if I thought it would do any good, but since that right there was the exact result he was hoping for, it would only add fuel—

"So. I promise you both, on my honor—such as it is—not to ever have D.B. killed. No matter how deliciously—"

Someone smart in my cerebral cortex hit the safety cutoff switch. No idea who.

Tom was silent.

Otis was kind. "It'll be okay, Allie. What did he say that…?"

Hot blood flooded up my neck again. My ears were itching.

"He insinuated that he knows where Rune is living now, Otis, and that he is 'concerned' for his wellbeing, 'if word gets out.' I know he wouldn't do anything like that. He's too self-serving to risk it."

"I have resources, too, Allie." Tom's voice was hardened to an ice-blade icier than mine, and, I noticed, his neck was flushing, too. "I'm not interested in killing anybody, but I'd be happy to put at least one-hundred-ninety-million dollars' worth of reputation-destruction and disbarment into play. What did you see in that guy, anyhow?"

"Geez. I wish I could remember."

● ● ● ● ●

"Well. I guess we're going to be back in hotels again, Tom." I shrugged my shoulders so as to communicate both resignation and *ennui* to Otis, while doing a happy dance inside my head. "Ritz-Carlton again?"

Otis gave me a look that said, "I'm ignoring everything you're thinking, Allie Harper." Then he dismissed my fantasies with a grimace.

"There's a serious matter we haven't been focused on because of everything else that's been going on. That changes now."

He had Tom's attention, locked and loaded. Mine was still struggling to escape. "Have you ever stayed at a Ritz-Carlton, Otis? It's sweet."

Stern Otis prevailed. "No, Allie. I'm looking forward to it, one day. But here's what we've got to talk about now. Yes, we need to be out of here for twenty-four hours starting at eight Monday morning. And yes, we'll need a place to stay. But, Allie. In case you haven't noticed, the security we picked this house for has let us down. Not merely Monday afternoon, but every day since we moved in here. Before we moved in.

"Clearly, we haven't ever been anonymous renters here. Clearly, you both haven't been safe. Clearly, our even being here could be the result of some devious goings-on. I don't know what. There's stuff about all this that's way out of my league."

I let Otis' "clearlies" wash over me and waited for Tom to have a question. Or maybe an answer, but he'd retreated behind his dark glasses and gone into his Thomas Bennington, PhD, Detective, information-gathering mode. Listening. Not talking. Not showing me diddly of what he was thinking. However, I could see he'd closed off our escape route to the presidential suite at The Ritz-Carlton, Cleveland, for now. Maybe forever.

Otis set aside his concerns about our safety and his competence. Temporarily, I knew.

"We should go with their plan. For right now. I don't think their twenty-four hours of do-over is going to make me feel secure about this place. But as far as I'm concerned Magna-Pro is the devil we know.

"However," his voice was all iced up now, too, "if Sandy thinks I'm going to let them roam around here unsupervised—" He let Sandy's foolish thinking die of its own embarrassment. "I'll be here. I'll be in the way. Those tech dudes will hate my ass, but I'll at least keep them from the freelance hiding of cameras or that eavesdropping crap. And it won't be only me. I'm bringing my own team to watch their team. Full court press. I'm done with this bullshit."

"But what about us, Otis? If you won't send us to the Ritz, where?"

Otis gave my face the once-over, as if he were trying to decide how much I could handle. I must have passed the "higher threshold of handle-capability test" because he narrowed his eyes and nodded. To himself, I think. Not to me.

"Allie. You know I'm—I like you. You are one wild woman with a hair-trigger temper. There's a whole bunch of Lee Ann mostly under wraps in there. Some of it works for you. Some not so much. But you got her guts.

"The guts come and go with you, naturally. Common sense goes out the window, too. A lot. And then comes back when it can't do you any good. Like it did ten minutes ago. But I know what you can do in a pinch. I've seen you kick a guy with a gun right in the—"

"Nuts, Otis. And right after that I saw you shoot that guy. And for sure save my life. We do okay. You and me. In a pinch."

"True. That's why I'm telling you straight on, Allie. Lottery winners, big winners, have it rough. You know this. They mess their lives up all to hell. Do hard drugs. Crash their Lamborghinis. Get killed by their enemies. And their next of kin. But as time passes, if they survive, they can move on. At least without looking over their shoulders all the time.

"Most of the time, they've very publicly run through the money in a couple a' years anyhow.

"But you and Tom are different. You two are celebrities in this town. You will never be anonymous citizens, not ever again. Tom is the Blind Mondo with the PhD in English literature. You're his…girlfriend. You guys are goddam fascinating. You're the stars of MondoSecrets.com. Or you were. Long enough for seven-hundred-fifty-thousand click-throughs or whatever.

"You're young, smart, good-looking, kinda glamorous. Well, Tom is, for sure. And you, Allie. You buzz around town in that little red car of yours. With the top down, for crissake. Looking cute. Sassy. People want to be you. Or hurt you. Or use you to get to Tom.

"I should probably move you out of here for good." He gazed around us at the dazzle of water and the simmer of a dozen upscale lounge chairs that cost more than my little red car when it was new. Plus the five "Shade Systems," all pristinely white. $2,029.00 a piece.

I'd checked. I'm materialistic that way.

Cute and sassy, though.

I glanced at Tom, oblivious to all this five-star eye candy. He was listening to Otis, attentive, open-minded, weighing all possible consequences. Unseduced by excess. Or, lately, even by me, as far as that went.

Otis, unaware of my runaway train of thought, continued. "But I'm pretty sure the danger here goes direct to your money. Not your persons. If these people, whoever they are, wanted to kidnap or kill you, it'd be done by now. Other less-sophisticated people would probably still do that if they could, but I'm not as worried about them. At least not for today."

I squelched the chill produced by *it* being "done by now."

"So where are you sending us, Otis?"

Tom spoke at last, "Not here."

"I agree. I don't think Otis believes we can stay, Tom, he—"

"No. Tom's got it right, Allie. I can't guard our every word, but I'm not going to tell you here— within range of this house—where you're going for the next thirty-six hours or so."

● ● ● ● ●

Five minutes later, we were standing at water's edge, getting spritzed by some modest-sized waves. Hiding ourselves and our words under the blanket of wave music. Not a roar, but a steady wall of sound. Rising. Falling. The wind was up, too, and singing its own song to protect us.

Susurrus was my perfect word for that wind sound. I admired that word, but I could never bring myself to say it out loud for fear of pronouncing it wrong in front of Tom. It was associate-professor-of-English-literature-level vocabulary, for sure.

"The whisper, murmur, rustling of water."

I usually delighted in the steady hush-hush susurration of the waves. Now, though, it was accentuating my anxiety.

Shush. Shush, Allie, it hissed. *Nothing to be afraid of. No one will hear a word while you're safe here with me.*

I shivered. Even I knew about directional microphones.

Creepy ear.

Now that we were away from the deck, Tom and Otis shed some of the tension that locked down their faces and shoulders.

I hoped Otis was not noticing that my Lee Ann Smith guts were sniveling like babies.

Tom was projecting some ice-blade left over from his rage at D.B. He'd stood down a touch, but he rarely stopped being on guard. I understood this, of course. Better all the time.

The rest of us could unwind sometimes, let our eyes take over and keep the watch for incoming threats. Tom rarely got the chance to shut down his internal security system. With Magna-Pro in disarray, he never really caught a break.

"This works," he said, finally. "We've got plenty of background noise and I'd say we're far enough from the house. Now you can answer Allie's question, Otis. Where are you sending us for the next thirty-six hours?

"I'm sending you back home, Allie."

That was a curve ball for me.

"West Virginia? Otis? Seriously?"

He grinned for the first time since before Sandy and Margaret showed up. "Your old house, Allie. I already texted Margo. And Tony."

Woo. Hoo.

Chapter Twenty-seven

On one of our darkest evenings of last summer, Tom and I fled to Margo's walled garden, mere steps across the street from the house I was renting from her—to hide out, eat her homemade spaghetti with meatballs, drink red wine—and be lectured by Margo, of course.

As my Italian/Buddhist landlady and undisputed BFF, Margo Gallucci had a lot of advice for us. Her advice, as usual, bordered on yelling and included a good bit of her signature swearing.

Tom's jackpot was barely a week old that night and already five people were dead. The circumstances of those deaths were ambiguous, but our situation was painfully clear. We'd sat around Margo's table in the shadow of a danger we couldn't comprehend, but could fear with no trouble at all.

Tonight, sitting in her garden, with lasagna and

wine this time, not a lot had changed. Finding out that the mansion in Bratenahl was not only insecure, but maybe a weapon in the hands of an unknown attacker? Well, that felt a lot like Square One. To be sure, we were more experienced in the ways of MondoMegaDanger, but still unnerved.

This time, though, we'd brought lots of backup. Plus, Margo was in a much more amiable frame of mind.

Tom, Margo, and I were the original trio. Otis was in the hospital on the evening of that earlier garden party, getting his heart bypassed because of the strain associated with his saving my life. Valerio was off somewhere, no doubt trying to nail me for one or another of my minor investigative infractions. Now there were five of us digging into the lasagna and arguing about who was entitled to more wine.

The sixth member of our dinner party was present last summer, too. Tonight she'd snuggled her immense black head into the crook of Tom's left elbow, thereby pinning him securely to the table. The Princess Vespa, vast, drooling mastiff bodyguard, was originally borrowed by Margo to protect us at last year's dinner. Overnight, she became Margo's forever dog. Princess was now feasting big adoring brown eyes on Tom who was, obviously, her soulmate from another incarnation.

In addition to providing us all with peace of mind and a certain ambiance of *eau de dog*, Princess' other main task appeared to be watching over the progress of each forkful of Tom's lasagna until it vanished into his mouth. She marked each disappearance with a small, sad doggie moan.

"I tell you what, Tom," Otis offered, "if you ever need a guide dog—"

Tom cut him off with a shake of his head, "If I ever need a hundred-seventy-pound guide dog I can ride, Otis, the Princess Vespa will be my girl."

Another reason Margo was abdicating her role of stern interrogator was the presence of three off-duty police officers. They were part of the detail Otis assembled in a matter of hours, using his vast network of former associates and Tom's money.

They were strategically positioned around the garden to save us from any of my former neighbors who might jump the fence to kidnap or rob us. So far it was working. The wine was helping me with my optimism about that.

When we arrived with our detail in tow, Margo went into Buddhist/Italian hospitality attack mode. She returned to her kitchen to start warming up another batch of lasagna, announcing, "I freeze in quantity. You never know when you'll be entertaining an unexpected number of officers of the law."

● ● ● ● ●

In spite of many troubling matters which none of us could dismiss, and the presence of Valerio, who was often a troubling matter for me all by himself, the conversation was lively. I was edgy, though. To my mind, a gathering which included Margo and Valerio within three feet of each other could turn incendiary.

Margo was in rare form. She'd cut through East Cleveland on her way to a grocery store on Green a couple of weeks before and gotten nailed by the speed camera. The ticket, which arrived in the morning mail, was ninety-nine dollars but according to Margo that wasn't the issue.

"The money is not the issue," she was saying. "I don't begrudge the City of East Cleveland. They need all the cash they can get. I don't even blame them for setting the speed limit at twenty-five-miles-per-bleeping-hour on every street in the whole damn city."

UhOh.

Tom laid a cautionary, if distracting, hand on my knee. We knew what was coming. Margo let "bleeping" stand in for her magnificent portfolio of swears, but only as she was warming up.

"I hate that little googly-eyed bastard."

Tom's face was a study in noncommittal, but I could tell by the twitch at the corner of his mouth that he was thinking, "This could be entertaining." Rather than the much more realistic, "This could be a fucking disaster."

"I hate his fucking, shifty, googly camera eyes."

Ah. So there we were. In the presence of four officers of the law. One at the table.

"The speed camera has eyes?" Tony didn't seem to be particularly shocked. He appeared to be almost grinning.

"Damn skippy. And he uses them to take stealthy photos of innocent bystanders." She thought about that for a second. "Motorists."

"But surely—" Tony began. His expression was bland, but I caught a twinkle.

Dammit! He was baiting her. No doubt appreciating the way the deepening rose of her flawless skin set off her dark, now flashing, eyes. I realized anew, and to my dismay, that Margo was lovely, amply endowed, young-for-her-age and—this was the extra-concerning part for my Margo + Tony equation—every bit as Italian as Tony Valerio.

He continued, unaware of my plummeting peace of mind. "Surely, if people speed, then they deserve what they get."

"A ninety-nine-dollar ticket for going thirty-one -in-a-twenty-five when everybody knows that the only reasonable speed limit in town—except for school zones and really busy business areas—is thirty-five? Which means forty to any normal person? So traffic can flow in a reasonable manner? And especially on that empty, abandoned, nothing stretch of road where they hide that little googly-head, flashing dumbshit in a fucking ambush of upstanding citizens who are merely driving cautiously around a bend and *bingo*! Screwed. As I was. Clearly."

Valerio had lifted his glass to his face to cover his expression and kept it there for the space of this tirade. Now he noticed it was empty and set it back onto the table. He then switched to gazing down at it intently. To make sure it was securely placed, I assumed.

"Well," he said, "since you put it like that."

I cleared my throat. "Great lasagna, Margo. As usual."

Tom released his grip on my knee which had ratcheted up to about forty pounds per square inch.

"Well said, Alice."

Valerio's head snapped up. "Alice?" He grinned. Extra happy for the diversion, I was betting. "Alice?"

Tom may not have been able to see the look I

shot his way, but I knew for a fact he could feel it aimed right into his ear. His smile waned.

Valerio was rolling now, gathering no moss. "Alice? Really? I never would have guessed. It's so…."

"Frumpy?" I shot back. "So old school? So…oh, I don't know, plain? While I, Allie Harper, am so unfrumpy. So trendy cool. So incredibly—"

Tom noticed a window of redemption opening in his direction. "Incredibly sexy and beautiful?"

Not so fast, smart guy.

"And you being the judge of beautiful, I suppose?"

"Point taken. But I can definitely bear witness to sexy."

"Enough. Stop." I was done being mad. "I concede the Alice. But Tony—"

"Yes? Al…lie."

"Employ it at your peril."

After that, everything got almost jovial, and my heart rate dropped below its customary 122 BPMs. In spite of Margo's having been completely herself at this dinner, Tony seemed—well, okay. He seemed enchanted.

Damn.

After a while, Margo caught my eye and said, "Allie, give me a hand in the kitchen?" Which meant, "Allie, I want to talk to you somewhere out of earshot of these guys."

I defied common sense and went.

Margo's kitchen was radiating the warmth and grace of Mable, her antique Maytag range. I adore Mable. She's been very, very good to me. As soon as we got in there, Margo started hauling stuff out of drawers and cupboards. Serving pieces. Cups. Cream pitcher. Cream from her fridge, a massive Sub-Zero that as far as I knew had no name at all.

I wondered what Mable and the Sub-Zero talked about in the wee hours of the morning. I figured Mable was probably filling S-Z in on the Truman administration. While I was musing, Margo was getting out her tiny limoncello glasses, limoncello from the freezer, plates, forks. Stuff. Arranging it all on trays.

While she was orchestrating the things of dessert, she was not meeting my eye because she was figuring out how to say what was on her mind without scaring me off. I can read Margo like a Doctor Seuss. Unfortunately she can read me like a romance novel. That's a good or a bad thing, depending on what's on my mind.

"Allie." She handed me the giant glass bowl layered from top to bottom with tiramisu, the fragrance of which neutralized my IQ.

"Margo. What?"

"Allie, Make me part of the T&A. You won't be sorry."

Sorry already.

Which was how the T&A got to be Tom, Allie, Otis, Tony & Margo. The last two were ex officio, but there it is.

Chapter Twenty-eight

After the coffee, the tiramisu, and the limoncello, we were not the sharpest detective agency in Cleveland, but we still had a couple of items to put before our expanded group.

I looked around the table at the new us. Tony already knew the details—and the name—of the T&A but was a handshake away from official membership. We planned to keep it like that. Margo would have shaken hands all around but we liked her at arm's length. Princess knew nothing of the T&A and didn't care. After the tiramisu, which she'd gotten at least one taste of, she'd appeared dazed with happiness. She was under the table snoring softly now. Tom had retaken possession of his arm.

Otis, I'd noticed, was abstaining from wine, limoncello, and tiramisu. He was, hands down, the alert-est detective on the team and therefore got to talk.

"Tony. Margo," he began. "We need to let you know about recent developments. As you're aware we have a case regarding Lloyd Bunker who we are confident was murdered back in February and dumped into the lake. His remains have been discovered now. Our charge, as an agency, is to answer questions and we've answered at least one for Loretta: Lloyd is not coming back. But we're still committed, at least Allie, Tom, and I are, to finding out how and why he was killed.

"Allie uncovered a significant link between Lloyd and CyCLE. It ain't computers or bicycles. It's scrap. The fact that Lloyd's house was scrapped may be incidental but it raised another flag.

"Allie and I paid Howard at CyCLE a visit and got two hundred dollars for an undocumented cat."

Otis caught Margot's expression which said, *A cat? You took a cat to a scrapyard? What kind of people are you?*

"That is, a catalytic converter," he tacked on smoothly.

Margo's face now said, *No longer appalled. Still clueless.*

Otis segued again. "As we know, that's a very expensive part of a car's exhaust system. It contains platinum. Howard Rexroad, the CyCLE guy we dealt with, was more than willing to take it under the table. No ID. No paperwork at all. In fairness, he may have been intimidated by a fear that I might be going to kill his ass."

I risked a sideways peek at Valerio. The brow was locked down for maximum security. I could tell he was wondering if the off-duty cop detail was getting even a syllable of this.

Me, too.

"One other piece of the CyCLE connection is that Lloyd was driving a vintage GTO when he disappeared and it disappeared, too. I suppose it might be in the lake—or somewhere else. Almost anywhere, as far as that goes—but our theory— which is based way more on intuition and hope than on fact—is that a guy, a guy like Howard, for example, might be given a car like that for scrapping and then have a tough time crushing thousands of dollars into a block of nothing much. Allie and I agree that scrapyard would be an excellent place to hide a car. There are about a billion in there."

Valerio was displaying his skeptical cop face, but I'd caught a microsecond flash of interest. He nodded. It was a conservative nod.

"Might be worth a look. How would you propose to get a search warrant for that?"

I grinned in a way that suggested I was at least partly joking. "I could rent a helicopter. For sight-seeing. And a bit of aerial photography."

"Probably not admissible.

"But then we'd know."

Margo was following our verbal tennis match with avid attention.

"Allie, if you do this? Can I ride in the helicopter?"

I had an eye on Valerio and I caught yet another microsecond flash. This one was for Margo. It looked a lot like approval. Damn.

Otis took another ten minutes to address the other direction of our investigation: Magna-Pro and the breach at our so-called safe house in Bratenahl. His description of his newly enhanced team, and the full court press he was planning, appeared to defuse Margo's need to give us any more advice. She liked how he talked like a cop, I could see.

After an additional half hour for delivering the dishes to the kitchen and cleaning up—a chore which Tom and Princess eluded by his being blind and her lacking opposable thumbs—and we were done.

It was after midnight. I was heading across the street. At last. Home. Bed. True Love.

Chapter Twenty-nine
Sunday, June 25

12:31 a.m.

My house. Musty from lack of human occupation, maybe, but all here.

The kitchen counter where Tom and I shared the chili that I made us from all the contents of his grocery bag that were not a winning five-hundred-fifty-million-dollar ticket.

The perfect spot in which I'd hidden the ticket. The window through which my first ever B&E climbed in. The couch on which we'd begun our first night's rest. The bedroom we'd retreated to after a giant storm thundered in to wake us up.

Oh, yes. That bedroom.

Margo had found a minute after Otis' call that morning to run across the street and make it up, all white and pristine. She'd opened the casement windows for the breeze. And found clean towels for the bath. What she hadn't planned for was the cop Otis posted on the staircase.

The open staircase with the no bedroom-damn-door at the top.

It didn't help that our own personal police officer was a woman. I caught the look she gave Tom, especially after he smiled kindly to her, unveiled the dimple, and offered his hand.

After that, I also caught the look she gave me, which, unless I misread it, said, *So you're the MondoMega…um…girlfriend? Who knew? Too bad about tonight. And possibly tomorrow night.* Then she gazed for a long admiring while at Tom again. I couldn't blame her but I wanted to hurt Otis. Just a little. Her, too. Just a lot.

At last. Tom and I were undressed and lying face to face. Surely we could at least kiss. Silently. Hungrily. Like teenagers with their parents in the next room. His hands caressing my face, his mouth warm and insistent on mine, our bodies….This was a mistake. The kissing was cruel.

A while after that both of us yielded to the temptation to touch, a slight, tiny bit. Lightly brushing. Here. There. Everywhere. That was another mistake. The touching was deeply unfair.

"Do you think she's maybe asleep now? Propped

up against the wall in the stairwell?" I whispered to Tom, resting my lips stealthily against his ear. Letting them linger there so he could experience how quickly and warmly I was breathing and to remind him of every passionate thing that happened between us last summer in that very stairwell. In this very room. In this very bed. In this exact position. With this same powerful sensation of sliding into inevitability. As if this moment on the brink was our law of gravity and we were fated to be in free fall together. Forever. At least all night.

I'd now cleverly moved all of me into alignment with fate. I was exactly where I'd been desperately longing to be. For days. Close enough to get everything I wanted us to do…done. And much, much more. Tom was right there with me. Matching me close for so close.

"We could be very quiet, Tom. They might all fall asleep. Guards in movies always fall asleep."

Tom groaned and pulled back. "I don't know what you have in mind here, Alice Jane," he muttered. "But what I have in mind here would not be quiet. At all. And they'll never sleep, any of them. Otis Johnson, peerless P.I. and bodyguard magnifique, won't let them sleep tonight. So we might as well."

He placed one last fabulous kiss next to my ear,

and murmured, "Besides, I didn't notice it that other time, but these bedsprings squeak like a maniac. We have to have breakfast with those people. And Otis. In the morning. And you'd have to make eye contact with them."

Sleep. To my vast disappointment, that's what we did. Or at least Tom did. He was breathing slowly and deeply within five minutes while I tossed and turned. And squeaked the dang bed.

For one thing, Otis was getting regular updates from his newly deployed Bratenahl mansion detail. This involved him asking and answering questions and saying "Uh-huh" a lot in his big, burly Otis voice. I loved my little cottage but little was not such a big advantage in any number of ways that night.

The breeze died and the lake went silent, so I didn't even have the pleasure of lying awake listening to the waves bounce off my old beach, the scene of my first kiss with Thomas Bennington the Third. Back in the day when some persons could make love in this house.

As far as I could tell from hearing every doggone Otis "Uh-huh," all was quiet at the mansion.

I was ready to go back there.

•   •   **●**   •   •

As it worked out, that's what happened. Sunday morning, when I came downstairs, cranky but resigned, change was in the air. All for the better, as far as I was concerned.

Otis had changed out his night shift, whose names I had not yet learned—one of whom I hoped never to see again during my entire lifetime—for a day-shift: Officers Alan, Edwin, and Julia.

Julia turned out to be an enterprising young person who'd taken it upon herself to pick up a couple dozen donuts on her way to her assignment.

I dug up a big bag of coffee beans that were in my freezer from last August. In spite of their possible archeological significance, they made us about a gallon of drinkable joe. No cream and a mere crust of sugar in the bottom of the bowl, but a donut will stand in for cream and sugar in my cup of coffee any day.

I was considering a medal for Officer Julia Perez. Moods rescued. Lives saved. I told her so. We were almost friends already. She was the one who told me—off the record, of course—that we were headed back to Bratenahl as soon as Otis cleared the way—her words—with Magna-Pro.

Then Tom got a call from Sandy, who was up in arms about today's Otis call to her about this radical change in our itinerary. I could see things from her perspective. We'd agreed to her plan. Even cleared out early. Now here we were coming back on Sunday with our bevy of off-duty cops, some of whom were already on the premises. And there we'd all be tomorrow when her team arrived. Underfoot and in her hair while her techs tried to fix the embarrassing mess they'd made.

Awkward and aggravating, I'd say. Like having your mom stand over you while you picked up every single piece of that broken glass. I could relate. It was pretty satisfying, though.

I relished Tom's end of that conversation. "Yes, Sandy," he said, "I understand. We'll do our best not to slow your people down. Give them free rein to get their work done. But, upon reflection, Mr. Johnson and I agree that given what we have learned about the original reboot, he—and his team—need to be present this time.

"No. No lack of confidence in you, Sandy. If it were only you running this…operation, I'd probably feel differently. But, to be honest, I don't trust every living soul at Magna-Pro right now, especially since what's at stake is the safety of people I…care about. And my own, of course."

I used my imagination to replace "care about" with some choice words I liked better. I also considered that I could stick "passionately" in between "care" and "about." That would work for me, too. By the time I tuned back in, Tom was saying, "That's fine. Your folks can start as soon as they can get there—Sure. This afternoon works. And however much time they need to get it right—That would not be a problem for us. But we'll all be there, too."

With all the finality of a slammed door.

Go him, I say.

Go us, too.

Chapter Thirty
Monday, June 26

Otis was sitting with his hands clasped in his lap and his shoulders slumped, a posture I identified as "I, Otis, blame myself. Like goddam crazy."

Inside the mansion, every dang thing was being aggressively observed and examined. Otis' Collinwood detail, now merged with a couple of his Bratenahl detail, added up to a detail of five. The Magna-Pro crew, a now undefined number of serious young men and women, who'd already been here for almost twenty-four hours, were quiet enough. But they kept popping up all over the place with no warning.

It was a zoo with no cages. Especially since the two teams related to each other like lions and cobras. Wary was the best one could hope for.

We'd tried to find some privacy for this discussion on the pool deck, but got driven in by a heavy rain shower. As far as we could tell the big, dark, ugly formal dining room was empty of observers. Human and electronic. Otis checked. And turned on some semi-intrusive music.

Distracted. Aggravated. Frustrated. Damp. That was us. And now Otis was bringing a big helping of self-recrimination to the fancy table. "I was spreading myself too thin. I thought I could keep track of everything. Just me."

He exhaled and let his shoulders sink another inch or so. "None of us comprehends how much money you've got, Tom. Not you. Not Allie. Not me, either. I've been arrogant. And stupid."

"Otis…"

"Allie, you don't need to comfort me about this. I'm not beating myself up. Not much anyway. But I'm more on guard now. I can see how big the whole thing is. So maybe I can make this place safe for you two. Cut the damn house down to size so it's easier to … to defend. And figure out how you both can move around town with something like freedom. *Like* freedom, Allie. Not the real deal.

"Because I'll tell you what. Whoever busted into your security system. That hacker with all the credentials. Either he himself or whoever planted him like a fu—like a mole at Magna-Pro, and then vanished him when the job was done? That person gets it. That person appreciates the value of a hundred and ninety million dollars—" He broke off.

"Tom?"

Whatever else Tom Bennington had to offer, a poker face, was not part of the deal.

I echoed Otis. "Tom. What's wrong?"

"Try two-hundred-twelve million, Allie. The jackpot's been invested, by some very savvy people, for almost a year. Maybe the hacker has information swiped from my statements, which were for sure on my computer backup. And probably living large in the cloud. That full amount is no secret to that person."

However, it was news to me. "What do you think they're going to do with that information, Tom?"

"Well, with any luck they could steal all the money and we could go back to being poor, safe, and happy again."

"No." Otis shut Tom's escape-route-of-choice down with a word. "It doesn't work like that, Tom. In the first place, you're too smart to go there. Safe is relative. If you were dead broke, there'd still be drunk drivers and Ebola."

Tom exhaled and nodded. I remembered him saying something very similar to that. In August when the bodies and disasters started hitting the fan, he'd invoked the name and inspiration of his hero, Helen Keller: "Security is a superstition."

"Anyway, the statements are one thing and they don't show your account numbers. The actual money is another. You've got that locked down and locked up. It's in the keeping of a whole bunch of left-hand-don't-know-what-the-right-hand-is-doing folks. The money's safe—as safe as that much money can ever be, anyway."

"Wow. Otis. How did you find that out?"

"Tom told your lawyer, Skip Castillo, that he could trust me. I talked to him. For about three hours. He told me all about it. He loves to talk about that shit. I think he was just waiting for me to come along and hear all about it.

"Not the actual security stuff for all that. I'm not sure even I'd trust me with that, but the structure of it. You are doomed to be one rich dude, Tom. And getting richer every damn day. I just didn't understand how much—which just makes my job all that much harder."

A small smile. "Also, I'm planning for you guys to send me on an extremely fancy vacation when all this dies down. In thirty years or so."

● ● ● ● ●

Opportunity knocked.

Everybody in the house had a job to do. Otis was watching his team. Otis' team was watching the Magna-Pro team. The Magna-Pro team was trying to get its work done. Things were tense. Everybody in the known world, it felt like to me, was constructively occupied. Except Tom and me. We were at loose ends. Trying to stay out of everyone's way.

Looking for something to do.

This was the sweltering, still part of the late afternoon. Even though the big air conditioning units were slogging away, it was way too hot to do anything productive. Too hot to think. Not too hot, however, to imagine the relief of shedding a few garments and sprawling on a big, wide, Einstein-sheeted bed under a ceiling fan.

Just for starters.

And what good fortune was here! The two competing security teams were totally done with their detailed inspections and scans of the master suite. Bedroom, bath, sitting room, dressing room. Clean, clean, clean, clean. Nothing that transpired there this afternoon would be showing up on YouTube.

A plan, unspoken but much on our mutual minds, evolved. After lunch, Tom and I drifted upstairs at timed intervals. Tom went first, muttering something about earbuds. I then followed, carrying a book about…dolphins, evidently…that I'd grabbed out of the house's official library. I figured Otis, at least, wasn't fooled by our staggered decampment. Once again, I felt like I was sneaking off to "study" with my boyfriend. Here was our second chance in less than twenty-four hours to be teenagers. Not the worst thing in the world.

I lay there for a minute under the speed-of-light top sheet, relishing as I so often did the freedom to admire Tom unabashedly without his being aware of it. Although he probably knew. The touch of premature silver at his temples had definitely increased over the course of our friendship. I brushed it lightly with my fingers. My favorite dimple appeared. I moved my hand to the top of his shirt.

"Aren't you hot in that?"

"I certainly hope so. You tell me."

"That's not what I meant."

"I know what you meant.'

I slipped my hand under his signature white tee-shirt, and skimmed up over his bare chest.

"You're cutting corners."

"I don't care."

"Me either." He turned toward me and copied my move, his fingers pausing as they reached my bra. "You have much too much undergarment for such a…" He paused as my breath caught in an insuppressible sigh. "Such a sultry afternoon."

"It is tropical in here. Isn't it?"

He kissed me for a while and my buttons must have unbuttoned themselves while I wasn't watching. I kissed him back for more of a while and the rest of my clothes fell away. "Who says you shouldn't multitask?" I whispered against his mouth.

"Not me. Never me."

And then his hands were all occupied so I helped him with his clothes. Turnabout. Fair play.

"Ah."

"My thought as well."

"When I think of all the payback the universe owes us for last night."

"It is exciting to think about. Now that there's hope of—"

He kissed me again and I pressed my whole self to his whole self. So that our souls could dissolve into one another and our bodies could set our untrustworthy mansion on fire.

The phone rang.

Not a chance.

Our souls kept intertwining. The ringing stopped. The machine picked up.

Chapter Thirty-one

Margo's voice, ragged and tearful, was a bucket of cold water. "Allie, I— I need you."

This was unprecedented. I moaned and pried myself away from Tom. He matched me, moan for moan.

I picked up.

"Margo, what's wrong. Where are you?"

"At my house. There's a policeman here. He says he's arresting me for assault and battery."

"No. He's not. Margo. Tell him he's at the wrong house."

"Don't be in denial. He is too. He says I injured and possibly killed…" Her voice crumpled into sobs.

My heart stopped. "Killed? Who? Margo. Who?"

"The flashy camera guy. That speed ticket machine. You know. The one I was talking about Saturday. The short, square, little googly-eyed, metal— "

"Margo." My heart eased ever so slightly. "Margo, don't finish that sentence in front of the officer. Answer me. Say yes or no. "Did you? Did you kill the googly camera?"

Tom, behind me on the bed, made a startled noise that was midway on the sliding scale between choke and guffaw.

"No! Well, yes, probably, but I swear to you not on purpose. Not even in self-defense. It was a total accident. It was pouring rain down on Belvoir. I was merely driving and all of a sudden the car just…just…drove itself right off the road and into the—into the speed camera…device. I braked so hard, Allie. No stopping. I think this man is taking me to police headquarters or somewhere."

"Let me talk to him."

There was a pause and a manly voice came on the line.

"Ma'am?"

I tried to picture this hardworking and well-meaning officer of the law. All I got was a big, blue uniform and a blurry face. I couldn't tell whether it was kind or implacable. And there was the regulation Glock, of course. Taser. Mace—

"Ma-'am?"

I blinked and my brain came back online. "Officer. This is Alice Harper." I gave him the

Bratenahl address, hoping to sound more like a solid citizen than Andy Reilly's squatter. "I'm a good friend of Ms. Gallucci. I can assure you that whatever damage was done was unintended and whatever it costs to repair the goog— uh…equipment. Device. Will be paid. By me, if I have to. You do not want to arrest this woman."

"I do not. But ma'am, there's paperwork. And we have her dead to…we have a photo taken by the camera." His voice was grave. "Its last photo."

"How was it—? What would be the charge?" I appreciated that this was a hard moment for Margo and obviously a serious concern for the policeman, but I was starting to get caught up in the way Tom was shaking the bed with barely suppressed laughter. It didn't help that we were both stark naked.

"Hit and run, ma'am. She ran him over. And fled the scene."

• ● ● ● •

What with the respectability of our address and the eloquence of my intervention on her behalf, and the fact that both the officer and I were hanging on to both ends of our phone call, trying not to laugh, agreement was reached.

Margo was not going to be hauled off to answer

the charge of hit and run on a speed camera. At least not on that afternoon. Which, from my perspective, was much more promising before the phone rang. The officer did not place her under house arrest either. I wondered where the Princess Vespa was during all this. Drooling on the cop, I hoped.

I didn't know what kind of reputation Margo had, but she was my BFF. So I didn't want her character besmirched by the charge of leaving the scene of an accident. Or even let her be ridiculed for killing the Flashy Camera Guy and abandoning him to lie alone and mangled by the side of the road. I was going to find her a lawyer. A good one. But not today. Today would be dedicated to the savoring of aggravation and frustration.

By the time I'd hung up, Tom was putting his shoes back on. I completely understood.

On the bright side, when I wandered back downstairs, not planning to avoid eye contact with anyone because there was absolutely no reason to do that, the Magna-Pros were all gone.

Chapter Thirty-two
Tuesday, June 27

It could have been an ordinary Tuesday with nothing more tension-invoking than the decision about what to have for breakfast and the general disquiet about Margo's current legal problems. That situation was leavened by our confidence that we'd get her off on the charge of hit and run on a googly speed camera and our impulse to laugh out loud every time we replayed our recollections of the fateful phone call. Only between the two of us, of course. There was so much Otis didn't need to know about that scene. We gave him the bottom line and stopped there.

So, yeah. Tuesday could have been a breath of fresh air, except for one tiny thing: The Magna-Pros were happily gone for little more than twelve hours when Otis called them back in again to help him knock some rooms off our mansion.

One of his plans to limit our current state of vulnerability and—okay—fear, was "I'm going to make this goddam house smaller." I saw his point. On the main floor, we used the kitchen, the breakfast room, and the family room off the kitchen. That was about it. These rooms were cozier and more human than the formal rooms at the front of the house. Plus they had the lake view. I liked to have my lake in plain sight, like a baserunner keeping one foot on third. Erie was home plate for me.

All those rooms had doors that gave us free access to the lake which, again, was a source of support and comfort to me. Otis begrudged it because he couldn't control the wide open spaces. And woe unto the person or persons who suggested they'd like a stroll in the moonlight. We were all adapting.

The back stairs, spiraling up out of the kitchen, accessed the two wings of bedrooms, ensuites, and sitting rooms, including my still-very-adorable-in-spite-of-everything study at the top of the grand staircase. We needed the grand stairs, of course, because they gave us access to the imposing front door.

Otis was ruthless, though. Every time he hiked along some endless corridor or gazed down another skateboard-worthy hardwood expanse, he'd shake his head in profound disbelief at the excess of it all. And make a note for the techs and the teams to shut it down. Risk-averse, that was our Otis. He did have a weakness for the second-floor kitchen, though. We didn't mock him for referring to it as rudimentary. "No double ovens."

The Magna-Pros, professional enough, but with a long-suffering vibe, went about the work of alarming those off-the-grid areas, from their leaded-glass windows to their majestic doors.

Otis even had the techs set up a special panel at the basement door. I was all about that. We needed access because of the HVAC, but for all the touted magnificence of the house, its basement was a basement. That high-priced heating and cooling was down there rubbing elbows with a bunch of well-fed spiders. Plus a hundred years below ground level? Next to a very great lake? Damp. Smelled like it, too. I enjoyed knowing that anything rising up from down there would set off a big old alarm. I watch spooky movies like everybody else. I was excited to see the attic go off limits, too.

Once Otis had identified everything we could live without living in, the Magnas armed it all—ballroom, living room, parlor, library, extra bedrooms and ensuites, musty basement, spooky attic, and much, much more. Then they packed up and left us alone again.

Getting used to the changes resulted in some scary moments of fine-tuning. Somehow the powder room off the hall to the front door got included in the no-fly zone. I set the thing off about six times before Otis could take it back offline.

I was fine with the Otis House Reduction Plan. I could see how keeping three-thousand square feet secure, was a lot simpler than patrolling nine-thousand-plus. Otis had knocked a ton of footage off our endless, empty spaces. Fenced them out. When darkness closed in now, it didn't come as far inside.

I liked that. A lot. But at the same time, the circling of our wagons made the wild, wide, wolf-and-snake-infested prairie of my mind bigger and more threatening. The warm, lighted spaces felt smaller. Shadows loomed along the borders. I noticed I felt safest in the downstairs powder room. Once it stopped screeching at me. But what really unnerved me was the closing off of what I was coming to think of as "the dark lands" that marked Tom's first nightmare. I realized then that he had some wolves and snakes of his own.

The man, in my experience which now covered almost a whole fabulous year—including intervals of terror and despair, of course—slept sweetly. The sound of his quiet breathing was the hush of wave music to me, lulling me to my own dreams in the most soothing way.

So imagine my shock when, on the second midnight of our newly smaller domain, he cried out and sat up fighting for breath. He sounded like a man who'd been running from a pack of ravenous wolves for a week.

"Tom." I didn't want to grab him out of some dreadful dream for fear it would turn into a dream of somebody grabbing him. "Tom," I struggled to control my voice. His panicked breathing was contagious.

"Tom. It's okay. It's Allie. You're dreaming. It's a dream. I'm here." I put my hand on his chest. Cautiously. His skin was damp. Chilly. His heart hammered against my palm. I exhaled. He exhaled. He fell back onto the pillows again.

"Sorry." His breath was still catching. "Damn. Bad. Stupid…"

"Tom." I eased myself down, leaving my palm in place. "Tell me. I've subjected you to every bad dream I've had since we met."

"I'm an idiot. I should know better."

"Oh, good. This my chance to be the sane, calm one. Please. Tell all."

He relaxed some more. "It's this damn house."

"The house itself?"

"Not all of it. Mostly it's the parts Otis and his team have roped off now. But from the day we moved in, those gigantic, gaping formal spaces have been—They're so unmanageable. You remember my house, Allie."

I did. All cozy, white Dutch lap siding, green shutters, big, romantic porch overlooking a scrap of sandy beach and a massive stretch of Lake E. The inside was a little wrecked up the only time I'd been there, following Tom's first B&E.

"I do. I want to live happily ever after there with you. When all this dies down." I moved a little closer to remind him that everybody here in this bed was still alive. He put his arm over me—

Footsteps approached. Otis knocked on the door.

"Sorry. Are you guys all right? Somebody hollered."

Super bad timing, as far as I was concerned. We both rolled back to our spots and I glared at the ceiling. I believed Tom did, too, in his own way, for solidarity's sake.

"We're fine. Thanks, Otis." I answered him. "I had a bad dream."

Footsteps retreated.

"Thanks for protecting my manly self-esteem."

"You're welcome. Invested interest there." I picked up the broken thread of a conversation I'd liked the beginning of, at least. "Your house?"

"It was small. Organized. Every space accounted for. Everything in its place. That's freedom for a blind man, Allie. Containment. Order. Put you and me on the edge of the Grand Canyon and you'd be hanging over, trying to find a donkey to ride down. I'd probably wet my pants. If you think less of me for that—"

"I think less of you for thinking I'd think less of you. You are the bravest person I know, Tom Bennington. The Third.

"I don't blame you for being creeped out. You may not have noticed I've been hiding in the powder room. It reminds me of the house I grew up in. About the same size and not as noisy. Comfortingly claustrophobic. So what in particular is the nightmare about?"

"The basement. And the attic. Of course."

"Of course. Works for me. That would be classic. Details?"

I was settling back into the comfort of the bed, relaxing for a bedtime story. My chest was getting peaceful and quiet now. Sleepy. I thought perhaps our libidos were dying out in this love-hostile environment.

"In the dream, the basement is this rainy place. A forest. Wet. Trees dripping. Moss hanging down. Everywhere. It smells green, full of…growing things.

The air is thick. Heavy. Bugs. Snakes. Kudzu. Like in the South. My Home Sweet Home."

"Ech. I get that. And the attic."

"Worse. The forest is awful, so I run. Because in dreams I can see. I see you sometimes, Allie."

"You never told me that. Does my hair look fabulous?"

I could feel him smiling. He's not the only one with the Blind Man Spidey Sense. "Sorry. I didn't mean to interrupt. So you run?"

"And I end up in the attic. Which is worse. Because it is crowded with stuff. Hoarder stuff. Dangerous scary stuff. Sharp. Ugly. Towering to the ceiling. Bugs and rodents up there, too. Threatening. And holes, naturally, to drop you into the second floor. Or back into the basement. I stepped into one of those. That's what woke me up. Thanks, Allie, for listening. And not making me feel stupid."

His voice was drifting toward sleepy as he told me. My hand was still on his chest and he clasped it gently, holding me to him. When his breath returned to its familiar susurration, I took my hand back.

I don't even remember closing my eyes.

Chapter Thirty-three
Wednesday, June 28

6:45 a.m.

Tom was sleeping off his midnight run through the forest and the plunge from the attic back into the basement. I was wide awake. An aromatic tendril of Otis' coffee was curling itself up the stairs, oozing under the door, and insinuating itself into my nose, exactly like in the cartoons. It was palpable. Irresistible. I slipped out of bed and grabbed on shorts and a tee-shirt that were mostly clean and tiptoed down the back stairs.

I was still tiptoeing when I got to the landing and stopped to savor the coffee smell, which at this point was so dense and rich, I could taste it. I was thinking, but not yet saying, "Mmm Mmm" when I heard Otis. On the phone. I grinned. Rallying the troops. I loved to hear him work. He was so fierce. My Otis.

Something made me pause. Maybe it was how hushed his words were. Maybe it was the inflection of haste in his voice.

"No. I can't do that. But you can. And if you don't, you'll regret it. Remember. I know who you are. I know what—no. Nobody has to find out. They won't. They can't. And there's money. Plenty. You can name your price. Okay. Set it up? Call me back."

My everything split open and fell apart. In my mind I hurtled from Tom's nightmare attic, down, down into his basement. Screaming.

Who would Otis talk to like that? Cold. Hard. All business. And how he'd said "plenty of money." Otis who'd saved my life. Who'd been guarding the money so it could keep us safe. My Otis. He had our backs. He was our peace of mind. Our insurance policy. When all else failed—If I couldn't trust Otis, it was a matter of time before the force that held my universe together let go and everything went flying—

I stood as quiet as I could. Afraid to try to sneak back up or clatter on casually down. Heartsick. Sick sick. Stuck. I closed my eyes and breathed silently for a handful of seconds. When I opened them, Otis was standing there, gazing up at me from the bottom of the stairs.

His face was not an open book.

"Allie." He stopped. Started again. "I know you heard that. It's not what you think. I need you to forget about this for now. Don't mention it to Tom. Or Tony. I know that sounds—but it's for them. You don't want them to be goin' through what you're goin' through right now. It'll make everybody crazy.

"I'm counting on your guts, Allie. This—what you heard—it's a burden. I know that. I need you to carry it by yourself for a little while. I've got to go somewhere. I'll be back. Trust me for now. Can you do that?"

I couldn't lie to Otis. Couldn't pretend. Be all cheery and "Oh, yes. No prob." Not to him.

"That's a big ask, Otis."

He nodded. "Good. At least you didn't give me the old, 'not trust you, Otis? Oh, my, my.' At least I know you'll try."

"I'll try."

He turned to go. To I-might-never-find-out-where. Or why.

"Otis."

"Yeah?"

"Be safe. I love you."

"There's coffee, Allie. Just made it."

"Yeah, I know."

• ● ● ● •

The dead of night again. Same time. Same place. Tom's nightmares weren't bothering him, but I was a million miles from dreamland. Otis had come back after dark, quiet and composed. Focused on his own thoughts. Keeping inside his own head. I let him be. I'd promised.

I sighed and thumped the pillow, not caring if I woke Tom. Maybe hoping I would. Wondering what I might break down and tell him if I did. He was out. The sheets were snarled. Well, me, too. I got out of bed, picked up my robe, and slipped into the hall. Headed to my not-particularly-secure little refuge at the top of the stairs.

I felt my way around the desk in the dark, trying not to break a toe, and stood at the window, staring down. Breathing in and out, telling myself, "There, there, Allie. There, there." The moon had dropped to the lake side of the house and was flinging white light all over the water. Erie was as flat and silent as a big restless lake is ever permitted to be.

Even the lake was calmer than me.

Sometime in the last ten months or so, I'd become a much more dedicated observer of my surroundings. My track record on spotting danger wasn't great, but at least I was trying. So I wasn't one to overlook a guy dressed all in black crossing the sand, slipping up onto the waterside deck, threading his way around the deck chairs.

He was a practiced threader. Made no sound. Tripped over nothing. Barely disturbed the still pools of moonlight as he skirted the flower boxes and crept toward the house.

He was tall, slim, athletic. Not young. Not old either. A man in his prime. A shadow cut out of the night, moving with fluid grace, disturbing nothing.

He stopped, then, and glanced straight up at my window. I was more hidden than he, but I could see him. And he saw me.

Caught.

His face was ebony polished by moonlight. Deep-set eyes captured mine. A lightning assessment. Which I passed. For him, I was not a threat. Not a target either, I didn't think.

He shot me a fraction of a smile and proceeded to walk into my house without raising the slightest peep from our one thousand hair-trigger alarms.

A shadow man.

Otis' early morning phone call.

I can't do that. But you can.

Can what? Cut a throat? Steal a fortune? Break something? Fix something? Save somebody?

I released the breath I'd been holding hostage.

I'd promised Otis I'd try to carry the burden of trust. I had it now. Or it had me.

In that sliver of time where our eyes met, I'd entered the same pact of trust and simple acceptance as Otis', shadowy intruder. Made myself subject to his mysterious power to help us—whatever that might be.

"Okay, then."

I went back to bed, and surprised myself by going straight to sleep.

Chapter Thirty-four
Thursday, June 29

My mom used to love to tell me "In the morning everything will look different." She'd be proud of this morning. It was different, all right. On a scale of one to ten, where last night's ten was crystal sequins of moonlight, flung out of a cloudless sky, and a one is crap? This morning was a one. Maybe a minus five.

The moonlit sky had been replaced by no sky at all. A thick layer of putty-colored cloud was roiling in low over the water, pouring out a chilly rain. Wind churned the waves. The waves slapped the decks. The Shade Systems were a sad huddle of tired, clammy umbrellas. For a final note of dejection, one of Otis' team members was standing out there with his head down and his collar turned up,

To compound the misery of the weather, I was

viewing this depressing scene from a treadmill in our lovely fitness room which, naturally, Otis spared from the house pruning.

I hate to work out. I'm fine with hiking, swimming, and biking because those are real things to do. Running in place on a bouncy strip of not-the-ground is not a real thing. The reason I was here was this morning's sixty-five degrees. Our fabulous upscale air conditioning system hadn't got the memo and was down in the musty darkness continuing to address yesterday's eighty-five. I'd dressed for summer. I'd been freezing to death in the kitchen. The treadmill was my only hope.

Also, I'd believed doing something active, even if it was working out, would help me stop obsessing about absolutely everything. So now I found myself obsessing in time with the pounding of my feet.

Annoying repetitive action does sometimes have a head-clearing effect. I was beginning to comprehend how unconscious I'd been when I was coasting along, believing our lives would get easier. That the murderous hullaballoo associated with Tom's accidentally winning an insane amount of money would die down. After a bit. Certainly by now.

Otis tried to warn me, but my fingers were in my ears all "la-la-la." I wanted to believe in a fresh, new summer. A more secure house. With some very-high-thread-count sheets, Tom and I would be safe and happy. He'd still be the irresistibly wonderful, smart, hot guy I'd always dreamed of. Hot, too, in case I forgot to list. Also hot.

We'd survive the Mondo. And move on…

Otis would live with us in our mansion by the lake and be our bodyguard to handle any minor disturbances that might arise. We three would become the ones helping other people solve their small mysteries so those people could be safe and happy like us. The T&A would be clever detectives "of the heart."

Crime Lite.

Not happening. Worse than not happening.

Tom's jackpot wasn't merely providing us with a bigger house, better sheets, and Otis. It was bringing us a more sophisticated brand of threat. Smarter, better criminals than ever before. It was growing every single day, way faster than we'd been spending it.

I kicked up the pace as if I could run away from these thoughts.

Not happening.

I ran on.

Even our protection was scary. Our security system needed a security system. Our mansion needed border guards. Now Otis had conjured up a shadowy, quasi-military expert. "Shadow Man," I'd decided to call him.

The T&A's first, far-from-solved case was a bona fide murder, spreading and connecting to petty crime, drugs, more murders maybe, and who-knew-what all. The more we uncovered, the bigger and more threatening it became.

Last but not least—I cranked up the machine again and pounded on—we had our very own mole.

The Mole from Magna-Protect. Who was he? Had he really "vanished" like Sandy said? Had he left the state? Or even the country? Or more likely—to my already overloaded brain circuits—was he so clever and talented he could hide in plain sight?

I pictured him as a younger version of Shadow Man. Or, of course, possibly Shadow Man himself.

Whichever. He could be walking among us, stripping us of security, privacy, and Tom's fortune. Then leaving us to all appearances still fabulously wealthy yet with no money for escaping or paying ransoms. Or maybe killing us to cover his tracks for good and always.

Was he in cahoots with one of our trusted teams? Was one or more of Otis' people not to be trusted? Was Otis—?

Stop it, Allie.

My thigh muscles were screaming. I told them to shut up.

So. How about old reliable Sandy? Even with Tom's endorsement, I was still squinting my eyes at her. I myself had successfully lied to Tom at least a couple of times. At least I thought so. And what about old silent Margaret? She was so far in the background of my memory I couldn't even picture her.

Allie. Shut up.

I ramped the treadmill back down, got off, and gave it a little kick.

Then I went upstairs, treated myself to a lovely warm shower, put on some refreshingly clean clothes, and started after the Magna Mole. I found Sandy's number in my personal copy of the Magna-Protect Trapper Keeper. When I reached her, she was sounding harried.

Otis on a roll can do that to a person.

"Allie. Hi. What can I do for you?"

"Sandy. I'm obsessed with the mole person at Magna-Protect—and here at the house for our reboot. What did he look like? Can you send me a photo and the file? There was nothing in our—"*Whoa.* I almost said "Trapper Keeper" out loud. I collected myself. "Binder."

I waited for her to answer. Silence. Big silence.

"You still there?"

"Well, that's the thing."

"The thing."

"Yes. The file. The personnel file. Got wiped from the computers. And the Cloud. From everywhere as far as we can tell. No hard copies either."

I waited some more. I was getting better at not letting my freak-outs escape by way of my lips. Not perfect. But better. I was the one who put the A in the T&A, after all.

"As for what he looked like— We don't actually know. Nobody does."

I gritted my teeth. Clenched my jaw for good measure. "Nobody? Seriously?" Freak-out slippage was occurring.

"Allie, I'm being as transparent as I can about this."

"Oh. Really. Transparent? And that's why you didn't mention any of this before? Feels like critical information to me. If you don't know who this dude is, Sandy, or what he looks like or anything, how do you know he's actually gone?"

She hung up.

On me? The significant other of her wealthiest client?

Bad sign.

Was this what Tom was hearing that morning on the deck? This small sin of omission. The part where he said she was holding back "something about the reboot." The slight rise in the pitch of her voice as she strained to keep her smallish kite of a lie in the air?

The game's aloft.

Chapter Thirty-five

I wanted to call Sandy right back and grill her like crazy about her unforgivable breach of forthcomingness, but I decided to let her percolate for a bit. At least long enough for me to unleash Otis on her about the mole.

In the meantime, I was energized by my workout being over, by the—possibly sarcastic— awe of Tom and Otis regarding my workout, and the prospect of an excellent lunch. The lunch was being delivered soon by a guest.

I'd explained to Otis about the lunch and we set up for it on the round table by the kitchen window. He was not all that happy about the guest, but the sun was coming out, which helped, and I was sure he'd be happier when he saw the lunch.

I was trying to figure out a way to get Lisa Cole on the T&A team. Ex officio, of course. She had incredible resources when it came to gathering information. Her connections were impeccable. She knew where all the bodies were buried. Plus she was so winsomely appealing she could worm information out of rocks.

I also wanted Lisa on the Tom & Allie ex officio payroll so she could use her gifts for good and not mere sensationalism. Maybe escape the clutches of her current well-paying job at Channel 16.

No matter how I sliced it, I owed Lisa for Tom. She was my FGF. Fairy Godmother Forever. If she hadn't let her impatience run wild in the crosswalk across from Joe's, I'd still be bogus-part-timing it at Mem-Nott. With an empty, lost place in my soul I'd never be able to figure out.

Lisa's current job was a poor facsimile of the super-hero fact-finding and truth-telling career she'd envisioned back in her "ignorant childhood." That touched my heart. I myself was always looking for some sort of transformation into my youthful dreams. Not the least of which was to be an extremely organized sleuth like Kinsey Millhone. I was in awe of her 3x5 cards.

I needed to walk softly with this Lisa idea. Tom was happy she'd honked at him, but he saw that more as a wacky twist of fate. Like when somebody throws a rock out of meanness and accidentally sets off an alarm that prevents a robbery.

Otis plain didn't trust her.

What pushed me over the edge was not that she'd sent Andy Doofus with the not particularly enlightening file, but that she was so great to Loretta. I, for most of the duration of our coworker relationship, was not so great.

I'd called Lisa to thank her for sending the file and to ask her if she'd like to "get better acquainted with key members of the T&A." And would she care to join us for lunch?

"Hell, I'll bring the lunch. What time do you want me there?"

I'd forgotten I was dealing with a woman who could walk, take a phone call, and make a mental note to send somebody something, all on the fly. And then send the thing. A person like that was always good to know.

Otis and Tom were skeptical. Especially about lunch. She won both of them over when she waltzed in with Slyman's "Home of the best and biggest corned beef" corned beef sandwiches, on rye, for everyone. Plus crinkle fries. And slaw.

I was particularly won over, even though I was mostly won already, that she didn't coyly suggest that "we girls" split one of the one-pound beauties. She ate hers, all by herself. No "Oh dear, I couldn't possibly." from our Lisa Čebulj. She was true to her roots. Had plenty of fries and slaw, too.

After lunch we moved out to the pool deck. The sun was warming and drying everything and glaring quite a bit. Otis raised the umbrella. Especially for Lisa, I could tell. The sandwich won his heart.

She further endeared herself to me by saying, "Holy crap. Is that one of those Shade Systems? Those suckers cost, like, two thousand bucks."

Tom, of course, did not know this and therefore looked surprised and appalled. Otis, who'd already demonstrated his appreciation of pricey vehicles and kitchen appliances, nodded his approval. "Yeah. It is. And they do. There are five of them out here. The guy who owns this place spent the big bucks. At least by the pool."

Lisa's pleased expression took a turn for the displeased. She grimaced. "That guy."

This was interesting. "That guy? We haven't met him."

"Lucky you. He's a total ass. He's supposed to be crazy rich, but rumor is he got over his head with this place. I bet you all are keeping up his house payment now. He should send you a fruit basket once a day."

"You know everybody in Cleveland, Lisa."

She grinned. "All the total asses, that's for sure. You want to meet a guy who has to tell you how much his shoes cost, I'm your girl. I know legions of those."

I wanted to interrogate Lisa in detail about "that guy," but I didn't want to appear mean-spirited in the wake of the dining room furniture dust-up. So I switched subjects. "Lisa, I never got to say thanks for the video and the file you sent over."

"Took five minutes. Did it help?"

"It did. Some. I appreciated that. And that kid? That Andy Reilly. He was very entertaining."

She frowned in that careful way of women who need to constantly remind themselves not to make wrinkles between their eyes. "Andy? Reilly? I put your envelope in the to-be-delivered tray. In the mailroom. I don't—"

"One of your interns. Completely unedited mouth?"

She shook her head, puzzled. "I don't—"

"Oh, come on. You'd remember Andy. Kind of cute. Drives a Jeep. Redhead? Freckles. About twelve?"

She was frowning for real now. The full Wrinkle-Maker.

"Wire rims? Bent a little?"

Her eyes flared wide.

I got a chill. "Lisa?"

"Allie. What else about this…Andy? What did he tell you?"

"Nothing. Geez. He was a complete doofus.

Couldn't get enough of the house. Couldn't believe I wasn't a servant—Lisa, please tell me I'm going to be happy when you explain why you're looking at me like that."

"Sorry. You're not. Give me a minute. I need to make a call."

Five minutes later, she stopped walking up and down by the pool—talking and shaking her head— came back, put down her phone and faced the three of us. A blind man could have read her expression, especially since she matched it with the tiny click sound a tongue makes when it's unsticking itself to say something complex and unpleasant.

"Lisa. Did something happen to Andy? Something awful you don't want to tell us?"

She dismissed my question with a sharp little laugh. "Not hardly. I wish that was it. I'm guessing your 'Andy Reilly' may be a young man with many names and faces. And many skills. Our 'Mark Fleming.'"

She made finger quotes I knew Tom could hear.

"He showed up at Channel 16, beginning of March. Heard we had 'an opening.' We did. Our tech department was three guys and the one girl who could run the whole deal. Lauren. That young woman got run down. Hit-skip. Crossing Chester in the slushy mess we had the last weekend in Februar—Allie?"

I shook off the big, flashing, "Last weekend in February?" bedazzling my brain. Coincidence. Had to be.

"No. Lisa. Keep going. I'll catch up."

"Anyway, she died. Our wonder woman…died? So that was awful. She was great. A lovely, bright, funny person. Everybody was just—But besides that, it became clear after about fifteen minutes that she was the whole department, and those dudes were mostly not geniuses. To be polite. Didn't I tell you about some of this at lunch when we were talking? It's still all top of mind at 16."

"I wouldn't forget something like that. Keep going."

I noticed Otis' eyebrows going up at my socializing with the press and/or collaborating with the enemy. Tom's eyebrows stayed level, though. I took that for a promising sign.

"Then this guy, this Mark Fleming, shows up. Like magic. Not from any of our go-to tech outfits. But I heard about his amazing résumé. Which we didn't look at too hard, or maybe at all, because I guess the first words out of his mouth were, 'I heard about Lauren. You're going to need your… scooby unbotoxed?'" She made a face. "Whatever. Only the tech guys understood him, but it sure lit up those server freaks. Mark was in without a second glance. No questions asked.

"I can't say I blame them. Lauren had been gone for a couple of weeks. The…talent deficit…was getting painfully obvious. People were pumping their lifeblood into the equipment and the only sympathy they were getting was, like, 'Don't bleed on that. You'll short out something else.'"

I was listening to Lisa, but making note of Otis' expression which was morphing from moderately interested to progressively more concerned. I nodded to keep her from getting distracted by the bad vibrations coming from his side of the table. "So, then?"

"So what's personally embarrassing, is that Mark was totally interested in me. He was young, like you said, and very earnest. He had the red hair but he was slicked down and dressed for tech. You know?"

I was busy collating a deluge of disturbing, only apparently unrelated, facts.

"Not so much."

"Oh, Allie. Trust me. It's a free-for-all. I hear the dress code at Google is "You Must Wear Clothes." That encourages these people. Mark was very young. You're right about that, but more like early twenties than twelve. Prodigy. Savant. Whatever. But I could tell he was working on not looking like a kid. He wore the same basic expensive jeans every day. Black. Black tee. Black hoodie sometimes. Black ratty-but-cool blazer.

"Backpack, of course, as he came and went. I swear, there was some kind high-tech readout badge on it. Could show all kinds of stuff. The time. Your turn signal if you were biking. His would have a smile-ly emoji sometimes. Creepy. Now that I think about it."

Tom had now either caught up with the Otis vibe of "Bad Things Here" or tuned in on his own. Lisa was still looking at March.

"Like you said, Allie. Those round, wire, smart-dude glasses. Bent up. No coat. Ever. And it was cold in March. Cleveland.

"But anyway. He was sweet to me. Had a kind of earnest, hungry-to-learn vibe going on. He flirted, too. I brushed that off. Too jailbait-y. And not my type."

She cast a "so my type" glance at Tom who was frowning but still handsome and attired on this occasion in techy black. I needed to warn her about Blind Man Spidey. And Otis wasn't blind so there was that. Me, either, as far as that goes.

She regrouped. "Anyway. Mark seemed okay. And boyishly unthreatening. Eager to please. He gave me this cool app. Put it on my laptop and phone and it lets me—oh. Allie. Damn."

"*Oh-Allie-Damn*" was right, but we were flying now and I wanted to see where this was going to land. "Never mind, Lisa. Not your fault. If he's my

Andy Reilly, he's very convincing. I tipped him ten dollars for bringing me your folder. But what happened?"

"He left. Went all 'my work here is done' and took off. Got himself paid on his way out. No forwarding. I don't know why he would have gone to the trouble to come here to see you, though."

"Ego." Tom's tone was bitter. "I'm only getting acquainted with this guy, but I'm pretty sure he likes to do outrageous, risky things because he can. He thinks he's brilliant. And unstoppable. Or maybe he needed to see something his surveillance wasn't showing him. I can't imagine what that could be. It looks like he was seeing and hearing quite a bit already."

Lisa was backtracking through her memories now. Checking. Rechecking. "How did he know you and I, Allie—? Where did he get—?" She caught the look I sent her. "Oh geez, Allie. You're right. Besides, what does it matter now? He could. He did. Now what?"

Time to hit redial on Sandy.

"Now we call Magna-Pro and ask them about their mystery guy. Surely they called him something."

Ted. They called him Ted.

As in Bundy.

Chapter Thirty-six

Ted's first name and his last name—something real common, like Stevens—was about all Sandy thought she knew.

I was getting better at prying, though.

"Sandy, try again. You have no solid information about Ted except his name? Truly? Did he just appear on the doorstep one morning in—let me guess—April?"

"Yes. No…Look. You're right. It was April but he didn't appear on the doorstep. He never appeared at all until your reboot day and never here at the office. I never saw the guy, Allie. My boss got a phone call from our new major investor. He was the one who'd set us up with this 'big mansion in Bratenahl.' Your job was a big windfall for us when we needed it. He said he knew your place was a challenge. And that he had a pretty good idea why…."

"And that 'good idea why' was what? Exactly, Sandy."

She threw in the towel.

"That the mansion was you guys. The lottery money."

"And that the security reboot was critical to the security of almost two-hundred-million dollars. And our safety. Yes?"

"Yes. But that was why he thought it would be the perfect project for us. I—" She paused to make room for an unwelcome conclusion.

"All right. Let's move on. We have bigger fish to fry. If you can imagine that."

"I can't really, but okay. I'm trying to remember every single thing now, Nobody has been able to give us much of a description."

"Nobody? The guys who were here with him? Doing the work?"

"I've talked to them. Every single one of them. Except for the one guy, Keith, who actually—"

Oh, crap.

"Where's that guy, Sandy? Keith. What happened with him? Sandy?"

"Nothing happened, Allie. He must have been a complete loser. He walked away after that day down there. Never showed up for work again. His wife was upset. Naturally. Kept calling. I'm pretty sure she went to the police, and nothing came of that. She was worried at first. Then super pissed off. Then she stopped calling. We asked the folks who worked with him. They all thought he was the sort to pick up and move on. Not all that happy at home. Maybe a girlfriend on the side. Always looking. Ambitious. Restless. You know the type."

"And he was the 'one guy who actually' what?"

"The one who actually stayed for the reboot when— Okay, here's what I got out of them. Finally. Ted was the investor's hot-shot guy, too cool for school. Young. Dressed all black. Wire rims. Arrogant smartass. You know. One of those guys.

"Ted threw our team out after about an hour for being incompetent. Told them he would never mention what idiots they were if we never found out they'd been kicked off the job. 'Win/Win,' they told me he said. So it was only Ted Stevens and Keith. Keith McGill. You don't think—?"

"We'll come back to Keith McGill. I promise. Let's don't get sidetracked right now."

"Allie, please. I can see where this is going. How we were played. How we're in serious trouble. We were just getting back on our feet after—

Flag on the play.

"After?" I made my voice as mild as I could.

"After a very tough patch. We were a terrific little

start-up, you know? Smart. Amazing success story. Doing good, careful work. Getting new clients. Favorable reviews online. But the overhead, the costs? They're tremendous in this business.

"And all of a sudden there was a shortfall. Didn't see it coming. Accounting error, I guess. Or something. Not my area. So now we were treading water. Drowning, more like it. And then our investor—angel, it felt like—came on board. Richard Tyler. Said call him Rich. Great guy. Sweetheart. Over the phone, at least. I think his headquarters are in Boston. Crazy busy. But he put cash into our operation. Got us your big contract."

"And sent you Ted."

"Yes. And from what our new team, the ones who were at your place this week, tell me, Ted was a genius, all right. As advertised. But not in a good way. A super-hacker. Set up surveillance all over your place. No cameras. Listening devices, though. Very sensitive. Everywhere. Like out on the deck where we talked that day? He could have could have heard it all. In the shower even, they said."

Score one for Otis moving us three down to the beach.

Score one for me, too. I wasn't so caught up in our current disaster that I couldn't silently approve "no cameras." Hurray on that. Yeesh on the damn shower.

Sandy forged on. "What's even worse, there was a…a back door installed into the system, too, so he could get in, remotely, whenever he wanted. Do whatever he wanted."

"And where is your angel in all this? What's he say?"

"I tried to reach him at his office today, after I….Damn. After I hung up on you, Allie. I'm sorry. I was so—But his secretary said he was at a big conference. Until next Monday. Unreachable."

I just bet.

"How about your boss here in Cleveland, Sandy? Can I talk to him or her. At least?"

"Oh, God. Allie. He's really sick. Got some food poisoning or something. A month ago. Then one of those super bug viruses. Awful. Still in the hospital with that. It looks like he'll recover, but he's—Everybody's— I can't find Margaret, either."

Alrighty. No boss on board. No answers for us. No Margaret. And no time for Margaret now.

Later, Margaret.

"Does the new team think it's fixed now?"

"They do. But Allie?"

"I'm right here."

"Don't count on it. Now you promised you'd say more about Keith?"

"Your guy who helped Ted with the reboot."

"Yes."

"Was this Keith McGill a total heartless son of a bitch, like those other folks suggested? Could he have gotten paid off, ditched his wife without a word, and left town like your guys insinuated? Or was Keith a halfway decent human being?"

"He's a decent guy, Allie. Not perfect, but, at heart, he's okay."

"Then I'm very sorry, Sandy. But I think he's dead."

Chapter Thirty-seven

The call ended with a few seconds of silence from Sandy, followed by her choked, 'I'll call you back, Allie. We'll figure this out."

Otis, Lisa, and I sat staring at each other.

Tom, on the other hand, was in a place of no staring where it was both quiet and very dark. No visual distraction to divert him from the mess we were in. We all kept quiet and let him think. The sun vanished behind a cloud and a breeze rallied some waves. I was getting goose bumps, but they weren't from the wind.

After Tom sat looking grim for a bit, he came back from there and told us what he'd seen.

"Seems obvious that someone's had access to our conversations in this house since we moved in. Who knows? Maybe before that. This just keeps getting more—And there are other possibilities. Phones. Anything you said to Lisa on her phone since March, Allie. And we've got no assurance that our own phones aren't compromised.

"We know that this Andy-Mark-Ted is one very gifted, impressive, calculating, ruthless person. A chameleon who can be many different boyish, likeable young guys. Who charmed you out of ten dollars, Allie. Who's likely caused the deaths of at least a couple of people. Your Lauren, Lisa. Sandy's Keith. Maybe that thing with her boss. So he could gain control of our information. And the money, of course. All of it. Somehow.

"We can be damn sure Sandy's 'major investor' is calling all the shots at Magna-Pro. They're not really in the security business anymore. At least as far as our security is concerned.

"We could try to go after that guy who I bet is no way in Boston right now. Try to find out more. But he's smoke, and I'd say we already know what he is. What he and his genius are up to. What's coming for us is coming too fast for…for research.

"At some point in the last ten months, somebody or a few somebodies turned a smart little enterprising company into a front for a—

Tom went very still, his hands lightly together, fingers steepled and pressed against his mouth, shoulders relaxed, breathing deep and even, while he considered what he was about to say.

"Magna-Protect's major investor is bankrolling an electronic heist. Of two-hundred-twelve million dollars. I believe our chameleon tech genius has been in his employ since—Well. Since sometime last fall. A guy like that, with an unlimited paycheck. And a passport."

He ended the sentence, full stop. Like running a thought into a wall.

I pursued that scenario into an afternoon back in January. Maybe a sun-blasted beach. Tom and me, drowsing in our deck chairs. Browned and lazy. Holding hands. Happy. But behind us, not far, a red-haired guy, wearing a lot of sunscreen and bent wire rims. Watching us through binoculars. Listening to us through our phones.

Making us his prey.

My skin crawled.

Tom was sorting his memories, too. Speculating.

"I don't know exactly where our Lloyd case figures in all of this, but everything we've been doing—it's all circling the same drain.

"And we're even more on our own. From what I could tell over the phone, Sandy is figuring all this out at the same rate we are. She can't help us now."

For a moment he considered what he'd said, his somber expression deepening.

"Maybe we should be helping her. Send one

of your team to Magna-Pro, Otis. Julia would be good. If Sandy isn't in on this, and I don't think she is—Just go. Tell Julia, or whomever you decide to send, to be careful. To take Sandy somewhere safe and stay with her until we can figure this out."

I chimed in. "Also, tell Julia to be careful about Margaret, Otis. In case she ever shows up again. Protect her. Tie her up. Who knows? Damn. Everybody we're looking at is either dead or dangerous."

Tom circled back through our unfolding situation, gathering up stray anxieties. "And, Otis, if our phones are not secure, and have not been since—And if some other device could be listening to us—right now—"

Wham.

That did it for me. Every avenue of escape from the threats that were careening through my head slammed shut. My heart pulsed fear all the way into my fingertips. *Run. Stop. Here. There. Nowhere!* All my impulses were frying themselves. I realized, right there, what would make a fugitive simply go back and turn herself in.

Tom was smart. He didn't bother to follow his train of thought into the chaos of its consequences. He did what he could.

"Go buy new phones for everybody, Otis. About

thirty." His lips compressed around an irony we'd noticed back at the beginning of our Mondo situation: It took a lot of his money to protect us from the manifold perils of his money.

"I'm fucking rich. I can pay for some phones. But let's figure out how to keep them clean. Otis, when you get a minute, do some research on that. Obviously the money doesn't make us bulletproof but it ought to be able to buy us a little clean."

I figured Otis had a man for that job. Somebody Tom still didn't know about…

Now would not be a good time, Allie.

Tom wasn't reading my mind right then, so he followed his own train of thought.

"And if anybody has a sudden revelation or a burning question that you think could put us more at risk? Take it outside. Or you guys write it down. We'll figure out a way for me to get those messages."

We were all being changed. Getting tougher, smarter, sharper as we came to grips with danger springing up from every direction. Right now, though, I was beginning to see that Tom might one day be the lead detective of the T&A.

But what I said was, "I suppose this phone problem means they know about my death threat, too."

"You had a death threat, Allie?"

I observed Lisa splitting her personality between "I'm your-new-good-friend-Lisa" and "Good afternoon, I'm Lisa Cole, 16 News. Reporter at the most scandal-mongering TV station in town." I snapped her out of it before I could find out which way the chips were going to fall.

"Me. I did it. I made the death threat, Lisa. D.B. You know how he is."

She unsplit herself. "You'll have to tell me all about that." A pause. "Strictly off the record, of course."

"Yeah, Lisa. On some distant day we'll talk. Off the record. You can swear by your mother's *žgan*—grits. I'm not worried right now about D.B. making trouble for me. He's ninety percent blowhard. This is more serious than that."

I was seeing a new angle to my D.B. meltdown.

"Somebody who wants to take me out of the whole two-hundred-twelve-million-dollar heist scenario, maybe permanently, might use my stupidity to hurt D.B. And get me locked up.

"No matter how much he deserves to be punished for being a terrible version of a human being, I don't want D.B. to die because of me. Or at all. As far as that goes."

Tom nodded. "When Otis comes back with the new phones, you can call D.B. Write down the numbers from your contact list now while you still have it. The new phones will have your old numbers, but you'll need theirs. Lisa, you, too. You may not be able to download from your backup for a while."

Lisa blanched. Then pulled herself together, grabbed her phone and a notebook from her bag, and started copying.

"A reporter *is* her contacts list."

• • ● • •

I didn't have to write down D.B.'s number. I don't have access to Tom's Blind Man Phonebook skills, but I'm good with numbers.

What's more, as it turned out, I didn't have to call him, either.

Chapter Thirty-eight

At four that afternoon, Tony Valerio was glaring at me from our front stoop. His squad car was parked in the circular driveway. It gave me a chill. As did the other officer waiting stoically in its front seat.

Huh.

The security system was disarmed at the moment in honor of the guards with guns we had roaming about, so I could open the door without ceremony. I assessed Tony's expression—still glaring—and went conservative with my greeting.

"Officer Valerio."

"Ms. Harper."

UhOh.

"Tony?"

He shook his head at me. Side-to-side. Slow, intimidating, and cop-like. Held up a cell phone in my face. Pressed play.

Oh, hello.

It was Allie Harper herself whose voice came out of that phone. Powered by a windchill factor of forty below. Freeze warning:

"I will have you fucking killed. I'm pretty sure I can figure out how to do that. It would give me great pleasure."

Tony raised his eyebrow at me.

Fortunately, my mouth was rendered inoperable for a long three seconds and by the time I got it working, I'd seen the pointlessness of lying, so I cut straight to the abject acceptance of responsibility.

"Is…is D.B. dead?" I braced myself against a lot of terrible realizations.

"Luckily for you, no."

"Is he okay?"

"He will be in a day or so. In the hospital now."

Whew for that.

"Tony…"

"There's an important lesson for you in this."

"Yeah. Otis and Tom pointed that out to me right after I clicked off. So, how bad is this?"

"Plenty bad enough. Could be worse."

"Yeah, D.B. could be dead. Other than that, I don't see any upside here yet."

"Well, there's this. He's refused to press charges."

"Seriously? Is it a head injury? Are you sure he's not dying?"

"He wants to see you. Today. This evening. He's at the Clinic in the fanciest room they could dig up. We've got an officer standing guard for a bit, in case your hitmen show up again. Also, you haven't been charged with anything. At this time. If your ex wants a meeting, I can't stop you from seeing him. We can't stop him from seeing you. We can't do much of goddam anything. I suggest you provide yourself with some reliable witnesses for the occasion."

I let the "hitmen" slide. I had that coming. "I'll take Tom and Otis. They already know I'm an idiot. And I think I'll need my lawyer present. Just in case."

"Yeah, that would be smart. For a change." He turned to go.

"Tony. Wait." I was still clutching my own phone from which I'd been trying to extract irreplaceable parts of my life before Otis could take it to phone prison. I held it out to him.

"I didn't beat up D.B. For one thing he's about six feet taller than me. And quick. Whoever did beat him up must have been listening in on that conversation. The one you replayed for me. My phone's been hacked. Hell, this whole house has been hacked. Our security people—But that's not as critical as this."

I pushed the phone closer to his face. "I think it is listening to what we're saying. Right now."

Tony's expression went from puzzled, to skeptical, to alarmed.

I answered that last face. "Yeah. I know. Imagine my dismay. But I know you law enforcement types have folks who can extract crime-related information from phones. Want to let them take a look?"

He put a hand out. I pulled the phone back. "Officer Valerio, if I hear any moments from my private life on, I dunno, WCPN—the CPD will be smoking ash. You understand. Right?'

I was surprised. He didn't get all up in my face about my making still another empty threat. Officer Valerio had shifted back to Tony. And he didn't seem to be worried that the phone might hear him.

"God, Allie. The whole house? The phones? Who—?"

"Somebody way smarter than me and you." I laid the phone down on the step and led him along the walk to what I thought might be a safe distance.

I lowered my voice. "Otis has got this, Tony. He has the whole picture. There's nothing for you guys to do. It's all supposition so far. Thin and flimsy. But serious. As in some currently-theoretical-murders serious. Could you take the phone?"

"God, Allie. Sure. I'll take it. But you guys need to be more careful."

I shrugged. "The place is crawling with the people Otis got us. 24/7. He's alarmed off two-thirds of the house. It's not us that's in danger, anyway. It's the money. And the money's not here."

I flashed on the Bank of Technology in the security room with its intimidating blinking lights and its feet of clay, but now wasn't the time—

"I get that, Allie. But you and Tom and Otis, and all of Otis' people—who are also my own people—are standing in the way of what they're after. So watch yourself."

I secretly added all the somewhat good people at Magna-Pro to that list. And Lisa. Plus. Oh wait. "Tony. Margo? Could you?"

If I wasn't so steadily vibrating with terror, I would have had a field day with the new expressions now playing themselves out on Tony's face. From "OMG, *Margo?*" to "Yes, indeed, Ms. Harper, we would inform Ms. Gallucci about that as a matter of protocol." As it was, I permitted him to say, "I'm on it." And let it go.

I did allow myself a moment's entertainment while I pondered whether he'd heard about her hit and run on the googly speed camera. I figured that, being Margo, she'd have vented all of her righteous indignation to Tony. And—understanding Tony better, as I did now—that he would have worked very hard to keep a straight face. And probably lost.

All I said was, "Tony, we'll do our best to keep all of us safe. I promise. We're not as young and foolish as we were last August."

Tony hesitated and then jumped in.

"You're not, Allie. Not at all. You've got focus now. You're actually thinking sometimes."

I bit my tongue.

"You actually have the makings—" He hit the brakes. "And, listen. Nobody would blame you for being blindsided last summer—"

He stopped himself on that one, too, and then started himself again without comment. Tom had trained Tony well on the "don't let's make a big deal about the blind man metaphors."

"You're smart, Allie, and you know it. Only… don't go overboard and try to—" He jumped back out. "Take care of yourself. Stay awake. And stop threatening to kill that idiot."

He went back and grabbed the phone off the step and strode back down the walk, holding it at a gingerly arm's length.

That may have been the moment Tony Valerio joined the T&A for real.

Chapter Thirty-nine

Skip Castillo, our friend, lawyer, and trusted advisor—as well as Otis' new, unlimited source of financial info—was overkill for the kind of legal advice I might need at the Clinic that evening. Or, as far as that went, to handle Margo's Googly Homicide in about another fifteen minutes.

I didn't bring Skip to D.B.'s hospital room to be my lawyer, although I agreed with Valerio that I probably could have used one or two of those on this occasion. I chose The Skipper, in particular, because, as D.B.'s fellow partner at GG& B, he was an unspoken threat to D.B. Also, it cheered me up to see him. He'd been an ally in the contretemps of last summer. A godsend, actually. He always made me feel sheltered from harm. And small and cute. That, too.

We were an interesting bunch gathered in D.B.'s

well-appointed room, all of us jockeying amongst ourselves not to get too close to D.B. Ever again. Tom and Otis were sitting on the couch that came with the room. Skip was lurking—no other word for it—in the corner by the supply cupboards and the little sink. I was standing at the foot of the bed, trying to look 1) at least in part responsible for his being here and 2) not all that sorry.

D.B., to put it graciously, looked like crap. First of all, he was wearing an embarrassment of a hospital gown with a busy design of unidentifiable little blue things. His meticulous grooming was out the window, too. The cowlick, which I knew he subdued every morning with industrial strength gel, had escaped at last.

There was a bandage across the bridge of his nose and a black eye with a hideous spreading bruise. A stitch or two in his lower lip. A padded sling on his right arm. No cast. I assumed someone dislocated it by trying to rip it off his body. I couldn't see any other injuries, apart from the air of general trauma written all over him. That and the deeply aggrieved expression on his battered face.

"You really did it, Allie. You hired someone to kill me?" His tone struck a delicate balance between mournful and accusatory.

I looked him over, from the cowlick, to the

bruises, to the sling. This was a complicated moment for me. He'd stirred me up by threatening Rune. That outrage was all his. But I'd somehow brought the wrath of this beating down upon him. I'd been out of control. He'd been injured. Not my finest moment.

I was relieved, for at least ten seconds, that Tom couldn't see the havoc I'd wreaked on this miserable excuse for a man. It troubled me to think that his blindness sometimes worked like gangbusters for the Allie Harper I knew so well and couldn't forgive for all kinds of malfeasance. I forbade myself to even consider what Lee Ann might yet have in mind for old Duane.

The D.B. was in a weakened state. I could see a side of him that hadn't been available to me for at least four years. There was a human being in there. Not much of one. This was always going to be D.B. Harper. But still. Its feelings were hurt. Wounded.

I took a step toward the bed. He scooched back against the pillow.

"D.B. Did you do any of what you suggested you might do? About Rune?"

"No. No, of course not. I was just yanking your chain. I figured you'd know that."

"Did you believe I'd actually have you killed, even if you did?"

"Well, you did sound pretty mad. But no. Like I said. I'd yanked your chain. You responded… appropriately, I'd say. You're still cute when you're mad at me, you know?"

"Don't press your luck."

"Anyway, they said, 'This is for Roo.' And proceeded to beat the crap out of me."

"Roo? Are you sure? Like Kanga and Roo? In the books?"

"What? I don't know about any books. But I knew about Rune. That's where this all started. Obviously. And they clearly didn't. They only heard you say…what you said. And meant to use that to make you a suspect for the beating. I wasn't about to let that happen."

"D.B. I didn't you know you cared—Wait a sec. You knew that if word got around your ex-wife went to the trouble of hiring a hitman, everybody would get focused on you. They'd ask themselves what was it you did to make an adorable little thing like me get so lethally pissed off. And it would be bad for you—?"

"At the firm." He didn't glance in Skip's direction. That right there took the discipline of a trial lawyer.

He shrugged with both shoulders and then grimaced. "The police are the only ones who have the recording now. As far as I know. If I tell them it was a joke, that you didn't want to kill me... You don't. Not really. Do you?"

He made his expression wistful. I was having none of it. He gave up. "Okay. I'd probably be lying to cops, but you wouldn't dispute it. Would you?"

"Not hardly. Then you could go away and not bother me ever again. And I might think ever so slightly more kindly of you. I'd shake on that."

I put my hand out. He took it and held it. His hand was warm. And bruised. I tried to remember a time when I wanted him to hold my hand. He did look pitiful. Up closer, his big old handsome face was lumpy and swollen from the beating. Even his smile was lopsided because of the little stitches in his lip.

Nope. Nada. I took my hand back.

"I'll hold you to this. And D.B. My promise about Rune? Think about the legal version of that. Look at Skip over there. Look at Tom. Think about his money. Read his mind. Consider your career. And then, please just forget about me. For as long as we both shall live."

● ● ● ● ●

When we all got back to the mansion, my new phone was put into my hands by Otis. He recognized my flash of "Oh, boy! A brand new iPhone. My life is back!" and wore an expression that was an admonition all by itself.

Too bad for me.

"Allie, this is not your camera, or your Facebook, or your music, or your e-mail. None of that. Nothing. It is a phone. I'm sure you can remember when a phone was a phone? That's what this is. It's secure. When people call your old number, it'll ring. Ring, Allie. Like a phone. Not play whatever tune you think expresses the caller's personality.

"It won't be eavesdropping on you all day long, not giving criminals your damn location. It won't be doing anything except allowing you a very occasional call. From people who have your number. To people you know. Or to 9-1-1, should the occasion arise. As it so often does for you."

I nodded to show compliance.

He sighed and sneaked me half a grin. "And no death threats with this one either. Voids the warranty."

"Otis. What's the point of a phone without death threats?"

No reply.

Valerio was one of a handful of people who knew my number. When I received his call, it didn't even show me his name. His ringtone used to be the theme from *Dragnet*. Very Valerio. I missed it already. But there was nothing frivolous about this call.

"The phone you gave me," he began in a rush. "Wait. Is this a secure line now?"

"I would surely hope so. I have the original phone from 1876 now. It's pathetic. It does nothing but let you call up and bother me."

"Well, it's better off than the phone you gave me."

"Why? Tony? What happened?"

"Our tech guy started to open it up and it melted. Sizzled. Got hot. Screen cracked. Stuff oozed out. He had to throw it out a window. Done. Allie, I hope you've got a plan for protecting yourself."

"I thought that was you."

"Nah. Protecting you is way above my paygrade."

• ● ● ● •

Ten-fifteen p.m.

It was a day of many excitements and now that I was reviewing everything that transpired, I had to hand it to the treadmill for helping me stay on the path. It warmed me up. Gave me time to consider how we were not yet out of the Mondo Woods and probably never would be. Maybe was the antidote for at least some of the prodigious weight gain usually associated with a one-pound corned beef sandwich. Kept me going long enough to focus on the mole—a focus that arrived just in time for our massive cybercriminal wake-up call. It saw me in and out of trouble about the D.B. death threat. And, finally, it knocked me out.

Today was a marathon and I wrapped it up by falling asleep on the couch all by myself in our cozy—and possibly, maybe, not-bugged—family room.

In case somebody might be listening from a cushion button or somewhere, I murmured as I nodded off. "Good night, Andy, Mark, Ted. Whoever you are. We're coming for you."

Chapter Forty

11:45 p.m.

In my experience, sleeping on a couch will put a crick in your neck for at least the next twenty-four hours. Especially if you haven't planned for it with a pillow and a blanket, at least. A body with any survival skills at all will wake itself up before too much damage is done. My body was enhancing its survival skills with every passing day, and they weren't all aimed at neck-crick prevention. One minute I was out and under. Next minute, awake, alert, and one good breath away from an earsplitting scream.

The breath and the scream were prevented by someone clamping a hand over my mouth and nose and then a very quiet voice saying, "Allie. Don't scream. I'm going to take my hand away. I need you to not scream. Okay?"

I didn't recognize the hand or the owner of the hand at first. He was a dark silhouette in the moonlight from the window. Oh. That was a clue. I nodded. He took the hand away.

"Shadow Man."

A soft chuckle. "That's not very original."

"I'm not at my best just now."

"You'll do. Can I sit down for a minute?"

"Sure. A question, though. How come Otis' team isn't all over you? Why don't I feel very protected?" *Again.*

He sat. A careful distance away from me on the roomy couch. His face shadowy. Just the way he liked it. Leaned back into the cushions. Made the sound of a tired man, taking a thirty-second break.

"Otis has released his team for the rest of the night shift so I could have free access. Like he did the other night when you saw me. He alerted the morning shift to arrive early. He'll cover any gap. It won't be long."

"Otis trusts you."

"He has cause. You should trust him. If Otis vouches for me. I'm…worthy."

My stomach seized up on the logic of that statement. It went round and round like the variety of snake which was probably a lie told to me by my brother Justin when I was five. He said it bites onto its own tail and rolls on down the road. Until it stops and spears you with its poison tail barb. This could be a moment when hollering would be a good idea.

I didn't believe anything Justin ever told me was worth a damn, so I let the hoop snake roll on.

"Who or what are you? Exactly?"

"No time for stories."

"Fine. Tell me what you're doing here."

"I'm doing what Magna-Protect should have done for you in the first place. Plus some other stuff that they couldn't have, even if they were legit."

"They're not legit." It wasn't a question now, but I wanted more information.

"They're...not...all bad. Their good guys have been manipulated by your bad guys. Or put out of commission. They didn't start out to be not-legit."

"But now?"

"You should fire Magna-Pro. In the morning. Everything they've touched is compromised by their hacker-genius. Andy. Mark. Ted."

"You've been listening to us, too."

"Yes. What Otis doesn't tell me, I can hear anyway."

"And he trusts you."

"Yes. And you should because he does."

"The security system?"

"I fixed it. Patched it, at least. I'll be back every night between midnight and dawn. Until it's all fixed."

"All?"

"All."

"And I should trust you?"

"Yes."

"Because Otis does?"

"Yes."

"This is hard for me."

"Understandable."

"I'm inherently gullible. I married an absolutely despicable man once."

"No redeeming virtues?"

"None I could find."

"Those are the hardest to identify. That's not me."

"Or so you say."

"So Otis says. And—"

"It never ends. I trust you. I'm in. Because, look. Shadow Man. I've got a decent idea now about what we're up against, what we're probably always going to be up against in one way or another. If Otis isn't trustworthy—if we don't have Otis—"

"But you do. And now you have me."

"You're a mercenary."

"I work for money. Like the guy who mows your lawn."

"But he's never killed anybody."

"How do you know? You tipped a for-sure serial murderer ten bucks for delivering a package."

He had me there.

"So I guess I'll keep calling you Shadow Man?"

"Works for me. And, Allie?"

"Uh-huh?" I was yawning again now.

"Go to bed. Also, Otis told me not to put the listening devices in the master bedroom. He wanted you to know, but not that he told me to skip the bedroom. You guys are all pretty funny."

"Ah. I guess now I know I can trust you."

I meant that. I'd been trusting Shadow Man since the night I let him walk into the house without sounding a peep of alarm. But I also made note of the permanent installation of a tiny chip of fear in my gut.

The one that said, "*Your privacy is dead now. You can count on that, too.*"

"Good night, Allie."

"Good night, Shadow Man."

Chapter Forty-one
Friday, June 30

Who'd have imagined the first, official, high-level, strategy meeting of the new and improved T&A Detective Agency would be, to all appearances, a séance?

Harsh truth: We'd recently discovered that the mansion in Bratenahl had been on-air more continuously than CNN. Since April. Even with all the precautions we'd now taken there, Otis and I agreed this gathering was best held offsite and in less than nine-thousand square feet of echoing huge. Plus he'd secretly deployed Shadow Man to secure tonight's location. Margo hadn't noticed.

The five of us were seated around a large mahogany table in Margo's darkened, opulently appointed living room. Tony had called this meeting. He sat in the twelve o'clock position with his back to the fireplace, which tonight was lit by a dozen tall, white, flickering candles.

Otis was at six o'clock. Margo, wearing a long purple dress and enveloped in a fabulous crimson shawl, was Tony's right hand, at nine. All she needed to complete the picture was a scarf around her hair and big hoop earrings.

Tom was at one o'clock. Me, at three, between Tom and Otis. The Princess Vespa was occupying one hundred percent of her usual spot by Tom's feet. And snoring.

Wooden shutters on the windows, a couple of officers from Otis' team stationed outside, and Shadow Man's mysterious magic, all guarded us from prying eyes. The atmosphere was heavy with the lingering spice of incense and the sheer weight of anxiety.

Tense.

The only thing missing from our séance was the damn crystal ball. I sure could have used one of those right then. Lee Ann would have liked it, too.

"Wow, this is so cool." Margo's enthusiasm level was amped up by all the drama. Maybe twenty percent higher than usual. Scary.

"Thanks for inviting me, you guys."

Tony grinned. "It's your house, Margo." He paused to let the grin depart and the lines around his mouth deepen. It didn't take long. Then he cleared his throat and rippled his fingers on the table—pinkie finger to thumb, an automatic, rhythmic patter. Tuneless scales on a keyless piano. "And we need a fresh ear on our half-baked idea. We need to bring you, Margo, up to speed on what we've been thinking since…not very long. About ten minutes, feels like. And we all need to be in agreement about some things that are already in motion."

He collected himself with a deep breath. Puffed it out through pursed lips. "Okay. We've all noticed that the more this whole Lloyd thing gets untangled, the more the connections show up. We've been talking around and about scrapping for a couple of weeks, but we're focused on it now.

"That first afternoon at Chloe's—after Lloyd's house—I dismissed the scrappers. I hate scrapping. It grates on me. It's such a stupid, nothing crime. Pain in everybody's ass. But it's a stupid, nothing pain in the ass that hooks up to much more serious crimes. Almost straight line. To dirty money for stolen goods. Money that pays for drugs. Drugs that lead to deaths. Many, many deaths. Dirty money. Drugs. Death. Not a whole lotta crime bigger than that. But the connections can be hard to nail down. Now, though, we think there's a new wrinkle. Something we might be able to work with."

Tony wandered off into his thoughts and Tom picked up. He gave Margo an encouraging smile. She beamed at him so warmly he probably could feel it on his face, but he kept talking.

"We think we're beginning to get a picture, Margo—albeit incomplete—of the criminal network that Lloyd Bunker was just enough into to get himself killed. We're thinking the scrapping of Lloyd's house likely wasn't random vandalism that happened because he was dead and his house was abandoned."

Margo nodded. "It's all connected? The scrapyard. The drugs." Her eyes widened. "Is that what this is about? Are you trying to trap scrappers? In Allie's house?"

My heart sank at the thought of my house looking like Lloyd's. Even if I was never going to be able to live there again. I groaned, "Margo. No."

Tony came back online. "No. Definitely not in Allie's house. And we don't want to set a trap for ordinary scrappers. They're a big problem and a lot of heartbreak—but we, the CPD, don't have the resources to chase them down most of the time."

"And how come is that? Scrapping ruins everything." Margo wrapped the red shawl tighter around her shoulders and glared at Tony. This caused her to look even more gorgeous. And also sexy. Tony noticed. Margo noticed Tony noticing. She arched her brows and flashed her dark eyes at him. He noticed some more but got enough of a grip to go back to talking again.

"It's tough, Margo, but when you're working a hold-up, a brawl, and a body in a burning car that all got called in three minutes apart? If some good neighbor hits 9-1-1? And says, 'I think maybe there's somebody in the abandoned house next door?' That does not bring two cars at high speed, lit up, with their sirens going. It's triage. Plain and simple.

"Also the homeowners, if there even are any, often have chronic difficulties, sometimes with the law. The perpetrators are miserable losers. There's no percentage in pursuing crime very far at that level. You could hardly eke a felony out of their profit. A day's worth can vanish into a guy's arm overnight. It sucks is all."

Out of uniform and into a faded work shirt and jeans, Tony was, I had to admit, not too bad to look at. He was sporting his Margo-Mellow persona, too. In spite of the gloomy news he was sharing, he offered it up to her with a smile before he continued. "But Lloyd's case has made us aware of something that's a bigger deal. I've been poking around into a new kind of crime that may be worth going after. And it's plugged straight into Lloyd's house: Scrappers-for-Hire."

Chapter Forty-two

Scrappers-for-Hire.

No wonder Tony wanted to get the T&A involved. Here was a target of worthwhile size and significance for the Cleveland Police Department's limited resources: Someone was turning scrapping into a temp agency. Their scheme was to organize scrappers for somebody's profit or gain. It worked every which way.

"If you wanted to cover up something, Margo," I said. "Anything. Like every single thing in Lloyd's house—"

Tony jumped in on that. "Or think about a great threat to keep somebody in line. Muscle. All you'd have to do to lean on the poor son of a bitch is show him a photo of a trashed house. 'Pay up or maybe you'll come home at the end of the day and…'"

"Geez, Tony. I understand what you're saying.

But from what little I understand about scrappers, I think sending them out on a—"

I knew Margo. I knew how her mind worked so I watched her making her way through the load of information we'd dumped on her. In spite of her noisy extemporaneousness, Margo would eventually settle down and veer toward the practical.

I waited.

She delivered.

"I mean, sending them out on…what? An assignment? Wouldn't that be like herding cats? I mean I can't get my plumber to show up on the right day."

"Yeah, Margo," Tony was nodding along to her logic. "You're right. But I'm guessing your plumber isn't an addict."

"Not hardly. He's just deciding whether to come to my place or take his boat out. The weatherman makes all that guy's decisions."

Tony gave Margo a look of admiration that made me feel uneasy and jealous all at the same time.

"What you're coming to, Margo," he said, "is how we can maybe close the loop on this whole deal. Scrappers-For-Hire links to Dealers-On-Speed-Dial. Addicts are unreliable about a lot of stuff but if they're conscious at all, they're zeroed in on their next fix. Suppose they know that somebody will show up at their location at the end of the day—well, night probably—with their payoff, which is maybe a small amount of money and the drugs."

He shifted in his chair and went back to playing table piano again. Both hands this time. Palms pressed tight against the edge, fingers flying.

"There's a web that connects it all. Scrappers for money and drugs. Scrap in bulk for participating scrap dealers. Money for the scrapyards. Drugs for scrappers. Money for drug dealers. And, depending how much organization there is in all this, money moving from all these sources. On up the chain. Higher.

"As we know, crime does tend to organize itself. Stupid, careless, and desperate at the street level. Ambitious, greedy, and trapped in the middle. Smart, ruthless, and…deadly at the top. Right now, we're aimed at the middle."

He stilled his fingers and dropped his hands into his lap.

A couple of days ago when Tony came to Tom, Otis, and me, Tony's plan sounded like good sense and good timing. Time we could spare right now. Otis' team and, of course—still unbeknownst to Tom—Shadow Man, were all working on making us more secure. For most of that, Tom and I were in the way and playing an uneasy waiting game.

Tom not teaching. Me not having adequate access to Tom. Both of us more-or-less trapped indoors. Scared, bored, frustrated.

Bad combo.

Otis thought it was a peachy idea. Helping Valerio with whatever he needed to do about Scrappers-for-Hire might keep Tom and me out of trouble. The four of us devised a plan.

For my own entertainment, I also developed a working mental picture of what Scrappers-for-Hire might look like.

Zombies.

Badly dressed? Check.

Dazed and hungering? Check.

Hordes of them, stumbling, yet relentless? Check.

Yup. Zombies. I needed not to say that out loud. Especially to Tony.

Tony had now laid the foundation. Tom tossed the ball over to me. "From here, it's Allie's story to tell. She's the lead on Zo— Scrappers-for-Hire."

Yeah, I'd told Tom. Big mistake.

Margo's sparkle had dimmed with every word out of Tony's mouth. I needed to check. "You still with us, Margo? T&A forever?"

"Yeah. I suppose. I thought it would be more fun, though."

Uh-huh. So did I.

"Okay. Tony has a friend, Margo. Actually Tony's mom has a friend. Very lovely lady. Widow. Not well-to-do. Lives in a tidy little house on what used to be a pretty little cul-de-sac. Friendly neighborhood. All that. Then the housing market took a dive. Helen and almost all her neighbors got caught up in one of the reprehensible mortgage scams. The neighbors are all gone. But Helen is hanging on. Isolated among all those empty houses. It's a scary place for her.

"So then—you know those ads that get stuck up on the phone poles?"

Margo's eyes lit up. "Sure. forty-nine-dollar weekend getaways to some skanky casino in PA? On a bus? 'Bed bugs? Call Larry.' I hope I never have to call that Larry. Geez." She shook that off. "Never mind. Without those signs what would we have for entertainment when we're stuck at a light? I always assume every one of them is some kind of scam, Allie."

"Well, Helen saw a sign on the pole at the corner of 152nd and Ivanhoe that said, 'Facing Foreclosure? We Can Help.' She was desperate so she called the number.

"And, you're right, Margo. It was a scam. But not what you'd think. It was different from offering somebody pennies on the dollar for their house.

Which is what I expected. That deal might work if you were hard-pressed enough to sell your whole house for five-thousand or best offer."

Margo nodded. "I've seen those. It's a shame."

"Anyway, assume you were that desperate. What if somebody told you that you could get eighty-thousand dollars out of your house, if you'd give them half? And maybe it's a bit illegal. But forty-thousand dollars? I know what I'd do."

Margo shot me a look.

"Okay, maybe not, but remember in this scenario, I'm desperate. End of my rope. Bitter. Scared. If I thought I could get forty-thousand dollars or so out of my house—my house that I knew I wouldn't be able to sell, like ever? And then blow town? With nobody caring enough to look for me? That's temptation."

Lee Ann would. For sure. Drop of a hat.

"So the Facing-Foreclosure woman asked Helen, 'Do you by any chance have an insurance policy on your home?' And she said, yes, she did. And the woman said. 'That might make a difference.'"

"I don't get it."

"Neither did Helen. She said, 'Make a difference how?'"

And then the woman asked her if her policy was paid up. And Helen said yes, but she was ready to let it go at the half year. And that's when she found out about Scrappers-for-Hire."

Margo's expression said, "I don't see—" But then her eyes widened. "I get it. They'd total the house to the max of the policy. Helen would file for the insurance. And get to keep half. So what did she say?"

"Tony's friend is a far more upright citizen than I might be in her situation. She said she needed to think about it. Talk it over with her daughter and son-in-law and call back. Then she called Tony."

"That's good. Calling Tony was the right thing to do. And then what?"

"Then Scammer Woman got a call from Helen's daughter. I made quote-y marks around daughter. "She's got a lot more of my, let's call it pragmatism, than Helen. Otis?"

Otis held up my other new phone. This one was way better than the bare bones replacement from 1876 he got me for my own beloved phone. The most expensive burner in the world, this one looked like an iPhone and worked like one from the perspective of the person getting the call. Showed the recipient a fake name, with my own photo, and recorded all the conversations, too. Easy-peasy.

I hardly recognized my own voice.

"Oh, honey. My momma is old-fashioned like

that. She will never do anything the least bit—well, you know—" My voice got defensive. "She grew up in a different time. Easier, like. More pleasant." I'd given "pleasant" a touch of contempt. "I sure hope she didn't put you off any. That sounds like a great opportunity to me. I'll handle everything."

Otis stopped the recording. Margo was looking at me as if I'd sprouted a multiple personality. Maybe she was right. Then she shrugged that off and frowned. "You taped the conversation? Isn't that illegal?"

Otis frowned, too. "Ohio regulations allow recording if one party is okay with it. That would be Allie in this case. I don't like it much but sometimes you gotta—"He broke off and stared past Margo into the glowing candles of the fireplace. As though there were better answers in there.

Margo was nodding and she reached over and patted Otis' arm. Tony's face was closed up tight. He hit play again.

The foreclosure woman's voice turned soothing. "Oh, my dear. These are terrible times. Your momma will thank you for helping her out with this. I'll look into the details and get back to you."

"Then what happened?"

Tom chimed in. "Then I got to be the proud owner of the about-to-be-foreclosed property at 211 Poplar. It's our bait."

Tony picked up. "Our guess is Ms. Facing Fore-closure's insurance scam is mostly a hit and run thing. If you did it very often, it would raise a flag, but as a one-off every now and again it would be real money. And a real, clear goddam felony.

"For my purposes, one bust of this ingenious little plan would make the news, be good PR for law enforcement. And it's hard to see all the way through, but the Lloyd Case could be in here, too. His house. The CyCLE connection. I believe it could work out to the sort of scenario we all had in mind when I agreed to support the work of the T&A." He paused to beat himself up for a second. "Ex officio, of course. Tom can give us the funding that the CPD doesn't have. He bought us a house. Otis and Allie are doing most of the legwork. And you, Margo, have skills and insights that help. It feels solid to me."

"I can see that," Margo's face was running an infinite loop from "I get it" to "I don't like it." And back. She wanted to make Tony happy. She didn't want Tom and me to be in any more danger than we already were. She wanted to hurt the people who were trying to hurt Helen. And so it went.

Hoop snakes were all over my life right now. I sat and watched Margo try to make up her mind about endorsing the plan. My stomach empathized like crazy.

In the end she said okay. Actually, she said, "Okay. Okay. Okay."

● ● ● ● ●

We'd agreed, and the business meeting was breaking up. Otis disappeared into Margo's kitchen where he, Margo, and Mabel had rustled up a slow-simmered Yankee pot roast. Margo provided her chewy focaccia and a big bowl of salad. There was a shaker of Otis' signature cosmopolitans for Margo and me, too. And some bottles of New Cleveland Palester for him, Tom, and Tony. The mood was comfortable but subdued. Margo, was uncharacteristically quiet. I thought maybe she was playing it cool for Tony, but I reminded myself that I'd never known Margo to edit herself down for anybody, anywhere. So I asked.

"Margo. You're a thousand miles away. You're picking at your dinner. And you haven't touched your cosmo. What's up?"

"Nothing. Well, something. That might be nothing. Or maybe a really bad—well, if not bad at least worrisome—"

"Margo! Cut to the chase. Please. Before I die of impatience. Or anxiety."

"All right. We're here for Lloyd. And for Tony,

too. And the scrappers thing, which is part of Lloyd. I understand that and I'm sure we don't want to lose focus, which I can. Sometimes. Not always, but—"

"The chase?"

"Well. Lloyd. He's our first case of the T&A: 'Who Murdered Lloyd?' And he's all connected. Everywhere. His house was scrapped. Maybe by hired scrappers? He's linked to CyCLE in his address book and we know they're into something that's at least fishy. Somebody broke into your mansion to steal Lloyd's book after they missed it. At Loretta's. How did they know…? They could do that because somebody hacked your security system. It's all too—"

I watched Margo bringing her experience and intuition to bear on everything that had been revealed around her table this night. She'd aged maybe a couple of years over the course of the evening. Tony, though, I could see, was pretty darned enchanted by Margo's tired, beautiful face. How the purple-dress-and-red-shawl combo made her exotic and the dark circles and softness of her eyes made her kind. My BFF—face it, Allie—my surrogate mom—was beautiful. And worried. That was the wrinkle between her eyebrows.

"For sure, Lloyd is in there, one way or another.

He's caught up in the—what do you call that scary swirly thing?" She circled her index finger in the air. "The eyewall? Of the storm. But, Allie, you and Tom, and Otis too, now. You guys are the eye. The hacker and the intruders knew. *They knew you had the address book.* Our case was never all about Lloyd. It's all about you. And your—"

"Yeah, Margo. You're right," Tom said. His voice was cool and contained. I knew better than that, but he was hiding it well. "We're figuring that out, too. It's all about our money. About the two-hundred-twelve-million-fucking-dollars. Again."

Chapter Forty-three
Tuesday, July 4

The T&A was moving at the speed of a lot of cash.

It was the Fourth of July. Helen had left her cheery red, white, and blue wreath, with a bunch of little flags stuck into it, hanging on the front door of her house on Poplar Street. A defiant spark of color.

Bright and early Saturday morning, Helen's daughter, "Lee Ann," moved her out, along with Tom's check for eighty-thousand dollars and the few treasures she'd gathered together. When the scrappers arrived at dusk on Saturday evening, Helen was well away, settling in at her cozy, well-furnished, brand-new condo, which Tom's money also arranged. I was happy about that. Also hoping that using the Mondo to make life better for somebody might take some of the jinx off it.

On Tuesday, the Fourth, the scrappers were done. When they were paid off at five-forty-five a.m., right out in the open at the front of the drive, with their money and drugs, three representatives of the T&A—me, Otis, and Tom—were there, waiting in a house across the street and two doors down.

We had it all figured out.

Here's what I understand now, that I didn't have a clue about then. When Pete, Jimmy, and Eugene got the bright idea to cut the gas line and let the gas flood out, like the water did at Lloyd's, the gas proceeded to fill up the empty house with itself.

That's how Pete, Jimmy, and Eugene were. As far as anyone could ever explain, they'd gotten half an idea, acted on it, congratulated each other for causing way more damage than they'd even been sent to do, and then promptly forgot they'd done it.

What they'd done, as it turned out, was build a humongous ticking bomb.

Tom's 211 Poplar was well-built and well-insulated. Helen and her husband worked hard to keep it tight against the weather and easy on their fuel bills. The basement was an enclosed space, underground with glass block windows and no door to the outside. So a lot of gas was contained in a not-very-large space. It separated itself. What was heavy, sank down, while the lighter components floated upstairs, seeping under doors and through cracks. Any opening it could find. The laws of physics are everywhere.

So there we were.

On Saturday evening, Otis and I had taken some good, clear photos and a very respectable time-lapse video of the four scrappers—Pete, Jimmy, Eugene, and Milo—being dropped off with their tools by a crappy van. They'd entered the house through the unlocked garage and on Sunday morning they set to work, returning to the driveway, again and again, loaded down with many trips' worth of destruction. Which they simply piled up there. All Sunday and Monday they came out and went back. In broad daylight and the dark of night. Dumping the metal pieces of infrastructure.

On Tuesday, by the dawn's early light, when the Lexus with tinted windows pulled up outside and handed over the goods, Otis got more photos and videos. Including a first-class shot of the license plate. The car departed. The scrappers divvied up some cash and some something else. After a bit, they wandered off down the street, abandoning the formidable pile of their handiwork on display in Helen's drive.

The neighborhood was dead quiet on this dreary Independence Day. The weather was chilly, with an eighty-five percent chance of rain in the afternoon. A lot of little kids were bound to be disappointed.

We were doing fine, though. Our plan was right on track. We were waiting around to see if the guys came back, but that was gravy, as far as evidence was concerned. As soon as we were done here we'd slip out the back door of our hideout house, through its yard, and onto another mostly vacant street where our vehicle was hidden in the empty garage of an empty house.

Later that very evening, I, The Lee Ann, would get into a beat-up old car Otis found for me and upon arriving "at my mom's house," discover the damage by opening the front door and peeking in. I'd been warned by Scammer Woman not to go back inside because, "Lee Ann, you don't want to see your momma's home like that. Just focus on what the money will mean to her. And to you."

I would then call "Helen's insurance guy," who was now in on our anti-scam scheme. After that, it would be a matter of the wait for my check, which the insurance company would cheerfully supply, especially since Tom was insuring the safety of the funds. And because it was an act of righteousness for an insurance agent to break up an outrage like this.

In the end, I'd sign my check over to Scammer

Woman, get "my share," probably find out it was not quite so large as advertised, and not be able to do a damn thing about it. Then I'd stomp angrily away from any ensuing peril, and let Tony and a couple of other cops pick her up on an eighty-thou-sand-dollar felony with ties to quite a few kinds of criminal activity. Woo-hoo.

What nobody figured on was the gas. And, also, that Milo would slump onto the stoop of an empty house halfway down the block for a long, long tiresome time and then, when the rain finally started up, sneak back to hide out and shoot up in the empty garage at 211.

The garage was attached to the house and shared a crawl space under its floor with the basement. If Milo hadn't been high already, he'd surely have noticed the smell and reflected upon what it meant. But all he wanted was to cook his brand new heroin. When he flicked that lighter, the flame must have flared way beyond his wildest expectations. We'll never know what Milo thought. The explosion about took out the block.

Everything that went on inside that house, right down to the big bang, is rough supposition about the stuff that happened in there.

Here's what I know for sure:

Otis and I had been keeping half an eye on the

dozing Milo while we looked through our photos and video. Gloating a little. Killing time by feeling smug. Talking about whether we could make lunch out of yesterday's dinner or whether we should wait and go someplace good. Like Otis' Kitchen.

We saw Milo go into the garage and agreed he might be a fly in our ointment. At the moment the gas flashed into fury, we were back at the kitchen table, trying to decide if we could get him out again without compromising our cover or the scene. Or whether we should just leave him there being his own little crime.

But then, Tom called out, "Allie? Otis? I smell…I smell gas—"

And in one bright, loud, hot instant, the world, the entire world, it seemed, blew up.

The window we'd taken our stealthy photos through blew in. If we'd still been next to it, the razor fragments would have shredded us. Plus, if it hadn't been pouring rain at that point, and if our hideout house wasn't at the margins of the annihilating wave, we would have been crisped.

So Otis and I were mostly saved. But there was Tom. Who'd insisted on being onsite for at least one night of, in his own words, "our stakeout of my house on Poplar Street." After the payoff excitement, which I'd narrated for his benefit, he'd gone to sleep in the upstairs bedroom, which still had something of a bed, and appeared for breakfast around ten. After that he'd pronounced himself bored with the tediousness of being staked out. "I remember about staking people out now. It's a form of torture. Don't ants come along and devour you after a while?"

I'd leaned close over him and whispered in his ear. "I believe you have to slather honey all over a person if you expect the ants to show up."

He'd grinned. "Will there be honey?"

"Nope. Not today anyhow."

So he said, "I'll be doing my staking out over here. Let me know if anything ever happens. He broke out his headphones, and started listening to whatever novel was on his phone at the time.

Of the three of us, Tom was the one closest to the blast. And he'd taken off the headphones.

My ears were ringing. I was dizzy. Disoriented. Daylight was showing through a ragged hole gouged out of the front wall. What was left of the storm door was swinging off one hinge. Outside, the world was swirling smoke and sparks. Chunks of Poplar's houses were still slamming down in the street. Debris buffeted around as it settled in the gray haze. I took a breath to steady myself. Checked to make sure we were all in one piece.

"Otis. Tom. Damn!" I shouted over the ringing in my ears. "We are lucky to be alive."

Then Tom, still in his chair, still clutching the headphones, cried out.

Pure terror.

"Allie. Otis. Say something. I can't hear you. I can't hear anything."

Chapter Forty-four

Otis drove us, as usual, but there was nothing commonplace about this trip.

All our lines of communication were severed. We could hug Tom and guide him. Period. When the sky stopped falling, we surrounded him from both sides, encircled him in our arms, and hustled him out the back door, through the still-floating ash and suffocating smoke, to the car.

As soon as we got in, I called the Clinic. I could barely put a sentence together. My ears were still ringing, but I could hear and talk well enough to communicate total terror and heartbreak over a phone. I was able to set us up with a hearing specialist for ten the next morning.

We'd decided—if a fragmented handful of sentences in the presence of a panic-stricken human being could be called a decision—to drive Tom to the Clinic's emergency room downtown. The Clinic's appointment person had recommended, "strongly" recommended, that we take Tom there. Otis and I had doubts about that, and we couldn't consult Tom, but that's what we were doing.

Tom was a human high-tension wire. He fastened his seat belt as always, but his hands had lost their usual smooth competence. Shaking fingers grappled with the clasp. Once Otis started up, every motion of the car was a threat Tom couldn't handle. He was startled by every turn, every bump in the road. Radiating alarm.

Ultimately, he sought out the handhold above the window, seized it, and braced himself in place by jamming his other hand deep into the smooth upholstery of the seat. Although I knew he could still could talk to me, and that he might believe I could still hear him, once he'd fixed himself into this more stable position, we rode in silence. Alone in soundless darkness, he didn't even bother to try his voice. After a few awkward attempts, I gave up trying to touch him, soothe him by being beside him. He was startled by that. Not soothed. At all.

My thoughts were darting frantically, trapped inside a monstrous fear that hammered my chest, chilled my trembling fingers, and tasted like iron in my mouth. I'd been afraid for my life and Tom's at least a couple of times recently, not to mention this very afternoon, but this was more terrifying.

There's more than one way to lose a person forever. I'd forgotten that.

After a few minutes, a residual fragment of Tom's sixth sense began warning him we were not on our way back to Bratenahl.

"Allie. Otis? Where are we going? Where is this?"

All I could think to do was pat his arm. *I'm here. Trust me.* He shrugged. Hopeless. Pulled his arm away.

When we got to the sidewalk in front of the street entrance to the ER, we helped Tom out of the car. He stood stock still. I tried to put myself in his place. Closed my eyes. Took a step toward the building. The automatic door whisked open. An air-conditioned breeze whispered over my face.

Tom felt it, too. He took a deep breath as if to brace himself, and something on that breeze must have said, "hospital" to him.

"Okay," he said. "Okay."

The emergency room was a nightmare on top of a nightmare. It was the Fourth of July, after all. The place was jammed. Nasty burns caused by sparklers. Bigger, bloodier injuries caused by shell-and-mortar devices. Drug overdoses. A couple of gunshot wounds and at least three possible heart attacks. Except for his gray pallor, the trembling, and general disorientation, Tom looked like the least of everybody's worries.

The intake person was unimpressed. When I said, "He's blind, and he was near a terrible explosion. He can't hear anything now," she muttered "fireworks" and signed him in.

My saying, "No, no, *gas* explosion" didn't compute. Tom looked too unharmed for something so large. The woman said, "I'll make a note."

Then she said, "Next."

It took hours. I made many trips back to throw myself on the mercy of the intake person. And the one who took her place. I would have tried a million-dollar bribe, but even if my better nature would have permitted that—which in my current state of mind, it would have—I knew for a fact that would have thrown us back to the end of the queue.

After a while, Tom put himself into a kind of stasis. He rejected my touch. And Otis'. He locked his hands together on his knees. Lowered his head. Sat motionless. Breathing. Every now and then he would startle and flail around for a moment. Then he'd gain control and return to his silent darkness.

When we finally got called, we waited in a room for another hour. The exhausted resident who arrived at the end of that time looked in Tom's ears.

"The eardrums seem intact to me. But I'm not a specialist."

"I made him an appointment with a specialist for tomorrow morning."

"Then why are you here?"

I said a couple of things I regretted right away. Then I apologized and cried. After that I made her listen to the short version of Thomas Bennington III, PhD candidate. Blinded by a stroke at twenty-five. Who did every goddam thing right, with courage and grace, finished his degree, and got himself an associate professorship at Case. The guy who had now been deafened this very afternoon by a gas explosion that was in no way his fault.

"Not by a fucking firework."

Exhausted as she was, she got it. Completely. Her eyes filled. She put one sympathetic hand on Tom and one on me. She had a kind and comforting touch. Tom didn't flinch. I forgave her.

She wrote us a prescription for Xanax. Like that was going to work.

Chapter Forty-five

8 p.m.

Back in Bratenahl.

I was experiencing, second by second, how much Tom relied on his hearing to orient himself. To move fluidly through the world. Every step was a precipice now, his hand clutching at my elbow. He leaned against me, feet stumbling, and with every broken motion, I felt his fear. His horror that this appalling loss would be forever. I saw it in the way he clamped his jaw against it. The tears that escaped before he could blink them back. The staggering disbelief.

At last we were in our room. He'd stripped his clothes off and let them fall to the floor. The man who never let anything be out of place. I scurried to pick them up. When I came back he was lying on his back under the covers, face rigid, eyes closed.

I dumped my jeans and shirt, slipped in close and

put my hand on his chest. He recoiled and then shivered, an involuntary reaction, but telling. Was Tom angry with me? He had to be. He'd followed me down the path that led us to that deafening blast. If he blamed me for this, half as much as I blamed myself, we'd never get past it.

I took my hand away and rubbed my palms together. Girl Scout kindling a fire without matches. When I put the warmed hand back, at least he didn't flinch. I moved closer to press my face into his chest. He put both his hands on my hair. I could feel the hammer of his heart.

"No. No. No."

He was moving his head side to side against the pillow to punctuate every repetition. I put my fingers on his mouth, realizing that with the exception of the shifting weight of my body, my every move, every touch would be a surprise. Possibly an unpleasant one. An intrusion into fear so overwhelming there could be no room for anything, or anyone, else.

First things, first.

I took his hand and touched his fingers to his own lips and then to my ear. Twice.

At least I can still hear you.

He nodded. And spoke to me. At last, a sentence that wasn't "No."

"Oh, Allie. That's good. That's something. I don't feel so—"

Alone. Helpless.

My whole body was vibrating in sympathy with the silent thoughts and emotions racing through him. Terror and sorrow had disabled his resourcefulness. His ingenuity. The brave spirit he'd used to replace his lost sight with his new gifts. The anguish of it was sweeping him away from me. He'd lost his bearings and crept alone behind a wall of darkness and the roar of silence. And I'd lost a voice to reach him there.

The explosion had blown us apart.

I had no plan. No hope. I was counting—however naïve that might be—on the fairness of an unfair universe to return to Tom every scrap of the world he accessed through his ears. "Soon," I begged, silently, "let it be now. Please. Oh. Please."

My entreaty fell on the Universe's deaf ear. Nothing changed.

So here we were. Side by side. Alone. I rested my head against his shoulder and pressed in against him. Warmth to warmth. *This is me. Allie. I'm here, Tom. All of me.* My body speaking for me, by its simple presence, to his. I splashed a tear onto his chest before I could catch it.

"No." Harsh. Breaking. He moved his head, side

to side again. "No, Allie, no. You can't. You don't have to—"

No yourself, Tom Bennington.

I shushed him with my hand. Gentle, but firm. Then, with one finger, I drew a big, slow heart on his chest.

"I love you, Tom Bennington," I whispered into that spot, counting on the small breezes of my breath against his skin to tell him that what I was drawing was what I was promising.

My heart to yours, Tom. Forever, no matter what.

"I know." His face softened infinitesimally, "I love you, too. Always. But, Allie…" I put my hand, firmly this time, over his mouth. I shook my head so he could feel it moving. Wrote "NO" on his chest. And drew the heart again.

He smiled the slightest bit and we both broke out sobbing. I slipped back into my place, trying to breach the walls of fear and loss that separated us, begging him with my whole body to let me in.

Come back to me Tom.

"Shhh," I whispered against his skin. "Shhhh,"

His body tensed. He drew in a deep shudder of a breath, willing himself back to control. With a brave remnant of his customary skill, he rolled us over.

His lips against my own ringing ear.

"Oh, Allie. Damn. I'm sorry. I'm so—damn this—just— Oh. Just fuck Helen Keller. That's all."

We held onto each other and cried. Made sorrowful, awkward love as though our gravity had failed us, abandoned us to float in a space where none of the familiar rules were in operation. Left us anchored to the one unshakeable truth we still knew. And then, exhausted by our waking nightmare—with our bodies still speaking love, skin to skin—we fell into sleep.

I woke when dawn brightened the room. Tom was sitting on the side of the bed, his back to me and his head tilted to one side. Toward the window, where the breeze was stirring the curtains. I sat up to touch him.

Carefully, I reminded myself.

He turned.

"Allie? I think I—can you hear waves?"

"I can. And they're not particularly loud today."

Chapter Forty-six
Wednesday, July 5

The ear specialist frowned. "A gas explosion? For mercy's sake. What on Earth? How...?

Impatience ambushed me. "Please. Will this get better? Back to normal? He depends on his hearing—"

The doctor dismissed me with a wave of his hand, disapproval spread all over his meaty face.

"So do we all, Miss Harper. So do we all."

I hated him with a burning passion. His hair was thinning, too.

"But Mr.—he glanced at the chart—Sorry. Dr. Bennington—"

He frowned again, squinting at Tom, adding two plus two hundred million. I saw the light of the Mondo dawn on him as the frown died and his eyebrows went up.

He turned to me. "Dr. Bennington no doubt understands that hearing, like vision, is something money can't buy."

Flame-thrower. Flames.

"I can hear you fine," Tom sounded as testy as I felt. "Some background buzz is all now. The explosion was an incident we were unfortunately near. Won't happen again, I assure you. Now. How much damage? How much loss can I expect?"

I braced myself. Tom braced himself. The specialist shrugged. For my benefit, I guessed.

"You don't have any structural damage, as far as I can see. The eardrums in both ears look normal. We're all talking at reasonable levels and you can converse."

The doc was done with us now. He closed the file and folded his fat hands. Moving on to his next patient who hopefully hadn't done something dangerous and inexplicable to her ears.

"I'll send you down the hall and they'll do a test. You'll get the results in a few days. But I will say, Dr. Bennington, you may have misinterpreted what you were experiencing as deafness. That would be unlikely, based on what you're telling me. A lot of static, yes. A roar that would drown out…well… almost everything. But total silence? Not so likely. Can't blame you. That must have been very—I'd say you should get back close to where you were. In time.

"I expect you're good at hearing. Good listener. Attentive. Have skills sighted folk don't get? That'll help make up for any deficit. You'll be more sensitive to how much your ears are worth after this, too. Try and take better care of them. Skip the rock concerts."

I clenched and unclenched my fists. *Take a breath, Allie. Do. Not. Strangle. Doctor.*

We all three stood up.

Dismissed.

Delighted.

Out in the street, Tom released a breath he'd been holding for almost twenty-four hours. And grinned all the way for the first time since then.

"Preachy bastard."

Chapter Forty-seven

Thank you, Ms. Universe. I owe you one.

Another half hour and we were well away from our hearing specialist and back in the Escalade with Otis. In spite of a whole list of things still unresolved, it was a day of unprecedented joy. Tom whispered to me in our secluded backseat. "You should know, I make much better love with ears."

"I don't believe I've ever experienced ear love. I can't wait."

Now that Tom could hear and had every expectation of improvement, we could be glad that having Helen's house blow sky high was working even better than the original crime-exposing plan.

All day long, the news kept pouring in.

Even down an abandoned street, the blast attracted a lot of attention with its sound and light. It was turning out to be a coup for the police department.

Having an investigation already in progress on Poplar Street. Putting the spotlight on the perils and plunders of scrapping. Revealing how scrapping connected the dots of all kinds of other crime in the neighborhoods. We gave Tony our video and photos. "Evidence from amateur neighborhood photographers." Plus, he thought they might even be able to nail Ms. Facing Foreclosure. We were ecstatic to have the CPD get all the glory.

The whole thing worked out every which way for the T&A. And of course Channel 16 adored the attention-grabbing story of a big, bright, ironic July 4th *Kaboom!* that focused attention on the problem of scrappers and drugs. Lisa never looked more big-time than on Wednesday evening, reporting from in front of a cratered house on Poplar. I was happy to provide her with the hot tip. She was happy to provide me with anonymity.

"I swear."

On her mother's *žganci*.

At that point, nobody knew exactly what had happened to Milo. Which, of course, was awful and also inevitable in about a hundred different ways. We knew he'd gone in, but not for sure he hadn't come back out. The wreckage was smoldering and hideously treacherous for quite a while. When it was all sorted out, days later, Milo got his own story, too. Lisa made it poignant. Since it was. In about a hundred different ways.

Many of our unanswered questions about how scrapping tied to Lloyd remained unanswered. For example, we weren't close to done with Mr. Scrapyard, the bigot-jerk Howard Rexroad. That was for sure. But this felt like a step in the right direction.

● ● ● ● ●

Distracting as the events of Independence Day were, I was now sufficiently back in my brain to remind myself I needed to find a good lawyer for Margo's court date, which was set for Wednesday, July 11.

Once again, I only knew two lawyers I could ask, one of whom I'd recently promised to forget about for as long as we both were alive. The other was Skip. As noted, both these guys were partners at Gallagher, Gallagher & Barnes. This would not make either of them a good match for getting somebody off on the hit and run of a "google-head dumbshit"—to quote the defendant. I called Skip anyway because it pleased me to hear his voice and I knew he was bound to have a suggestion.

Sure enough. After he stopped laughing the inimitable Skip Castillo laugh, he said, "I'll send you one of our summer associates, Allie. This guy is sharp as a tack and probably fixing to steal my job. It'll be pro bono, of course. Though I may have to charge him something for the experience."

When the guy showed up, he looked like a slightly more mature Harry Potter. His name was Trevor Something and he was "third year at Yale Law." The glasses were very Harry-like, but his haircut cost at least eighty dollars and the eyes behind those four-hundred-dollars-and-up round black frames glinted with high-test intellectual acuity. His suit could have been his only suit, but it was an excellent suit. He set to gathering facts with a scary intensity.

I felt we'd be ready when the time came to face the court. Margo, of course was supremely confident in her innocence and her "defense team." I went ahead and put the whole thing on the back burner.

Minute by minute. Hour by hour, Tom's hearing was improving.

I wanted to send the Universe flowers.

Chapter Forty-eight
Saturday, July 8

What is the name of serendipity's evil twin?

Fate, maybe.

The theme of the evening was "Art & Artists On The Road." I would have preferred to theme the night, "Tom & Allie At the Ritz-Carlton, Cleveland." I'm irresponsible like that. But we'd promised. Or at least RSVP-ed. For a party. Fancy, too. Our thought, several weeks back when we checked the "Will attend" box, was to give Tom's jackpot—tarnished by murder, mayhem, and a sleazy rogue website—at least a veneer of respectability by coming to an upscale benefit "for the arts." Also, we hoped we might be able to make ourselves feel less guilty by giving some of the tainted winnings away, where it could do some good rather than kill people.

Tom's jackpot weighed heavy in so many, many ways. Apart from the evil scheming weasels who were ready to commit all manner of skullduggery to get at it, there was the relentless tug of about seven and a half billion kinds of human need that might be improved by a healthy chunk of two-hundred-twelve-million-and-still-growing.

I'd read the names of Cleveland philanthropists on many large and magnificent edifices about town. Those lovely hospitals and university buildings, those wings at the museum, the plaques that remind the sick and those hungry for culture, learning, and food that someone had thought of them—in a big way. One day, I hoped Tom and I would be together on the Tom & Allie Bennington III building at The Clinic or somewhere. We'd be married, for sure, and for posterity then.

Otis was with us that night, of course, locked and loaded, in an excellent tuxedo. A couple members of his team, also formally attired, tailed us at a discreet distance, holding, but not drinking, their champagne. Julia, back from her assignment to secure our now former security people, was pure dynamite. Red dress, small satiny purse, and vertiginous shoes. I figured any gun she was packing this evening would have to be strapped to her inner thigh.

"Hello," I said. "I don't believe we've met. You look fabulous. Who are you wearing?"

A demure smile, a murmured, "Julia Perez, T.J. Maxx."

"Yes, ma'am. Some of us got it. Some don't."

I referenced, with a downward glance, my expensive but inevitably nondescript dress. It was little. It was black. It fit. In my opinion, that was all.

She smiled and moved away. Relaxed but alert.

The evening was dazzling for a small-town girl. I could hear Lee Ann, a couple of paces behind me, saying, "Holy wow."

The big, formerly industrial, building was converted into workspaces for artists, performances, and special events. Art was everywhere. All glorious color, texture, and design. Plus the creators were right there to talk to me—and, yeah, about five hundred other potential philanthropists—about their work. I had to stop myself from saying, "This is way cool." Loud enough for people to hear. I was chanting it in my head, though.

I loved the paintings. In particular, the ones that, by merely standing in front of them, I didn't need to understand anything except that I could feel their spirit pressing into the center of my chest. I watched Otis looking, too. The center of his chest was getting pressed by some of it, I could tell.

Sculpture was the whole shebang for Tom, naturally. You can't keep handling a Monet or whatever without doing it damage. Sooner rather than later. But sculpture is often not so fragile.

I was struggling to keep my hands off the work of art that was "Thomas Bennington III. In a tux." A sight I'd never before seen. Lord almighty, he was something. And I wasn't the only female in the crowd noticing, I noticed. I was hoping to be the lucky girl who'd get to help him take it off later in the evening.

But back to the sculpture.

Tom had secured Jacob Foster's permission to touch one of the pieces, and he was enjoying the additional benefit of having the young sculptor as his guide.

Unlike the rest of the tuxedoed and sequined crowd, the artist was dressed in jeans that showed signs of frequent laundering, and a soft, well-worn shirt topped off with a battered leather jacket. The privilege of being a headliner, I figured. He was thin, almost frail, and I wondered how he managed to wrestle and subdue the large pieces displayed there.

"It's Jake, Dr. Bennington," the kid was saying. "I don't go by Jacob. It feels weird how everybody's calling me that now."

"Tom. Ditto on the 'Dr.'"

He followed Jake to the plinth where a compelling sculpture glared out at party-goers. I tagged along, hoping Jake would include me in the invitation to lay hands on its beauty. I was drawn to the rich and varied colors and textures of the metals, but something about the shape sent a little shiver down my back. For all its abstractness, the thing seemed alive. And sinister.

Tom let his fingers play over the sleek form.

"It's called—" Jake began.

"Don't tell me, Jake. I'd like to see it for myself first."

"Sure, Tom."

I was experiencing it right along with Tom. Under his touch, the shape resolved itself out of abstraction into mighty wings and an intimidating beak. Two exaggerated lengths of steel defined the creature's legs. Its sharp talons, Jake said, were black masonry nails hammered through the metal and then bent into claws. I winced as Tom's searching fingers reached the sharpened points.

I checked the nameplate: *Predacious*.

I'll say.

"It's a bird, Jake?" Tom ventured. "You think it would be too simplistic to title it *Scary*?"

Jake rested his hand on his creation. Possessively. Carelessly. I saw the scars of his art on his fingers and wrists. "If that's what you feel, Tom, then I'd say I got my job done. Sometimes the metal works itself, you know? And I never am sure whether the darkness is in the material or in the sculptor."

"Probably both. That's the way it often is with art. Whatever kind. Ask any poet."

"Jake?"

"Yes, Ms. Harper?"

"Oh, wait. If Tom can be Tom. And you can be Jake. I can definitely be Allie."

"Okay then. Yes, Allie?" His grin warmed his grave young face and lightened his blue eyes.

"May I touch this, too?"

He nodded and the grin brightened him even more. "As long as you're with Tom, Allie, of course."

"I'm your free pass, Allie."

"In so many ways, Dr. Bennington III."

Jake brightened again. "Now you're the one being formal. Is Allie a nickname?"

"Do not go there, Jake," Tom warned. "There be dragons. Keep an eye on her for me. I'll be back."

He drifted away, moving carefully among the other sculptures of metal, pottery, and glass. And the other guests. Extending a hand to discover and touch, innately sure of himself. I figured "you break it, you bought it" would hold little terror for Tom. Even among these rarified objects. But they were secured and he was alert and respectful. As always.

I suppressed a shiver at the thought of Tom moving through this space without his hearing. We'd dodged a bullet. That made me grateful. Jittery, too.

I ran a tentative finger along a gleaming ribbon of metal that poured red-gold blood over the predator's breast. It reminded me…

"Where do you get the materials for your work, Jake? This is copper, isn't it?"

Jake's eyes sharpened but his tone was light. "I didn't strip that out of a transformer station, if that's what you mean."

Damn. My one evening away from the scrappers and I open my big mouth.

"No. No, of course not. I was only wondering. Is it tough to find what you want?"

He softened. "It's easy. I find it everywhere. People throw out the most amazing stuff. I just love metal, you know? It's the framework, the skeleton, maybe, of our made world. How it's strong and beautiful. And sad, too, when it's rusted and worn out. I can bend it and cut it and give it a new life. Make rust its history, its provenance, rather than calling it some old junk.

"There's a place I go sometimes. You should never go there, Allie. It's gross now. Smelly, dark. Dangerous, too. But for years it was an observatory. Looking into the stars. You can see them there now, that's for sure. The dome is disintegrating, but the frame is mostly intact. The bones. It's an odd choice to be somebody's favorite place, but it's mine."

"Did you find metal there? To use in your art?"

"A little. Mostly it's empty and trashed.

"So to answer your question without being a dolt about it, if you don't need to make money from scrapping, if metal is your medium, not your—" An expression near panic skittered across his face. Veiled itself in his eyes.

"Jake?"

Defiant now. "Oh, you know, Ms. Harper. If you don't need it to get your next fix. Everybody's got some kind of addiction. Heroin just happens to have been—to be—one of mine."

Our eyes met. My scalp tingled. Truth was in the room.

The elegant crowd circled, ebbing, flowing, murmuring, unaware of the word that had crashed through the wall of polite conversation.

A woman in a smooth-sculpted dress, more cream-colored armor than second skin, paused, captured by the aura of *Predacious*. I started to move back, to let her look. To diffuse the moment.

"Allie."

"Jacob, I'd love to talk with you about…that." I

gestured to the sculpture. Covering tracks. "Maybe we—"

The woman, now being uninterested as hard as she could, pivoted gracefully to check me out. I returned the look with a smile that said, "My nephew."

She volleyed with an eyebrow that said "Sincerely doubt it."

I yielded to her judgment and went back to Jake. "Jacob, maybe we could meet for coffee. Six Shooters on Waterloo? You know it?"

He grinned and the ghost abandoned his eyes. "I do. I love that place. And art is what that street's all about. You buying?

I am only ever always buying.

"You bet. Tomorrow morning. Ten? It's a Sunday."

"Works for me."

"When Tom comes back, show him something that won't stab him. He's in the market for a piece that will make our rental a little more 'us.'"

Jake gave me a grateful smile and turned back toward the woman who was carefully appraising everything everywhere.

I went looking for more champagne. Stumbled into, then grabbed onto, and ultimately stepped on a tall stranger wearing what struck me as very likely a four-figure tux. He accepted my stuttering embarrassment with a polite, if condescending, word or two, and moved away.

I escaped to the ladies room and splashed cold water on my face.

Are we having fun yet?

Chapter Forty-nine
Sunday, July 9

8 a.m.

Sometimes you gotta get out of the house and drive around until the racket in your head dies down. The last ten days were jolly-jam-packed with high-test danger, heart-wrenching fears and sorrows, plus multiple unsolved puzzles. I had a date with Jacob Foster at Six Shooters at ten, but right now there were a couple of hours just for me. I read somewhere that the process of staying in your lane—between the lines—encourages creative thinking. Clarity. Maybe. This morning, I'd be happy if I could drive some of the gerbils out of my gut.

Otis was the winner in the battle of the cars, so now I had a new vehicle. Per his insistence, I was giving up my salsa red WV bug. Leaving her to sit, along with a substantial chunk of my former identity, in the mansion's fancy garage. In that hulking space with room for five cars, my Flying Tomato looked diminished. Small. Forlorn. Like a good old dog, panting to go for a run in the park. Wistful. And someone says, "Stay."

Buck up, Allie.

Even getting to my new ride was a challenge. Otis drove me from our car auditorium to the repair place in Collinwood where he was keeping it "for now, until I know nobody's tracking you." He watched me get in and steer it—carefully, under his eagle-eyed gaze—until I was out of sight. I checked my mind. It wasn't clear yet. Or calm either. Maybe the gerbils needed another couple of blocks.

My Otis-approved vehicle was the perfect disguise for a hooked-up-with-an-über-rich-Mondo-winner woman such as myself. Inside, luxury leather, excellent sound system, new car smell, the works. Plus it would warn you of anybody passing in your blind spot, tell you if you were about to back over someone, and park itself. The tinted windows blocked glare—and stares.

Outside? Ha.

On the exterior, this baby was a wreck. Dented. Filthy. Otis commissioned one of his minions to drive my pristine new Range Rover Evoque through mucky vacant lots and down gravel roads. Scrape it against something unforgiving, like a concrete divider, then beat on it with a baseball bat. Or a jackhammer. And, for good measure, get it super dirty.

It was a sin and a shame. I bet the guy who did it had to go home and have three beers to soothe his soul.

I was delighted with the whole deal. Because sandwiched in there between the "teardown" exterior and the "hot ride" interior, security ruled. GPS out the wazoo. Listening everywhere. If I sneezed, one of my guardians would know. I needed to remind myself not to say "Help" in any context, or swear at stupidity, my own or that of others. Or sing along with anything.

I'd filed my flight plan with Otis. It was vaguer than he liked but he let me go. I just plain wanted to drive around. Visit old neighborhoods and scenic locations. On my own. Breathe some air. Like I used to. And then go meet Jake. Clearly, my days of driving wild out into the winter night with the top down were over, at least for a while, but this morning I could ignore the listeners and trackers and enjoy the leather seats. They were sweet.

A downpour at dawn and the summer sun, now blazing away, had steamed up the neighborhood.

Foggy wisps floated up off the wet streets. The play-ing fields behind the Collinwood Rec Center were knee-deep in mist. I'd cruised along Grovewood and pulled over to watch a couple of kids tossing a football. Cracked the window to savor the seductive smell of mowed grass, wet and crushed underfoot.

Ah, the freedom of being out and about on my own.

Heads up, Allie.

A big gray elephant came lumbering toward me through the fog.

Trash truck, looming.

Out of place on a peaceful Sunday morning. Nobody around here got their trash picked up on weekends. The kids stopped tossing to watch it approach and my own tranquil vibe evaporated into avid curiosity.

As it got closer I could see it wasn't one of the newer trucks. Those were all automated and smooth. This one was well past retirement. Its general demeanor of grime and abuse made my Evoque look new. And not inherently smelly.

Here was a little mystery I could handle. Harmless and kind of fun. Who could be driving a used gar-bage truck up Grovewood before nine a.m. on a Sunday? I peered up at the approaching windshield to see—

Howard Scrapyard.

I pressed myself back into the seat. Blessed Otis for tinted windows. Howard Rexroad and a guy I'd never seen before drove past my dirty wreck without a second glance.

Lee Ann whispered in my Otis-proof ear. "C'mon. Let's follow this dude."

So we did. To my credit, I waited till Howard and his truck had a decent lead before I made a U-turn and fell in behind him. I was guessing he'd be heading to the yard. I'd catch up a bit, wait for him to turn, then hurry up and cut through on the next side street, hang out at its intersection with Villa View, and follow him from way back.

I got there, waited. No truck.

Wild goose chase.

Take a breath, Allie.

I explained to myself and Lee Ann that we were about to blow many thousands of dollars' worth of custom-designed anonymity and my ability to go free-range around town, so I backed up and disappeared us into the neighborhood.

I figured Howard must be heading to the scrapyard from another direction. Where else would he drive a trash truck? Spotting him where I did provided me with a juicy little chunk of information to share with the guys. Carefully. I didn't want to get me and Lee Ann grounded.

The fog was rolling up now, hiding the sun, turning the day to overcast. After a few more minutes of aimless driving, I surrendered and steered the vehicle—she needed a name, but would have to earn it in some kind of tribal ritual to be determined later—over to Ivanhoe and let her point me, slowly, over a lot of bottomless potholes, toward Waterloo. She'd done all right.

We had lots to think about.

Like, for one: If I had a house-size load of scrapped-for-hire junk, dumped and left in somebody's driveway, maybe a trash truck could come in handy. It would look official and not criminal. Unless you noticed that old, nasty Howard Rexroad was driving. I would mention this to Otis. Otis would tell Valerio. Valerio would tell whoever he usually reported to at the Fifth District. Then we'd see. Or we wouldn't. I could deal.

Another idea that came to back mind was, "Helicopter?" You'd be able to pick out a giant trash truck like that from the air. Even in a scrapyard full of trashed metal.

Lee Ann approved.

The rain started up again. Like it does.

Chapter Fifty

At ten a.m., on a rainy Sunday morning, there was a long line for coffee at Six Shooters, but most of the drinkers were taking it to go. Jake and I carried ours and some muffins up the stairs to the comfy sitting room, which was unoccupied. Lively conversations from the main, street-level space covered what Jake wanted—needed, I guess—to tell me.

I was a semi-disinterested party, not likely to get in his face about anything, not sufficiently put-together myself to be judgmental. That was my take on why he'd agreed to meet me. As it turned out, I would have preferred to be even more dis-interested. It was a hard story to hear.

"Look at me. I'm a real athletic type, right?"

I looked at him. No answer required.

"So my dad, who is in many ways an okay guy, figured I could be more of a…something he wanted me to be. I never put my finger on exactly what he had in mind. Just more. He bought the football coach a fifth of Jack Black and sold him on some fantasy he had about me rising to the occasion and being the star field goal kicker.

He rolled his eyes. "At least you don't have to be six-foot-two and two-seventy or whatever. I know who I am, Allie. At least who I was. Even then, I knew. My work wasn't academics or athletics. It was making things. Shaping things. Bending them. I'm lousy at talking about it. For me it's taking rough, confused, broken metal and bringing out what is true inside of it. Spirit, maybe."

"That doesn't sound like someone who's 'lousy at talking about it,' Jake."

He shook me off. Had a story to tell. Was bound to tell it.

"No. I wasn't an artist. Not then. Not yet. It's always hard to claim something for yourself when you hold it so—I don't know…holy, maybe. But I could understand—fucking comprehend my own dream.

"I tell you what, Allie. Maybe you already know. It takes guts to stay different all the way to high school. Be okay with yourself when maybe no one in your life is really okay with you?"

He looked at me. Inquiring. I nodded. He had

me there. Lee Ann would have agreed, but she'd wandered off somewhere. Lacked the stamina for this kind of conversation, I figured.

"I hadn't found my real work yet. Even the art kids didn't see me for real. Loser hiding out, is what they thought. They were decent about it, at least.

"Anyhow. My dad said to the coach, 'C'mon, Frank. Let the kid try.' Coach got out a couple of glasses and said okay.

"Me? I said no. Absolutely. Systematically. Up until the moment practice started in August. It was ninety-two degrees that morning. The grass was, like, shimmering. When I tried to breathe, the air was too thick to support life. We weren't wearing all the gear, but I got a helmet. Felt like eighty pounds set up there for the purpose of snapping my head off my neck. Medieval.

"Coach was already screaming about how terrible we were before we even started. He had everybody running around doing things. Exercises, I guess. Training things. My training thing was tires in rows and you were supposed to lift your legs up high and run through them.

"Second set of tires, I didn't lift my right leg up high enough and my foot caught in the edge of the tire. I had time to think, Allie. I thought how crappy I was at this, and how I should be anywhere else, and I tried—I tried really hard—to recover my balance but it was all over from the moment my foot got caught. I was just along for the ride. I went down. In among the tires, in the heat, and the fumes of rubber the sun was melting. And the pain was—I'd never realized that could even be possible."

He broke off. Looking at me. Not seeing me, I don't think. I could see, though, that saying what happened doesn't always free up all the associated guilt and despair like shrinks and gurus tell you.

He was back there in the shimmering heat and the blackened fumes, and he'd taken me with him. I saw it all. His disbelief of the betrayal dealt him by his untrained, unwilling body, by the coach who should have clapped his dad on the shoulder and just said no. By his dad who should have been…a dad, while he was at it.

He closed his eyes. I wanted to close mine, but that would have given my mental picture a bigger, darker screen.

"Jake," I said. "Jacob."

He shook off my sympathy and came back to himself. "My dad said I'd done it on purpose. That I'd wanted to get out of the whole deal so bad."

He grinned. Wry. "I might actually have considered that. Especially since I didn't have a clue what pain was. Real pain. Until right then.

"I was in the hospital for the time it took for the ER, the gurneys, the imaging, the discussions, and the surgery that lasted for five hours. I didn't have to be present for that, no biggie. And then recovery and overnight. Three days, total.

"And that's where I found Oxy, the Jesus Christ Himself of all drugs. Oxy was everything. It lifted me up. It took away my pain. It forgave me for never being good enough and ripping my leg apart on purpose.

"The first morning I was actually awake, my leg was screaming and the nurse came in with this cute little white paper cup. I swallowed its contents with plenty of water, like she said. And in about ten minutes, Jesus was right there in the room with me. Kind. Powerful. Healing. I was born again. Yeah, I know. Don't look at me like that.

"Born again and lost. All at the same time. But you don't know all about everything, Allie. You weren't there."

I tried to make my face neutral, free of sympathy and any possible judging. Jake didn't need my approval or disapproval. Just my attention. But I thought he was probably telling me the truest truth he was capable of. I nodded, remembering my own short tango with Oxy, "my fairy godmother." After my minor collision with a bullet. It's hard to be righteous when you haven't been all that virtuous. My brush with opioids ended in a couple of days when the pain got better all by itself and my prescription ran out.

"I needed the Oxy for my recovery, Allie, for the therapy. The PT guy kept saying, 'Be sure you take your medication, Jacob. Otherwise you won't be able to do what you need to.' He didn't have to tell me twice."

He stopped. I nodded again. He shrugged. I thought maybe I was a disappointment. Not what he needed from a good listener.

"When I got home, my dad was pissed. Disappointed. Maybe, embarrassed. Or sorry. Wanted me to shut up and not bother him. My mom wanted me to be happy. Oxy got the job done for them, too. I didn't know I was hooked. I didn't know I was anything. I just wanted to feel better, and about every six hours I was getting a double dose of great."

My mug was cooling in my hands. I could hear people coming and going, the street door opening and closing. And feel the little draft it made. They were grinding the beans. The dark, roasted smell was intoxicating. As always. I'd tried to quit coffee about a hundred times.

"People get the risks a lot more now, but back

then they hadn't really begun to figure things out. When my mom told the doc I was doing okay but she thought I'd handle the PT and getting back on my feet better if I could get one more prescription, he made that happen.

"After that, it was a joy ride down the slippery slope everybody likes to talk about. I'd be sore. I'd be down on myself. I couldn't do my art. I was behind at school. And here was my vacation in a bottle. And guess what? After my doc cut me off, I dipped into my personal savings account from my after-school job I didn't have anymore. I could pay for my own little white vacations. And the travel agents? They were just around the corner.

"Still. It got expensive. Hell, it was expensive all along. And then one day, one of my new best friends said. 'Y'know. H costs a third of what Oxy'll run you.'

"That's how I found the Almighty Holy God of all drugs. The one that all the other drugs bow down to."

I'm sure my face was shouting out how sorry I was feeling for him. How empathetic I was trying to be. He cut that off with a sneer that transformed his face from sincere to feral.

"You should try it someday, Allie. If you can afford it—and you surely can—it's…the best thing."

I recoiled from his tone. "What do you want, Jacob?"

"What do I want?" Anger tracked red up his throat and into his cheeks. "I want what I always wanted. The time and attention span to do my art. And enough money to keep my habit quiet and under wraps. It looks to me as if that's the best I can hope for now."

Hold on a sec, Allie. U-turn.

My pretty idea about being a philanthropist slammed on its brakes. "The Tom and Allie Bennington III Center for…Heroin Support?"

He read my face. Shook his head. "I know. I'm so—I'm sorry. I didn't come here to say that. Or ask you for anything. I needed—I wanted someone to know. My parents are in denial when they're not freaking out. My drug friends don't have to be told and don't care anyway. I wanted to tell someone who'd understand. Who'd care and not judge so much.

"That's you, Allie. I can see that about you. But I'm an addict. Me? I would never trust an addict. You shouldn't either. I just want the feeling. The calm feeling I used to get back when I was learning my work, getting better at it. When everything clicked, and my hands didn't shake. Not ever. And, at the same time? All the time, I want more—

"Can I just—? Can I have your phone number, maybe?" His eyes were pleading. "I promise I won't ask you for—"

He pushed back from the table.

I dug in my purse for a scrap of paper. Wrote my number on it.

"Jake. Please. You can call me anytime. And when you're ready to go somewhere, Tom will pay. The best, the most, the longest. Whatever. Tomorrow. Tonight. Please. Just call. Please call."

He took it and stood up. I couldn't read his face. Fingers crossed.

"Thank you, Allie. I promise. I'll use your number. Swear."

Chapter Fifty-one
Monday, July 10

Jake used my number.

I got a call the very next afternoon. It wasn't from him.

He'd written "Call Allie Harper" on my scrap of paper. Put it in the pocket of his shirt. And gone straight to his favorite place.

"Is it Jacob Foster?"

"We need you to tell us. Can you come?"

"Is he—?"

"Just come. As soon as you can."

I went. I didn't go alone, of course. Otis drove. Tom held my hand.

The observatory was as I imagined it when Jake described it to me. The filth. The smell. Destruction and graffiti everywhere. But I could see why he'd loved it and perhaps why he chose to come here this last time. The big telescope had been gone for years, but the empty space kept on pointing its blinded eyes towards the heavens. The vision of the designers and the skill of the engineers were all there, in the soaring power of the arched ribs and the few remaining panes of shattered dome.

Jacob called 9-1-1 when it was too late. Too late for Narcan. Too late to turn back. He'd left my number and a note addressed to me. Apologized way more than he needed. Told me to fill in the blanks for the cops. Asked me to tell his parents he was sorry. To tell his brother not to waste his life. Tell his dad not to blame himself for anything. Tell his mom he loved her.

He wrote, "This is on me. I'm just not strong enough. So tired."

I gave the officers information from Jake's website so they could handle the notification. I'd talk with his parents. After a time. When they were ready to hear what I had to figure out how to say.

The squad car from Lisa Cole's video was rolling down the drive for them now. They'd never be the same.

We stayed until the officers were done. Vigil. Bearing witness. Otis stood talking quietly with the guys as they collected what evidence they needed. He'd found us an okay place to sit. Where the wall was fit to lean on.

After a while some other guys came and took Jake away. All that talent. All those dreams. Zipped up. Gone. Nothing here for us to do now.

Otis was waiting.

Tom and I sat for another moment in Jacob Foster's favorite place, our shoulders touching, sharing warmth and consolation. Nothing to say.

I looked up. The bare bones of the metal dome let patches of the bright evening sky shine through. Broken shards of blue. No stars.

Chapter Fifty-two
Wednesday, July 12

In spite of catastrophes, sorrows, and losses big enough to crush your soul, you still have to keep your court date.

Otis drove Trevor, Margo, and me to the East Cleveland Courthouse on the appointed Wednesday morning. I was reasonably optimistic that there'd only be a fine and a lecture, both of which Margo could manage without feeling bad about herself or going all contempt-of-court.

Trevor was able to determine, by gathering weather information and reports of other accidents on that stretch of road on the day in question, that it would have been a clear-cut case of hydroplaning. This constituted loss of control of a vehicle, of course, especially in a city as cash-strapped and fine-hungry as East Cleveland, but not such a big deal since no one, at least no person, was injured.

Margo used her spotty computer skills to look up hydroplaning on Wikipedia.

"Listen to this!" she crowed. "'If it occurs to all wheels simultaneously, the vehicle becomes, in effect, an uncontrolled sled.' Everybody knows that nobody on Earth can control a sled. That should get me off the hook right there. And also, you can call it 'aquaplaning.' If I have to plead guilty to something I want aquaplaning. It sounds graceful and maybe a little sexy."

We all agreed that Harry Potter should accompany Margo into the building while Otis and I waited in the car. We dropped them off. They walked away looking young-and-sharp, and middle-aged-and-radioactive, respectively. We then parked in the shopping strip across Euclid Avenue to wait.

"Do you think she'll be all right, Otis?" The worry was all over my voice.

"Oh, I think so, Allie. It's not a big deal. She may have to pay for the equipment damage. That could be a lot. And we have to remember that this is Margo we're talking about. If she gets mad—"

I should have known better than to ask Otis. He could be as straight as a stick about legal stuff. I folded my arms, clamped them tight into my stomach, and prepared myself for unexpected outcomes.

Thus, I was surprised and delighted when after a few minutes they reappeared. We picked them up. Margo came out bouncing around. Beaming unbridled triumph.

Trevor seemed both delighted and confused.

"Ha!" That was Margo's first word as they piled into the backseat.

"Ha, what?"

"Ha!-somebody-moved-the-googlehead-dumb-shit's-body-before-the-cops-could-pick-it-up. That's 'what-ha!'"

Otis made a tiny, unintelligible sound.

I peered into the leathery cave of the backseat. "Trevor, what is she talking about?"

"Well, they said that before they could go collect the er…remains of the speed camera to use as evidence, it was scrapped. All they have that pertains to this case is the photo of Ms. Gallucci's vehicle coming toward it. They didn't feel that was enough. They dropped all charges."

Margo patted his arm. "Trevor. You don't do yourself justice. No pun intended."

"Allie, he was wonderful. He suggested that no harm was intended and that I and the googly-head flashy camera were both victims of aquaplaning and an act of God. And that if it got out about their losing their valuable equipment, the city and the police would look bad. I would have said, 'worse.' But I'm not a hot young attorney." She patted his arm again. "No disrespect."

Trevor gave Margo a look that was part admiration and part pure terror. "Ms. Harper, that's kind of what happened, but I hope you understand that I did not at any time say, 'googly-head flashy camera' or 'aquaplaning.' And I was wondering?"

"Wondering what, Harr—Trevor?"

"What is 'scrapped'?"

● ● ● ● ●

The reoccurring theme.

I sat quietly and allowed Margo to explain scrapping to Trevor. I could see that the concept, though not particularly complex, was as alien to him as not making Law Review. I checked the mirror to see how he was taking Margo's colorful explanation. She was using her hands. A lot. He was nodding, but he had "uphill climb" written all over him. Learning curve ahead.

Trevor was smart, though. And a decent person. Margo's colorful descriptions were making their mark. He was shaking his head. As far as I'm concerned, disbelief is a good place to start. This was a good thing.

A less good thing was the call Otis got when we were all back at the house. He'd been popping the top off a celebratory beer.

So close.

His phone rang.

A.J., Otis's young detective-in-training from the "no-fingerprints-on-the-Escalade" episode over on Ridpath Avenue, had hung on to Otis' business card ever since the very first day of the Lloyd case. He was calling to let Otis know that something was up on his street. At Lloyd's moldering house, to be specific.

Otis passed the beer over to Trevor. Said, "Trevor, good work. I woulda hated to see Margo in jail. Jail woulda hated it, too. Stay right there, Allie. Tom. I got this. Save me a beer for later."

A lot later.

It'd been hours since lunch. The sun was good as gone. We'd ordered in Thai food. Plenty of extra for Otis. And made sure there was still beer. We knew what was good for us.

"Otis. You missed lunch and dinner."

"Got all complicated. I ended up calling Tony. And I'd promised A.J. a ride in the Escalade. He asked his mom if it was okay and she said yes. And came along. Took a while. I enjoyed that part though. A.J.'s a good kid.

"Lloyd's house, though? I'll tell you what. It's the dead center of this whole investigation. And scrappers are piled up all over it. They're freakin' everywhere."

I watched Trevor's face. He'd have an advanced degree in scrapping by the time this day was over. Crash course. I wondered if he was picturing zombies.

Otis was into it now. "Remember that junker car with the funny rust on it the day we were there, Allie?"

"The car with the rust mustache? I've got that mental picture stored, Otis. Forever. Also notable for being parked facing the wrong way on the street."

Even Tom was onto that car. I'd described it to him in loving detail later that day because I'd thought it was wacky fun. He'd liked it, too. Not as much this evening.

"Yeah. That's the one. A.J. said it was a regular on the street, came and went all the time there but didn't belong to anybody on Ridpath. Juanita, his mom, does the block watch thing. After A.J. told her what we'd found at Lloyd's, she got all over it with the neighbors. Nobody would claim it. Juanita called the cops to have the car towed. Still there for maybe three or four days and then, one morning, gone. She'd figured it finally got picked up. But no. I talked to Tony. He said it was so far down the pick-up list, they coulda hung lights on it for next Christmas. No problem.

"Anyway, it was back. Parked in Lloyd's driveway. Close in to the garage. A.J. checked it out. From a distance, he assured me, but I doubt it. Said it was full of trash. Clothes, too. So then, he said, he took a closer look at the house. 'Closer-but-still-from-a-distance,' he said. I doubt that a lot, too.

"I get the sense that A.J.'s been poking around the house ever since we were there. Looking for clues, maybe. And a ride in an Escalade. For sure. Not to mention, it's a spooky, empty, dangerous house. Therefore, fascinating." Half grimace. Half grin. "Kids."

Whaddya gonna do?

I was watching Tom listen to Otis. Composed, attentive, and focused—he was stone. Handsome stone, no question. Michelangelo's-David-stone. The contours of his face. The line of his beautiful jaw. Fully clothed, though. Unfortunately—

"Stop that, Allie."

Right there in front of me was why Tom could be transformed into our detective with the secret super powers, and I might miss the entire boat. He was tuned in all the way. Again.

Me? I was using my eyes to make myself distracted

and unreliable. Focusing at least twenty-five percent of my undisciplined attention on admiring Tom, twenty percent on the nearly empty container of Pad Paradise I had not had even a bite of yet, and five percent on Margo, who was also thinking about the Pad Paradise. At least I could read an evil mind.

There I was, halfway out to lunch, while Tom was simply listening to Otis and thinking about what Otis was saying. Plus employing all the other components of his Spidey sense. When Otis got to the crux of his story, Tom began to nod along.

"It all fits." Otis was saying, as I hauled my brain back in. "It all better-than fits."

It did. Exactly as we were hoping, Lloyd's house was yielding the link to Poplar Street. To be more accurate, three links: Pete, Jimmy, and Eugene. Survivors of the Scrappers-for-Hire explosion. Freaked out. Hiding out. Out of ideas. Ready to cooperate in whatever way would work best for them.

I snuck a glance at Trevor. He was staring at Otis, and thinking '*Explosion?*' so loud I could hear. I suspected Skip mentioned to him our sweet "mysteries of the heart" project when he stuck Trevor with Margo's case. This was clearly not that.

Welcome to our nightmare, Mr. Trevor.

Otis was on a roll and therefore oblivious. "A.J.

told me stuff around the house had been moved," he said. "I checked it out. And yeah. The front blind was up a couple inches on one side. Like somebody was peekin' out. The back kitchen door was open a crack, too. I found it hard to believe that anybody could be in there after how it was when we—"

He answered himself. "Desperation, I guess. When I checked around, it looked enough like a break-in that I called it in. To Tony, to be specific. He was on duty for the first part of the investigation. When his shift ended, he stayed on. Hung out. "The T&A Shuffle," I guess you could call it. But that was mostly after everything was handled."

I saw that last couple of sentences register with Trevor, too. He blinked. Guy was never going to be the same.

"Anyway, a couple officers went in. Sure enough. There were the guys. Names of Pete, Jimmy, and Eugene. In there. Scared shi—uh— Badly scared. Because they were the ones who understood that the Poplar house did not blow up all by itself. Turns out, there was this other guy."

Now we were hearing the whole story of Milo. With his drugs. And his lighter. Pete, Jimmy, and Eugene had figured it out pretty quick, though. For one thing, they knew *but exactly* who had cut the water line at Lloyd's place. That was great fun at the time. And smart, too. Gas line was a reasonable next stop after water line, as far as they were concerned. Then, of course, after the blast they asked themselves where Milo was, and came to the most likely conclusion.

"Because," Pete had explained to Otis, "where else would he be?"

Milo was reliable in a druggie kind of way. You could count on him, Pete said, to show up in certain places. Regular. Milo never showed up in any of his places again.

So now, instead of an easy, scrap job with no one knowing or caring, there'd been this mega bomb blast. Bad. Milo was missing and about to be presumed blown up. Extra bad. The guys didn't have a clue about much, but they could make out some problems arising. For them.

So they took themselves in their interestingly rusted junker car to their hiding place. The house they'd found empty, available, and full of good stuff, way back in March, after Lloyd didn't come home. The same house they'd destroyed when somebody found them there and paid them to make it look scrapped. By scrapping it.

Inside my mind, I was sorting the story and shaking my head in disbelief. Scrappers-for-Hire was turning out to be "A Tale of Two Houses." The worst of times. Times two. Geez.

Lloyd's wasn't as comfortable now, they told Tony, but it was dried out some and not too terrible. Except for the smell.

They could have hung out there for a long time.

Too bad. They were about to get a new address. Unless somebody made their bail. Odds didn't look great on that.

Chapter Fifty-three
Thursday, July 13

When I was a kid trying to learn enough stuff to look good in class, I believed for a long and ultimately embarrassing while that June 6, 1944, wasn't D-Day, but "THE Day." Made sense to me. I wasn't paying all that much attention at the time.

In so many ways, July 13th—which started out quite satisfactorily as the day after Margo and Trevor's triumph over injustice and the resolution of the mystery of who scrapped Lloyd's house—turned out to be THE Day for us.

It was barely lunchtime when I heard from Skip. He sounded serious and also dazed. Not your ordinary Skip.

"Allie, I'm so glad I got you. I'm sorry if this scares you, but it's concerning, so—Somebody's made a serious assault on your money, Allie. Even though it was all spread around—"

I heard an echo of Tom: *An electronic heist. Of two-hundred-twelve-million dollars.* This was a zap to my solar plexus, but I was calmer than I'd might have expected. At least now Tom and I could maybe—

"Skip. Did they get it all?"

"That's the funny part, Allie. Odd. Weird." Skip was definitely dazed.

"Odd-weird, how?"

"Brace yourself. I'm about to talk about a cyberattack, and you know I have trouble with a spreadsheet. Without my admin—"

"Go for it, Skip. I wouldn't understand a complex explanation. Dumb it on down. I'm right here."

"Okay, pretend Tom's money is behind a door. Actually, behind many, many different doors. And you're standing on the inside of one of the doors, staring at the doorknob. And it's slooow-ly turning. From the outside. And if you could see all the doorknobs? *All* of them? At once? You'd see them all moving. At the same time."

Geez Louise. I could visualize *that*, no problem. I'd be the woman in the old black-and-white movie, staring at the door, pulling the covers up to her chin and screaming bloody murder so big you could see that rubbery thing at the back of her throat quivering. Only this was a bunch of women screaming at a bunch of turning doorknobs....

Snap out of it, Alice Harper.

"I'm with you so far."

"And then? They all stop moving. All at once. It's like whoever's turning all those doorknobs got totally vaporized. Vanished."

Ah, now it's sci-fi. This explains a lot.

"And the money's safe."

"Dead safe. And it's spread out behind more and different doors now. Every penny."

For reasons Tom, Otis, and I discussed many times, losing all the money would be bad. Also, "bankrupt" is too weak a word to describe the financial mess we'd be in. Merely paying next month's rent. The security team. Let alone…

Therefore, I felt relieved. But then, for a couple of seconds, sad. As if Tom and I were about to run, hand in hand, out an opened door into one of those green meadows with the romantic music. And the flowers. Birds. Blue sky. A lake…

I closed that door, too. It wasn't a smart door for us and I knew it.

"Skip, you're wonderful. We'd be…a lot less stupid rich if not for you."

"But that's just it, Allie. It wasn't me. Or anything our people were doing. Somebody else used…um… the vaporizer gun? On your attacker. Do you have any idea who besides my people might be working on your money's security?"

Oh, yes. Indeed. His initials are S.M.

"Not off the top of my head. I'll check with Otis and get back to you, but Skip?"

"Yes?"

"That doorknob explanation of yours. It totally creeped me out. That's every haunted house movie I ever saw. To about the tenth power. If you ever have to explain this sort of thing to somebody else, try a less hair-raising analogy."

Before he could answer. Or laugh at me. My almost entirely useless phone blooped in my ear.

Incoming.

"Skip. I've got to answer call waiting. I'll get back to you." I took the call.

"Allie, It's Sandy."

"Sandy, are you okay?"

"I'm fine now. I used to be in security, remember? Witness protection couldn't hold a candle to how safe I am right now. Thanks for Julia, though. She was great.

"But Allie. I'm calling about you. And Tom. And Otis. Even after you fired us, I kept our monitoring going. Minimal, but I felt bad about everything. You're the one who's not fine. At all. Your entire system is collapsing. Rebuilding itself and collapsing again. I don't think it could even dial 9-1-1 if your lives depended on it. Have Otis get you out of there. Do it now."

● ● ● ● ●

I knew a guy back in high school. Stoner. Big into mind alteration. He always said if he was ever in a plane crash, he was pretty sure he'd hear "A Day in the Life" from the Sgt. Pepper album playing in his head. The getting-louder-and-louder-and-scarier-and-scarier part right before the silent-dying-away part. All the way down.

As we hurried, grabbing the few things we needed, on our flight from the house, I understood what he'd been talking about.

It was loud. And scary. The soundtrack of panic.

Oh. This must be THE Day.

Chapter Fifty-four

Otis walked us to the front desk at the Marriott. Said he'd be back in a couple of hours. Said Julia would be in position outside our room in twenty minutes or less.

"Hotel security will have you until then. I threatened them. A lot."

"No worries, Otis. We'll just…kick back and get some rest. No rush. At all."

No eye contact.

I closed the door and set the security lock. Oh, boy. That great soapy, bleachy hotel smell. I could breathe in here. The bad feeling that chased me all the way downtown was dissipating. The Beatles were letting up some, too.

"Alone at last." I leaned into Tom and he slipped his arms around me.

Home.

"Oh, Tom, I'm so tired. And confused. And only about twelve percent less terrified. Who would have thought a mere two-hundred-twelve-million dollars could be such a pain in the ass?"

"Me." He pulled me closer. We were almost dancing. I could almost hear music.

"Me, too." I was starting to cheer up. We were here, after all. In our own special Marriott. Like the very first night we were on the run from the Mondo murderers. On the very top concierge floor this time, though. Upgrade.

He must have read my mind about that first night. He found my mouth with his blind man magic.

Some time passed…

"How do you do that, exactly?"

"Triangulation. And blind man radar."

"Radar, huh? I thought it was magic."

"Believe whatever you like. Mojo, maybe. It could be blind man mojo."

"Be serious."

"All right. We blind magicians are very particular about who we share our professional secrets with. But since it's you."

"I believe it should be 'whom' all you magicians share those with—and there's the preposition, too—but I'm in a bit of a hurry here. Go on."

"I can hear you breathe. I love that sound. He kissed me again. Long. "I know how to make it go faster. See? Anyway, your mouth is right there, directly under your nose."

He was right about the breathing thing. Also there was the rush of tingle.

"Well, that's disappointing. Like finding out that Santa is really—"

"Shhh. Don't spoil the magic." He kissed me again. "Or the mojo."

I reached up on tiptoes and entwined my arms more about his handsome shoulders, to better enhance the mojo—

Somebody knocked on the door.

"Mr. Bennington?"

Not a chance in two hundred million years.

I covered Tom's mouth with my fingers and whispered into his ear super softly, "Let's be real quiet. They'll go away."

He nodded. We waited. No breathing.

A chirp.

A click.

A clunk.

The door popped open.

Our intruder had three first names.

Andy. Mark. Ted.

Chapter Fifty-five

Amazing. All those aliases, and I was looking at a grown-up, dressed-up, slicked-down version of Andy-the-Intern. Andy who was also Mark Fleming, the cyber-genius, the cocky savant who'd come to the aid of Channel 16 and wooed Lisa Cole for information about Tom and me. After he engineered the sudden, untimely death of their wonderful Lauren. And, of course he was "Mr. Nobody-Ever-Saw-Him" the Magna-Protect mole, Ted Stevens. Who'd no doubt selected, flattered, and then murdered Sandy's mostly decent Keith McGill at the end of Reboot Day.

Who else had this one guy been since March? Who else had he killed for Tom's money?

Without Lisa's warning, I could pass this version on the street and not recognize the original Andy Reilly, but he was permitting Andy to peek through his brand new wire rims. Demonstrating for my benefit how clever he was. How much trouble we were in.

How did I ever miss the icy steel in those blue eyes?

My funny doofus was a brilliant sociopath. I wondered where he was hiding his gun.

Fear was everywhere. In my ears. High-pitched. Like bees. A zillion furious, threatened bees. In my whole body. A total, vibrating paralysis.

I was immobilized, but even with all the buzzing and vibrating, a piece of my brain still functioned. I couldn't help noticing my maniac was all cranked up, too. It takes one to know one.

Something or someone was scaring the pants off Andy-Mark-Ted.

Could I put this to work for Tom and me? Or was it our death sentence?

Tom knew trouble when it broke into his hotel room. His voice was steady. One arm still tight around me. "Let me guess. You must be the hacker."

A smirk. A shuffle.

"The genius hacker who's got your number, dude. All your numbers, to be more accurate. Good guess, though, Mister McGoo. Or perhaps I should say, Professor McGoo. The Third. PhD."

His fidgeting hyperactivity was all Andy, but

this energy was skittish. A definite touch of suppressed hysteria. The dude was in major trouble. I was betting the trouble he was in was due to Otis' Shadow Man. Skip said the heist—this guy's heist—went bust.

Andy had a boss to answer to. Magna-Pro's wonderful mysterious benefactor was my current leading candidate for that job. Richard Tyler. Rich. You wouldn't want to piss off this boss. No way he could be happy.

I smothered a flare of hope.

I could feel the anger in Tom's chest, thrumming against my back, but his tone was bland. "Associate Professor McGoo will do fine, thanks. And do you have a human alias, Mister Genius Hacker?"

Now anger was thrumming all over the place. I stayed very still, representing the spirit of quietly terrified conciliation in our meeting.

"Tom." *Please don't set this guy off.*

Andy heard the fear in my voice. He savored it. I could tell.

"No worries about your Tom, Ms. Harper. Y'know, you may look like the maid, but you're pretty sexy. I suppose a blind man could—"

I leaned more into Tom to remind him we were better than this impertinent murderer. He returned my lean. We agreed.

Deep breath.

I decided to think of the guy as Andy AssHat, for simplicity's sake.

"Look. Andy…Whatever. Why are you here? You should have your share of two-hundred-twelve-million tax-free dollars and be on a beach by now."

He dismissed me with a shrug. "There's more than one way to get some passwords. Based on things I overheard back in the fantastic, free-for-all days of your first security system override, I'm pretty sure you've memorized them all, Tom. 'Blind Man's Phonebook.' Right?"

No. Not happening. No way. Not good.

Tom memorized a lot of stuff, but only Skip had access to those passwords. Tom was about to tell this guy he didn't know them. Because he didn't. And because they were different now. The guy would think he was being stonewalled. Stalemate. That was a recipe for dead.

The electricity of fear pulsed its way out of my heart and down into my elbows. I fought to look composed.

"I'm sorry, Andy." Tom said. "Those are not in the book."

Tom was upping the ante.

I found out where Andy kept his gun. Under his jacket, in the back waistband of his khakis.

He got it out of there, showed it to me, and described it to Tom.

"I tell you what, Dr. McGoo. I have here something you may have noticed made Ms. Harper tense up her very serviceable body. My brand new Sig Sauer P320 Compact nine-millimeter pistol. Modular. Polymer. She is looking at it now, and I am describing it so you may comprehend how unintelligent it would be of you to mess with me."

"I'm not—" Tom began. I felt a slight shift in his posture. It telegraphed to me that he was about to put his body between my body and the Sig Sauer. Not happening. I resisted the shift and stepped forward. Tom came along, too, and his hand grabbed onto mine. Both our hands were cold and slippery. Now we were side by side. Holding hands. Facing Andy's gun.

My vocal cords were swarming with panicking bees. I swallowed hard and did my best to talk around them and sound calm.

"Andy. Listen. Seriously. He doesn't have them. If you shoot one of us, you'll have to shoot the other one. We're a package. You'll get stuck with a loud, risky, double murder and nothing to gain.

"Plus—" I was babbling. Trying to outtalk the dread that was unraveling me. Holding on tight to Tom's cold hand. "I bet your fabulous compact nine-millimeter makes a crap-ton of noise. You're twenty-five stories up in this Marriott. Slow elevators. Jammed with guests. Stairwell full up with security guards, hiding out and smoking. I wouldn't—"

"Nor would I."

Huh. Just like that.

Chapter Fifty-six

A big, tall, well-dressed, dark-haired man shoved open the unlatched door and walked in. Casual. At ease. As if he'd booked the reservation. When Andy turned and saw him, he lowered the gun.

Okay.

Four of us now. Less space. Less air in the room. Less room in my chest.

The guy looked at Andy and said, "You fool."

Conversational tone, sharp edge.

Hello, alpha dog.

Was this better? Worse? I liked not having the gun in my face, but the buzz of fear was not improved. My bees were as frantic as before.

Poor Tom. He must be adrift in all this....

Tom gave my hand a hard, warning squeeze and said. "Mr. Ricci."

Like the guy was arriving for tea.

"Tom. How—?"

"I've met this gentleman before, Allie. And he— what are the odds of two tall men I've met before wearing the same extremely distinctive cologne?"

Cologne? "You're joking, Tom. Right?"

The man smiled. Not warm or friendly.

"He's not joking, Allie. It's '1872.' One of the world's most expensive fragrances for men."

Okay. A wealthy, well-dressed man, who knew both our names, and who'd slapped on quite a bit of his fancy cologne. An expensive fragrance that smelled like every flower, herb, citrus fruit, and tree on Earth took a shower together. I shifted my focus from Andy, and the gun he was still holding, to Mr. Ricci. The real boss of this fiasco.

I was no Tom Bennington, but my memory was getting jogged, too. That voice. Deep, smooth, but not one hundred percent uptown. A trace of big city, rough neighborhood, maybe. It jogged…

Ah, now I'd located him.

At the "Art & Artists on the Road" benefit. Where I was fleeing the knowing look of the woman who was sure I was no way Jacob Foster's aunt.

Heading for a glass of champagne.

In my haste I stumbled and stepped, full-weight, on the foot of a big tall man in an upscale tux.

"Oh, sorry. Sorry!"

I wanted to get away. Far.

"No damage. Don't I know you?"

"Sorry. No. I...."

"Don't worry about it. We'll probably run into each other again sometime, and be properly introduced."

He drifted.

I hustled to the ladies' room to splash cold water on my face and get a grip.

So, yes. Here in this hotel room that reeked of fear—Andy's, Tom's, mine—and that flamboyant aftershave, I recalled this guy. His voice. The four-figure tux he'd been wearing. And the fragrance, too. Now that Tom mentioned it.

"You're starting to remember me, I see." This afternoon, his words were grating with barely suppressed fury, but his smile was still arrogant. Smug, too. As he dropped his bomb.

"Really, Ms. Harper. You both should know me. You're renting my house."

Holy. Shit.

Right. Of course I should. I did know him and his goddam pretentious dining room furniture.

My despot. The Grade-A dick.

"Cut the crap, Tito." Andy was vibrating all over the place now. "You're here. Make him give you the passwords. We can—we can still—"

"No, actually, Nathan, we can't. We only had the

one shot. You know the one. 'The piece of cake?' And you? You dropped the cake.

"Mr. Bennington III doesn't have the passwords. For real. He's not lying. Although I'm sure he would to protect his millions. But you should know, better than anybody, the money is tied up in multiple accounts behind multiple passwords. By now new codes have been redistributed among multiple trustworthy people. Your way was the only way. For now. It was promising. I invested…that's not important. You've been out-geniused, Nate."

"No, Tito. I can—"

"No, Nate. Not this time. Turn around."

Alarm in blue eyes.

"Like she said. You can't shoot me, Tito. The noise?" A high-note of fear.

Ricci sighed. Tired. Resigned. Bored. "I'm not going to shoot you, Nate. Just turn around for a minute."

Andy—there wasn't time for him to become Nathan to me—considered the gun in his own hand but let his arm fall slack. Turned away, still anxious, but still confident in his sociopathic brilliance.

Ricci slipped something out of his jacket pocket. Deft. A syringe in his hand. Uncapped in one smooth motion. A second later, he'd dispensed its contents into Andy's neck.

Andy gasped, recoiled from the needle's sting, and turned back to face Ricci, shaking his head, fighting confusion. He raised the gun partway. Lowered it again as if it was suddenly very heavy for polymer.

"*No*," he choked out, "Tito. No. Not. *Don't*—" A sharp intake of a breath got trapped in his heaving chest. Realization and terror chased each other across his face. The gun slipped from his hand. Thumped on the rug. His eyes widened and rolled back.

Dead man standing.

Gone.

I saw a man die from a gunshot wound last year. This was more horrifying because it was so fast. Ricci caught Andy up from his awkward, boneless collapse. Laid him, carefully if not gently, on the floor where he lay jerking for a few endless seconds.

Ricci stood and brushed himself off. "Getting better all the time."

He laughed at my frozen face, this so-called "Tito Ricci." Who I was pretty confident was also Sandy's Mr. Great Guy—"Just call-me-Rich."—Richard Tyler. Our biggest mystery yet.

A good looking, well-tailored man who with one smooth, careless gesture disposed of the brilliant, ruthless boy genius. Now that death had wrenched

Andy's unconscious body one last horrible time, he lay silent, eyes staring. Discarded like trash on the Marriott's attractive rug.

I braced my wobbly knees and clutched at Tom's hand. He clutched right back. He could hear a murder as well as the next guy. Not the method, maybe, but the madness? Crystal clear.

Andy-Mark-Ted-Nathan, hacker mole and merciless killer of innocents, was dead, and now Tom and I were alone in a hotel room twenty-five floors above Public Square with someone even scarier.

A villain who looked like any other wealthy, powerful, well-dressed guy. A man with a driving need to win. Who would, without a moment's reflection, kill anyone who got in his way. Who'd found nobody aware enough, or brave enough, to stop him. The two of us sure didn't have a plan for that. Or this…whatever was about to happen next.

Ricci laughed again at the question on my face.

"Not today, Ms. Harper. It's tempting. Might even be smart. But I can't revisit you and Tom and your money at some point unless you're alive. I am still quite interested in your money."

"This kid." He glanced down at the lifeless body of a young man maybe named Nathan. "This *boy* made a sloppy mess of things because he believed he was way smarter than everybody. That's always a mistake. I remind myself of that. Particularly today.

"You, too, Professor Bennington. You're a regular smart PhD, aren't you? And very...observant for a blind guy. Don't get too cocky. I'll be back around sooner or later. The world never runs out of opportunities for entrepreneurs like me."

"Wait." If he wasn't going to kill us right now, I wanted to confirm the last of our theories. "You're— You were Flotilla. And Flotilla was—"

"Yes. A pity. We were raking it in for quite a while. And I thought that was a brilliant name for an interrelated group of enterprises. We've closed the Cleveland branch. Time to change the name and the venue. Only takes a click."

A click? My worldview was wrecked. Real was false. Solid was smoke. Alive was dead—the click of keys? The touch of a finger to a screen?

Anything could vanish.

Okay. Good to know, going forward.

I couldn't help myself.

"Richard? Rich? Ricci? Kind of a theme with you, huh, Tito? And your name isn't really Tito, either, is it?

A chuckle. "No. Tito is a handmade vodka, Allie. As I'm sure you know."

He bent down, picked up Nathan's gun, and stood for a long moment with his foot poised to kick the corpse he'd made. Thought better of it and left Tom and me with the still-warm body of a genius-hacker-killer and a lot to explain to the hotel manager, the cops who showed up for the 9-1-1, and the homicide detective.

The overpowering echo of the citrusy, floral, fruity, woodsy fragrance lingered with us, too. It costs three-hundred dollars for the economy size. I checked. But not until a long time after that terrible day.

Chapter Fifty-seven

We were on our way back to Bratenahl by dark. The two of us. No sign of Julia. No Otis.

No Otis anywhere.

Our calm, deliberate Uber X driver was determined to obey the speed limit. I kept pressing my foot down on a phantom accelerator. Willing her to hurry. *Go, lady, go!*

Tom was radiating worry, too, but he hid it better. I slipped my hand into his. Both our hands were still freezing. I longed to lean against him, press my face into his shoulder. I thought he might feel the same. But my next move would be to cry, and breaking down was not in order right now. We needed to shore ourselves up. Not let go.

I was frantic about Otis. I'd called his phone. The house phone. Julia's phone. No answer. Then I called all his security guys' phones, and they all said the same thing. "Our shifts got changed today. I'm not on."

They were on now, though. I sent them all. I called Tony. No luck there, either.

Here was yet another bad thing: Nobody could reach Julia Perez, who might or might not have been outside our door when Nathan arrived. She was missing, too.

My world had been hacked. Again.

The Uber driver delivered us to the front gate. The first batch of Otis' team had beat us there. A couple of them met us in the drive.

"Otis? Where's Otis."

A shrug. "In the kitchen. Pissed, of course. He was freaked about you guys until we told him you'd called everybody."

Relief.

It felt good to inhale and exhale like a normal person. Not possible after I realized Otis hadn't ever made it back up to the twenty-fifth floor.

"Oh. And there's a guy with him."

I'd relaxed too soon.

"Come with us."

The mansion was dark. We trekked along the side and around to the back. I wasn't ringing the front doorbell. Not then. Hopefully not ever again. We were so done with this place. All this time, all this every-bad-thing. The answer was simple all along. "*You're renting my house.*" Not much longer, I told myself. And not paying this month's rent either.

You son of a bitch.

The artful stone walkway, snaking among the designer shrubs and flowers, made the going challenging. Tom had my arm, him guiding me. Steady.

The kitchen shades were down. A trio of shadows shifting.

One. Two. Three.

The door was locked. I glanced at our guard. His hand was resting on his weapon, but his face was placid. Walk in the park. Probably not a good idea to scream at him.

This is serious. Be more scared.

I knocked.

Otis answered—Shadow #1 as seen through the window. Thanks again, Ms. Universe. Close behind Otis stood Julia Perez—Shadow #2. Another cause for rejoicing. Out of uniform, though. Slim and beautiful in a pair of jeans that used to belong to me. She did them justice. I couldn't fault her for that. And fading away again, down the long darkened hall away from the kitchen, I could see my craggy night visitor, Shadow Man—Shadow #3. Ever the phantom.

All shadows accounted for. I couldn't tell what

I should be feeling. Relieved? Angry? Scared? Betrayed? My brain was worthless so I checked my heart. In there, Otis was still Otis. And Otis was someone I trusted. All day, every day. We were good. That probably kept Julia and Shadow Man grandfathered in. Under the protection of my trust in Otis.

"Tell me everything, Otis. Where have you been?"

"I didn't want to go, Allie. Leave you guys there. After—"

Julie rescued him.

"My fault, Allie. And we had to drag him. You and Tom were surrounded by Homicide, and they didn't appear to suspect you of anything. That's about as safe as it gets in this town. They—Otis and…the other guy—found me in the service room. A little messed up, aggravated, and tied up with my own uniform, but I was fine. We needed to—"

Tom raised his hand. "Stop. Wait. Who the hell is this 'other guy'? Allie, why was he here? Why did he take off like that when we came in? Why haven't I heard about him until right now?"

Otis to the rescue. "Not Allie's fault, Tom. This time it's on me."

"Do I have to yell at you now, too, Otis? You know I can handle bad news."

"Not about Allie, Tom. And we both know it.

But this wasn't about her going...rogue...like she used to do. A lot more than she does now. She would've told you if I—"

He stopped himself. Rubbed at his face. Hating everything about this moment. I got it. Totally. Otis was nothing if not loyal to Tom, and now Tom had a question about that. It was my bad moment, too. Tom's trust was everything to Otis. And me, of course.

Otis straightened his shoulders and started again. "Allie found out about him, Tom. Accidentally. The guy is a....very talented...uh...security guy. He has powerful...connections. And access to a... very big...network. She calls him Shadow Man. I contacted him when I realized Magna-Pro was worthless. She overheard me on the phone. I asked her to trust me and not tell anybody. I was never sure who might be listening, Tom. Or where. Or through what device. Everything was moving so fast. The—the guy was our secret weapon against them. The less said to anyone, anywhere—"

I searched Tom's face. This right here was a couple of giant sticking points in our whole relationship. His fierce independence. Not wanting to be protected because of his blindness. His obsession with my safety.

I thought that obsession might be the index to how he felt about me. I searched his face.

Unsearchable.

He relaxed his shoulders and smiled. "Okay, Otis. Since it was you. I'll forgive her."

Oh, look. He was getting over worrying about me. Not. Good. That put a catch in my throat.

Be cool, Allie.

● ● ● ● ●

An hour later, Julia was vanishing, too. Shadow Man had found her some of that sharp, black, lightweight spy attire that looked good on him. It looked better on her. She gave me back my jeans. I was sad to watch her go, and I thought those jeans were probably disappointed not to be following the Shadow Man wherever he might lead.

As far as we could tell, between the hundred or so now disabled doorknobs and Shadow Man's fresh repair of the non-protective Magna-Protection, we could at least spend another night or two under this upscale, untrustworthy roof. The nine-thousand-square-foot mansion was a learning experience. Hell, everything was a learning experience.

Two-hundred-twelve million dollars and still growing was the fast track.

We needed to move somewhere smaller and more manageable. Also safe. Safer. It was going to take a few weeks to turn this hulking aircraft carrier of mediocre security around. In the meantime, I didn't have any problem enjoying the decks.

Chapter Fifty-eight
Friday, July 14

On Friday morning, the day after THE Day, Otis brought a couple of coffee mugs out to where I was sitting. On a fancy deck chair. Under a fat-cat umbrella. Counting my arms and legs and feeling almost okay. I wasn't asking him any of my questions. Especially about Shadow Man. Especially since I mostly didn't want to know. I needed to be able to live without answers. My ducks were never going to be all in a row, but I could deal.

Otis and I looked like a mini-vacation. Me in my cutoffs, flashy red top, and big, floppy hat. Him in a screamingly loud tropical shirt. Celebrating being alive, lakeside, on a glorious Friday. As best we could.

"Morning, Otis. *Coffee*. Perfect. Thanks."

"You want to know more about the guy, don't you?

Damn you, Otis intuition.

"I always want to know more about every single thing, but I'm okay about the guy. Better than okay. Grateful to him. Grateful to you for bringing him. You're more than meets the eye, Otis Johnson. You always have been. Works for me. No questions asked."

"You've earned an answer, Allie. I'll keep it short and try not to compromise anybody's security. Only gonna tell it once. Trust you not to repeat it....

"Except maybe to Tom. He's tryin', Allie. Tom. You're a big deal to him. He—but I'm not here to talk about that." He sipped at his coffee and squinted at the horizon. The long, low shape of a freighter was out there, hauling something from somewhere to somewhere else. Slowly. I waited.

"Before I was a cop, Allie, I was Navy. My dad was Army. MIA. Never came back. Period. Not his body. Nothing. I enlisted to prove something. Find something out—I don't know. For something that didn't make much sense. Any sense. A mistake, of course, but not a disaster. I was a kid. Learned a few things. Never saw action. Only made one friend-for-life.

"Military wasn't all that inclusive. Every third guy was that racist, scrapyard dude of yours. Howard. Only more in-your-face about it."

Understatement, I knew. I nodded. Waited.

"But there was a bar in the town where brothers would meet up. Where that was more important than the insignia on your shirt. I'd talk with a guy there sometimes. I was drinking way above my rank and talking out of my wheelhouse but we weren't stuffy about all that.

"We'd trade lies. About the job. About the ladies. Sailor talk, y'know? Oh. I guess you don't. Never mind. Anyway we'd talk and were sort of buddies. Even after I left the service we'd talk sometimes. 'How's it goin'?' The usual. Anyway, this guy, Pin—

"Pin? What kind of name is Pin?"

"Don't interrupt. Nickname."

"Shadow Man forever for me."

A laugh. Short but sincere. "I know. He got a kick out of that. More accurate than Pin, probably. These days. But back then he stayed in for as long as he could stand it. And then he went private—"

"Private. Like Blackwater?"

"You don't miss much, do you?"

"We bogus-part-time librarians read, Otis. And watch the news."

"Got it. No. Not like that. Not as—never mind. You're in the ballpark. When he got out of combat stuff, he built up his mind. Turned out he had skills. Was gifted at...Let's just say he adapted to 'the new domain of intelligence.' And he learned from the best of the best. And, of course, now he has a 'loose working arrangement' with somebody bigger than you and I."

"I see."

"I can tell you do."

"And my Andy—?"

"Your Andy. Somebody's Nathan. Nobody's more details. 'Nathan' was the only other thing I could find about him. He erased himself. More than he meant to, no doubt. Gives new meaning to 'dead and gone.' He was a formidable talent. But, in the long run, no match."

"For Shadow Man."

"Him. Yeah."

"Then when Andy went to collect the money, he found…?"

"Let's just say, 'a door he couldn't open.' And that kid was very good at doors."

Holy cow. Those damn doorknobs again.

"Hurray for Shadow Man. Pin. And how do we ourselves access the money now? To pay for your vacations?"

"I'm proud of your cool in this matter."

"Hey, I'm Tom Bennington's girl. I understand the limitations of money. Somewhat."

He grinned. My Otis was all the way back.

"I talked with Skip this morning. It's all there. All safe. Except for one-hundred-thousand dollars. Well spent, I'd say. The jackpot's a little more complicated to get to now. And even more…distributed, but it's there and it's as secure as anything ever is."

"And Pin?"

"On his way. Not likely to be back. He thinks he's got your security locked down. If not, we can always contact him."

"And he took Julia with him? I thought she and I were about to be friends."

"Yeah, she thinks highly of you, too, but Pin…."

"I get it. And she's special. I could see that. More valuable to herself and the world in general if she's with him. Bigger field of operation. More good to be done. I should let you go with him, too."

"Nah. My world is here. I wouldn't trade."

"So Otis? Seriously? Pin?"

"From *pinniped*. Scientific family name of 'some semi-aquatic marine mammals.' Means 'fin foot.'"

Ah. Seal.

"I see. I get it. All right. I'm good. I'll forget all about it now."

In the mist at horizon's edge, the freighter was keeping on keeping on.

"And Otis?"

"Uh-huh."

"Trusting you took some guts. Like you said. But I'd never call it a burden."

Chapter Fifty-nine

Otis left.

And, like the next float in a parade, Tony Valerio hove into view. In uniform. Looking official.

I reviewed my last twenty-four hours. No crimes or misdemeanors. No more of my death threats against D.B. Or anyone else. A lot of surviving.

I waited.

Tony took over Otis' vacated deck chair and stretched out his legs. Crossed his ankles. A good sign. He sighed. That could be good, too. I considered how frequently Valerio's conversations with me began with that exact sigh. The sound of a man reluctantly letting go of serious reservations and all common sense. The Tony Valerio Signature Allie Harper Exhalation.

I waited some more.

"Margo will be disappointed. You, too, I suppose.

We're gonna skip your helicopter ride. Officers operating on a tip found the GTO at CyCLE."

No helicopter was not terrible news for me. Lee Ann wasn't cryin' either. She and I wanted answers more than we wanted more thrills. We'd had an oversupply of those. We were all about answers now.

The T&A's Lloyd Case began with Tom, Otis, me, and a map of the City of Cleveland. All we had when we started was an intersection and a flashy camera ticket: Euclid at Mayfield. '67 Pontiac GTO, headed west, at 11:52 p.m., on Friday, February 24.

The case started as guesswork and reconstructions. Vague ideas of what it was all about. Missing connections. Connections we'd not understood. Evidence that filled in some blanks but left us guessing about ones that were likely going to be blanks forever.

Valerio and I were watching the freighter now and not looking at each other. That freighter was getting to be a regular at these awkward discussions.

"I promised I'd tell you whatever we found out about Lloyd."

I could see Tony was still working on stopping himself from telling me anything, but another impulse won the battle. He cleared his throat.

"You did some good work. Took some stupid chances. But on that score, I'd say you're improving.

Maybe a B-minus a couple of times. I feel obliged to say that it only takes one stupid chance—"

We gazed at the freighter. I guessed she might be the *Federal Bristol*, one of the regulars on our horizon. Long and low, with maybe a flash of red. There's an app for that.

Meditating on distant ships unruffles my feathers sometimes.

"Otis gave us your tip about that Howard Rexroad guy over at CyCLE. Him and his old trash truck. While you were occupied with your so-called 'security glitches' and that dead Nathan guy I don't much want to hear about, we went over there looking for this Howard. But he was gone. Everybody except a guy named Stan was gone. Even the dog. They were under new management, he said. Didn't know anything, he said.

"The place was packed up and cleaned out, except for a busted coffee machine. Scrap still there, of course. But no records. Somebody destroyed all of it. But Allie. Here's a kicker."

He was squinting at me now, all self-satisfied, waiting for me to beg him for the kicker. I was feeling generous and glad to be alive so I didn't make him wait more than thirty seconds.

"What, Tony? What kicker?"

He nodded. More satisfaction.

"Tell you what. A big old trash truck is goddam hard to hide. It was full of stuff. Scrapped stuff. More than one job, it looked like. Your theory about how your Howard Rexroad was using that truck to pick up metal and fixtures left by Scrappers-for-Hire? Right on the money. And here's how I know for sure. Some lady called us last week about scrappers at her house while she was out of town. She was royally pi— hacked off."

That mention of Scrappers-for-Hire transported me straight back to the detonation that ended our stakeout—a moment that will occupy a bright, loud, searing spot on my soul for the rest of my life. This chilled my happy dance of self-congratulation for spotting that truck.

Tony noticed.

"Don't worry, Allie. Tom seems fine to me. I don't see any difference and he says it gets better every day."

He put that behind us and continued with his tale of triumph.

"Anyway, we gave the lady a ride over to check out the trash truck. She identified some of her stuff like she'd been married to it for forty years. She told us a woman has a personal relationship with her kitchen sink. That she would have recognized it anywhere. Gave us its identifying marks, scratches, and one stain she'd 'been after since 1996.' She could stand up in court, if it ever comes to that.

"Now we can see that operation. All the way along. Not that there's anybody much left to get. Except Pete, Eugene, and Jimmy. Small potatoes. Milo's out of the picture due to being blown up, of course. The foreclosure insurance scam woman you talked to, we've got her. She'll do some time, I hope, but she's a cog.

"Less clearly tied in, but in there somehow, you can bet on it, is your mole guy, Andy or Nathan or pick-a-name. And also your Mr. We-Don't-Know-Who. Mastermind of way too much of this. Owner of this actual house. Whose name is nothing like Tito Ricci. Those guys. One dead and gone. One just plain gone. Both wiped off the face of the world as far as anyone can see.

"We think your Ricci got his hacker to make him a new ID, as a precaution. Passports, too, no doubt. God knows what else. That genius shoulda been smelling a rat right about then."

"Ricci's gone, Tony? And we can't do a damn thing about it?"

"Uh-huh, Allie. The three saddest words in Cop Land. "He. Got. Away." And for right now, I'd suggest you let him go.

"This so-called Ricci was the big dog. Everybody

was working his plan. Everybody in this whole train wreck—from the saddest, scrapping druggie, to a guy who turned his nice, legitimate security business into a spy machine, to your smart, dead hacker. Every damn one of them was your Mr. Ricci's lackey. And those big clever dogs are slippery. Escape hatches everywhere.

"You're right. We didn't catch Mr. Not-Ricci. Not this time. It sucks but there it is. And it's not good news for you that occasionally those guys circle back to pick up what they missed. I wouldn't hope for that if I were you. On the bright side, he's one powerful, arrogant dude. That's a trap all by itself. Those guys like to show off. It gets them caught. Or maybe dead sometimes."

"Look, Allie. You need to put this one down. You got what you came for. You found out about Lloyd. Loretta has some truth to get used to, but at least she has the truth. She can move on."

He read my face.

"I know that's a cliché and not much. But, Allie, moving on is what makes life possible. Like me and Margo. I couldn't have Margo if I'd never moved on from about ten-thousand things. And believe me…" His grin broke free and lightened up his face. He looked ten years younger. "You would *never* want to miss out on Margo."

I had no viable argument for that. Cliché or not, I moved on.

"Stanley is the sole survivor of CyCLE? And Flotilla?"

He nodded. "Yeah. He was a total pawn. Somebody needs to tell guys like him not to—Tell them not to throw it all away out of pure—I don't know, inattention maybe?"

I nodded back. Encouraging, but not interfering with the flow. Eyes on water.

"That guy, Stan, was a ride-along with Howard Rexroad when he killed Lloyd, Allie. Down by the last bridge over MLK."

A jolt to the chest.

Answers.

"Howard? *Howard* killed Lloyd? Tony, Tom needs to hear this."

"I stopped in the house on the way in. I gave him the top and bottom lines. He sent me to you. He's a born detective, you know. And a team player."

Ow.

I wanted to defend myself on both those scores, but I wanted Tony's information more. It took me a second to get my voice back and be a team player. "What did Tom say?"

"He said this was more than you both hoped for. Would you maybe like to hear it now?" A pause.

"Alice Harper, for crissake. The man is batshit crazy about you, and you know it."

I blinked.

"Tell me all of it, Tony."

"What I may not have mentioned is when we found the GTO, we found Howard, too. They'd crushed it with him behind the wheel. Two birds, you'd say. Bad. He was maybe still—anyway, we were sure, but we needed to be a hundred percent. We waited for DNA. Didn't take too long, for a change. Crushed-alive-in-a-car captures everybody's imagination. It's him.

"Then out of the blue, Stan shows up at the Fifth District like a herd of drug dealers was after him. Looked like he'd been hiding out under something dirty and rusty for a while.

"Something woke him up big time. He may have been an eyewitness to the smashing of Howard. He knows about it, I can tell. He's not talking about that, though. Not yet. But he's talking. He probably believes gross stupidity is 'extenuating circumstances' for every damn thing he was an accessory to. We are cutting him a deal. Somewhat.

"You were there? When he confessed about Lloyd?"

"Not at first, but when the detective doing the interrogation saw the direction—she invited me in. Lloyd was not mine per se, but he was my concern. I guess everybody knew that. I watched from behind the two-way."

As Valerio told me what he'd seen and heard in the room behind the mirror, I patched it together, using pictures I'd been collating in my head since the beginning of the Lloyd case.

It was a fiction created by me out of theories, guesses, and flashes of light. Scraps.

It satisfied the spirit of the T&A, though. To answer questions that leave gaping holes in people's lives. I began with the scene we'd worked out for ourselves that first day of the case when we'd closed our eyes and put our imaginations to work on the Ouija Board map of Cleveland.

As Valerio recounted the details of Stan's confession, I watched the story of Lloyd's last run come to its end.

Chapter Sixty
Friday, February 24

From the passenger seat of the car following Lloyd, Stan detonated the bubble-gum-size lump of C-4 Howard had affixed to the GTO's distributor cap. The explosion was muffled. A thump. A small backfire maybe. The steering and brakes went stiff and unresponsive.

Lloyd's whole attention was focused on keeping the car in control long enough to get it stopped. Then he sat and stared at the bridge ahead, disbelieving, heart hammering in his ears, waiting a beat for his composure to return. His perfect run was toast. The car behind him had already passed him up like a ghost, in a swirl of white. Going on to claim glory that should have been Lloyd's. *Shit.* But maybe he could try again tomorrow night.

He turned the key in the ignition. *Nada.* Not even a goddam click. What the—? This was bad. No. Wake up, Lloyd. This was very bad. He was getting back in touch with his assignment. The package. The money. People were waiting. Wondering. Important people. He needed some road assistance. Pronto. He'd left his cell phone in the console, as instructed, when he'd gone into the warehouse. He flipped open the lid. What the fuck? The compartment was empty.

The flare of headlights sluiced over his windshield, which had already built up a thin coating of snow. Car coming. Should he wave for help? Was that a good idea? Hell, they probably wouldn't stop anyway—this time of night.

He gave a tentative wave. They slowed. Stopped. Was this good? Was it bad? Should he lock the doors?

Okay. Let's see. He wiped the fog from the side window. Here were two ordinary-looking guys. Nodding. Smiling. Good Samaritans. Maybe it was even his pals from the joyride downtown. Lucky they'd been back there. Seen him in trouble.

One of the guys, the taller and wider of the two, jerked open his door. Well, that was unexpectedly aggressive. Guy put his big hand on

Lloyd's upper arm and pulled him up and out of the GTO in one effortless motion. Cold air hit Lloyd like a hammer.

"Hey!" The stammer from the sudden chattering of his teeth made it come out, "H-H-Hey." Embarrassing. The guy appeared not to notice. "Look, here," Lloyd started over, "You don't have to—"

His tongue failed him again. He couldn't finish a sentence and it felt critically important that he say exactly the right thing. The other, shorter guy—still taller than Lloyd, though, Lloyd noticed—had him by the other arm now and they were propelling him toward the edge of the creek. Lloyd could hear water whispering and gurgling. He could hear his shoes and the guys' shoes crunch-squeaking in the snow. He could hear everything so clearly that the clarity of the sound and the glaze of terror over his brain were interfering with his ability to say this right thing, this critical thing, whatever it was.

When they were standing at the edge of the stream, Lloyd could see, by the glare from the city, transfused through the milky brightness of the snow-filled sky, that there was a layer of jagged ice at the edges of the water.

It came to him, then, what he should say.

"I have money," he blurted, filled with hope. "I have money in the car." He peered into the smooth, impassive face of the tall man.

"We know," said the tall man in a soothing voice. And he shot Lloyd a couple of times with a gun Lloyd didn't even know was in the world. After about twenty seconds, when Lloyd was dead, the two guys dragged him between them and let him down over the edge until he was stood up with both his feet in the water. Then they jackknifed him over and in.

He floated up, the current tugging at him, but the shorter man got a heavy stick and the two poked his body until it was jammed under the ice by the bank's edge where it was thickest. They exchanged a glance that asked, "Is that enough?" And the tall one shrugged as if to say, "Who cares? What does it matter?"

They walked together, almost companionably, back to the GTO. The tall man opened the passenger door. He took out the envelope, fat with money.

After that, the tall man, whose name turned out to be Howard Rexroad, waited patiently, as if he didn't feel the cold, while Short Guy whose name was Stan pulled their SUV around and hooked it to the GTO. "Nice," he remarked.

"They'll never make these again." When a car passed and slowed, both men waved genially in a "we've got it handled, but thanks so much for rubbernecking" way. It snowed harder.

They both climbed into the SUV, and Howard said, "I don't know why he came down here. Based on where he was supposed to end up, he was miles out of his way. This worked out a-okay for us, though. I told you the C-4 would come in handy. Don't forget. Control of the situation is key. And you know what's weird? He didn't have to stop for a single stoplight the whole run." He laughed softly, a little "huh-huh" that jerked his shoulders up and down.

"Yeah," Stan said. "But what was all that money for? It doesn't make sense."

"The money's for us, moron. Four thou for me. One for you. Poor SOB was carrying our payoff and didn't have a clue." Another little laugh, shoulders hitching.

"But what about the package? It's still in the GTO. We're dragging it?"

"Wake up, Stan. There was no package. Lloyd was the package. Stop asking so many questions. Stay awake. Unless you like swimming in ice water."

Stan pulled out. Howard looked back. Their tracks to the creek were already fading.

"You never know what the wrong question is going to be," Howard said. "Ask Lloyd about that. It's hard to tell what'll make you start looking like a loose end."

Stan swallowed hard, dismissed any objections to the inequality of his share, nodded, and kept driving through the falling snow.

When they came to the bridge, the light was red. But nobody was around, so he ran it anyway.

●●●●●

I told Loretta the story as gently as I could, with none of my horrible details. I'd made a lot of it up anyway. Or Stan did, maybe. She cried and hugged me.

I was for sure never telling her that she set off the whole damn scary mess by bragging to Lloyd that she'd worked with the MondoMegaJackpot winner's girlfriend. I said nothing about how Lloyd was not the night watchman of Flotilla. That he was their night accountant. To the regret of the Magna-Protects. In the end, Lloyd Bunker was collateral damage from the Mondo. Like so many others.

The Mondo. It never stopped giving.

The first case of the T&A was all about us.

Whatever. It made no difference now. It was a useful instruction for us detectives. Understatement.

Chapter Sixty-one
Sunday, August 6

On a Sunday afternoon in early August, we took Lloyd on the *Linda Mae*, the day-fishing boat that runs out from Wildwood Marina, and we poured him with love and care upon a Great Lake. The last thing, before we gave him to the water, I added a handful of grindings from the Linden Green Pontiac GTO into his urn. I thought Lloyd would have liked that. I sure did. And if there was a scrap of Howard Rexroad in there with Lloyd? That's justice for you.

Lloyd's official wake was a fine affair. Otis hired "the best caterer I could find in Cleveland. You guys can afford it, right?" The spread was lavish past the point of decadence. The guests were scattered around on the fancy deck chairs under our pretentious umbrellas. Drifting off to worship the lake in thoughtful silence.

Murder to the Metal   397

Everybody was drinking Veuve Clicquot from real glass glasses and snarfing up the "Caramelized Onion, Apple & Squash Quesadilla Bites" and "Petite Hummus-Stuffed Roasted Fingerling Potatoes" being graciously offered about on trays. The Lloyd I'd come to know would have loved it. The Lloyd who believed he needed more cash and more class to tell Loretta the simple truth that he loved her back.

Margo and Valerio were there. Too close for comfort, in my opinion. Lisa Cole. Making mental notes but not writing them down. A friend now, I was pretty sure. Skip and his beautiful wife.

The library crew gathered for Loretta: Velma, Quentin, the part-time-not-as-bogus-as-Allie-Harper librarians, and one of the library security guards, not in her uniform. I noticed Otis noticing Velma. I told myself to quit noticing anything that might disturb my peace of mind on that evening.

After toasts to Lloyd, we raised our glasses to Loretta. For being Loretta—Loretta who whispered in my ear "Oh, Allie. Everything you did for Lloyd. Two wakes! He would have been so proud."

● ● ● ● ●

The sun settled into its nest of cloud, painting everything with an unnatural ruddy glow. It blazed over Jacob Foster's sculpture, the predatory metal bird we'd installed, for now, on a high perch that commanded the whole sweep of the water. I better understood tonight what I'd seen in its glowing eyes at the benefit, barely forty-eight hours before the artist's death. Burning dreams. The ones Jake could see and touch but never realize. Poised for flight into darkness, claws sharpened against fate, its bloody ribbon of copper burnished by the dying rays, *Predacious* waited, in eternity, for the chance to soar.

The library guests made their good-byes. Loretta and Lisa went with them. After-party at the condo, perhaps. A Manhattan in honor of Lloyd, maybe.

Margo and Tony departed, together. Out of my jurisdiction.

The caterer's crew cleaned up and whisked themselves away and there we were, the three of us, with one last toast to the first case of the T&A. In all of its vast, subterranean connectedness. I clinked my glass against Tom's. Then Otis'.

"To us. The T&A. Who would have guessed we were set up to be the victims of our own first case?"

"I should have, Allie."

"Otis."

"I know. I have to let it go. Doesn't help effectiveness to be beating yourself over the head all the time. Next time, though—"

I hid a sigh of relief. Otis really was in for the long haul in spite of everything. I picked a spare bottle up from its ice bath and got myself a couple of glasses.

"Night, Otis."

No eye contact.

"Night, Allie. Tom."

Chapter Sixty-two

At last the night was down to Tom and me. Almost too worn out and too intoxicated by the sorrow and the lovefest of the evening, by the mostly successful end of the case, by the not dying because of the case, and, of course, by the Veuve Clicquot—

Almost too worn out by all of that, for love.

Not quite, though.

We were creating a new tradition. Our cases would always end in bed.

"Tom, last summer at the Ritz-Carlton, Cleveland, could you have seen all this coming? Even with your blind man skills?"

"Allie, a blind man might have predicted some of this, but no. Not all, by a long shot."

"Are you sorry? Sorry that we—?"

"About the T&A? No, Allie. Most of this wasn't the T&A's fault. The Lloyd Case actually woke us up. Saved us, maybe. I still blame almost everything on the MondoMegaBucks. And, remember, I'm trying to stop beating myself up for everything that's happened because I bought that ticket to show Rune it doesn't pay to play.

"It's awful that Lloyd and the other people are dead. The Lauren 'everybody loved' at Channel 16. Keith from Magna-Pro. Gone since reboot day. Still missing, but we sure presume—no closure about him. And Jacob…Jake. It'll take us a long time to get over that, Allie."

I moved closer and put a hand on Tom's chest to comfort us both, but he was moving on again.

"My, God. Poor dumb Milo. Vaporized? Howard Rexroad crushed in a GTO? Not very sad, I guess. But that was a horrific way to—And Nathan, I wish he'd lived long enough to grow up and go to jail where he belonged for the rest of his life. Plus the stupid people who are probably going to wind up in prison. Hard to feel bad about them."

Tom's fingers were tracing a long, absent-minded path up and down my bare arm. I noticed, though.

"One thing. I'm totally bummed that the Flotilla guy got away.

"That part? How it just burns my gut he's out there? That his threat to us is still alive. And the destruction. He had a hand in it all. The drugs. The lives ruined. Ended. Most of the people we're talking about here, one way or another. How ruthlessly he went after the money. How he murdered Nathan. Casually, Allie. Like he barely noticed he'd done it. The way he annihilated Magna-Pro."

Magna-Protect. I flashed back to a recent moment. I was holding the Magna-Pro Trapper Keeper, giving it one last look before filing it away. My fingers traced the embossed logo and my eyes focused, at long last, on the very tiny tagline. "A Flotilla Company." That simple, closer look, a little earlier, might have saved us some time. And trouble.

Understatement.

Tom was oblivious to my flashback re: Tito Ricci's Web of Evil.

He continued, "And his fucking cologne, too."

I nodded, letting Tito lie for now. Wherever he might be.

"Mmm. Don't forget his reprehensible dining table and chairs."

"Yeah. Of course, your chairs. I guess how mad I am about all that's still unfinished. How unsatisfied—" He sighed.

"That's a clue I'm more onboard with your 'We solve mysteries of the heart' scenario than I was last year, when I had no idea how messy it was about to get. So, yes and no. You know I loved—love—teaching. I'll get back to it.

"But the T&A? I'm all about it for the foreseeable future. We can't stop being detectives, Allie. That's clear for now. The money is a magnet for crime. If we've learned anything, it's that we detectives need to be on our own case. All the time.

"One thing I'm not sorry about, though."

"One thing?"

We were lying on the big bed, in the warm, lake-smelling breeze. Me with my unruly hairdo against his handsome chest. His fingers still tracking my arm. But now his arms were gathering me in. This was better.

"Us. This. Also the about to be this—"

I permitted some minor unbuttoning, but I didn't pitch in. My eyes stayed fixed on his face. Searching for something that might be lost.

"Tom."

"I know. I know what you're thinking."

"No, you don't. I'm not thinking anything."

"You're thinking why did I propose marriage to you before…before Rune…and then drop the subject?"

Damn you, blind man intuition.

"Okay. Uh-huh. Yes. I wondered. But I figured—"

"I also know what you figured, Allie. You figured that you, Alice Jane Harper, small-town girl, divorced from the Jerk of the World, broke, a little lost, and a lot impulsive, are too ordinary and possibly too aggravating to be married to a MondoMegaMillionaire. And that I was hedging my bets with you until someone more appropriate comes along. Someone whose name could go on a hospital or a library next to mine."

Crap. He knew every single thing. I nodded my head against his shoulder and buried my face there, breathing him in. Inhaling everything that whispered "Tom" to me whenever I was in his arms. He still smelled like good soap.

"That was not what I was thinking," he said. "Not ever. Not once from Day One. Now, you use your 20/20 vision and tell me what in your heart you know I have been thinking. What you've known about me all along but were too yourself to admit it to yourself."

Tony Valerio would have been amazed and, no doubt nonplussed, if he knew that at this critically naked moment, it was his voice I heard. *"Alice Harper, for crissake. The man is batshit crazy about you, and you know it."*

I blinked. "It's not that I'm too ordinary. It's that you're afraid—"

"Good for you. How many times have we talked about this? How many different ways do I have to show you?

"Allie, when that house blew up. I lost everything. I had nothing inside my head but screaming panic. All that kept me from screaming out loud was the hopelessness. Total despair. The 'how quick can I figure out a way to kill myself and make this stop' kind of despair. Like that, Allie.

"I'd lost my world. My rebuilt world. My functioning world. Everything was gone. Even us. I couldn't hear you. You and I vanished into the roar of that blast. That was a blackness infinitely deeper and more lonely than mere blindness—" This pulled him up short. "*Mere* blindness? Perspective is a fabulous gift, Allie, if you survive long enough to get it back.

"But you found me. You came into that devastated place to get me. You brought me back. You made me willing to keep living—at least for one more night—even before I got my hearing again. You, Allie. The woman I've never seen with my eyes."

His voice hardened. "I am so terrified that my ridiculous money will steal you from me. That if you're Mrs. MondoMegaJackpot, there'll be a target on your back forever—and I'm going to lose you. This. The whole world that is us."

He traced his fingers along the notch in my collarbone, and down from there, slowly, through all the swells and hollows. Caressing, Exploring. Questing. Down. More down.

I yielded. Opened. To everything. All of me to all of him. All of him to all of me. I could see—like waking up to a revelation I'd always known—that when Tom Bennington put his sentient hands on me, more than our passions awakened with his touch. When we met in the warmth of his palms, hands spoke to skin. Skin answered hands. We became everything we were together.

One.

Eye contact paled.

He'd known all along, of course. I'd been afraid to let it—to let him—in the rest of the way. He sighed.

"You really are clueless, Alice Jane. You and your doubts. And I am, too. Me and my fears."

He moved to close all the gaps between our bodies, his words a caress. Said what I was thinking.

"When I touch you. When you and I make love. When I cross the border between us, and bring you, all of you, into my darkness. In here with me. It's sex. Yes, it is. I'd wager nobody on the planet—but let's not go there...."

"Oh, no, Thomas Bennington the Third! Go there. Please. Feel free. Let's go there. And keep your hand there, too. So you don't lose your place."

I closed my eyes. He put his mouth on mine. The skin between us was consumed by righteous fire. Oneness. Gladness.

Time passed.

• ● ● ● •

"So," he said at last, holding me, his voice clear and sure. "Listen to me."

"This is us. Alice Jane Harper and Thomas Bennington. For better and worse. In darkness. In light. In silence. In words. For as long as we occupy these bodies.

"Here and now. I promise you…us. No matter what. Along with the clandestine possession of all my fabulous, annoying, lethal worldly goods. Do you take us, Alice Jane? Us together until death do us part? What do you say?"

I lay against his chest, sharing the rhythm of our breathing, listening to his heartbeat promising all of himself to me. My heart answering him with every beat. I *do*. I *do*. I *do*.

For as long as we occupy these bodies.

"Yes," I said. "I say yes. And now, Thomas Bennington III, you may kiss the bride…."

Author's Note

"Murder. Mayhem. Romance. Cleveland."

Writers often describe setting as a character in their books. Well, count me in. I can't imagine *Too Lucky to Live* or *Murder to the Metal* without their Cleveland roots. This gritty, funky, cool old town jumps out at me, grabs my imagination, and leaves her fingerprints all over my stories.

I love my city, and I know it's not a walk in the park. Not all landmark buildings and cultural icons. Not impeccably manicured. Sometimes not even survivable. But it sure is alive. Cleveland people and places, created from scraps and memories—a little bit real, a lot imaginary—bleed into my plots. I want to be respectful, acknowledge everything I don't know, pay tribute to the beautiful, mourn the terrible, and tell a rollicking good tale. That's my challenge.

Clevelanders tell me they love finding themselves in familiar places with Allie and Tom. They wonder if the people are real, too. Yes. And no. Much as I've renamed some locations, made some up from scratch, resurrected scenes from the past, I've also swiped bits of people I have known and added a liberal sprinkling of creative license. I love them all.

The Memorial-Nottingham Branch of the CPL is my very own library. I've never seen Loretta there, but the strong, kind people and warm welcome are real. I've always loved libraries but, as a new author, I've rediscovered librarians. They rock. Bookstores and bookstore people, too. New friends.

Chloe's Diner? Gone. Leaving only a fond memory of the peach pie. The mansions of Bratenahl? Spectacularly real, though Allie and Tom's is my fantasy. The Beach Club Bistro pizzas? They're as real as the numbers on my scale. Ditto, Slyman's corn beef. Bob Sferra of Culinary Occasions shared his fall menu a little early—and all the way from Florence—so some characters could take comfort from a beautiful feast. Skip Castillo is an homage to a smart, handsome guy who graciously puts up with my Skip. My husband, the lawyer, is not in any way at all represented by D.B. Harper, "Mr. Tall, Dark & Unfaithful, Esquire." Ridpath is a real street. Grovewood, too. Six Shooters Coffee? Yes, indeed. The wreck of the observatory on Taylor is majestically and dreadfully true. Lake Erie is actually Great. Scrapping is present and accounted for in the neighborhoods. The opioid crisis—in Cleveland, as in many other places, urban and rural—is crushing hearts all over town.

If you're a Clevelander reading this book, you're bound to say, "Oh, yeah. That's my Cleveland." And also, "Wait a sec! That's not right—" If you're a Clevelander reading this book and you see a villain? That's not you. If you see a hero? That's you, no question.

Oh, and one more thing: About the flashy speed cameras of East Cleveland? Margo and I are on the exact same page.

To see more Poisoned Pen Press titles:

Visit our website:
poisonedpenpress.com
Request a digital catalog:
info@poisonedpenpress.com

CPSIA information can be obtained
at www.ICGtesting.com
Printed in the USA
BVHW04s0402170518
516508BV00001B/10/P